This Time

C. M. Burdell

This Time

Copyright © 2025 by C. M. Burdell

Published by

 BurdellMedia

Burdell Media · Atlanta, Georgia

ISBN (ebook): 979-8-9987559-1-0

ISBN (paperback): 979-8-9987559-0-3

ISBN (hardcover): 979-8-9987559-2-7

Library of Congress Control Number: 2025908883

Cover design by Getcovers

For permissions or inquiries, contact: **info@burdellmedia.com**

For my sister, who has listened to my stories—both the wild and the ridiculous—for more years than either of us will admit. Thank you for laughing when I thought I was funny, for indulging my craziest ideas, and for always believing in this dream.

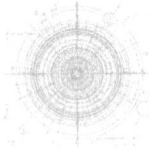

CURRENT – Borrowed Hour

AUGUST 2023

The smell of fresh paint mixed with the unmistakable old-building odor in the dorm was resurrecting something uncomfortable from deep in my brain and conjuring memories that were almost too much to bear. I had loved this place intensely when I was a student, but after what happened to Will all those years ago, the guilt and regret were still overwhelming.

I hurried down the hallway from my son Sean's room, where he and his roommate Zach were still unpacking and getting settled. Aiming for the exit sign in the distance, I fought my way through what looked like hundreds of parents and students talking in little clusters. I felt as if the walls were pressing closer to me, and I had a nearly overwhelming urge to burst out of the press of bodies and into the fresh air.

Then, above the din, I heard the old campus steam whistle begin to blow. I felt a sweet twinge at the familiar sound. A beloved tradition stretching back over a hundred years to when

Tech had been a trade school, the whistle blew at five minutes before each hour during weekdays to signal the end of class periods, as well as when the team won a home football game. To most alumni, the sound would have been a happy, vivid reminder, but it only deepened what was growing inside of me. If I ever got out of this building, I felt like I could never come back.

Skirting the crowd and hugging the wall, I noticed a narrow, old-looking door on the right, a few feet away from my hand. It was painted an institutional yellow and looked like it had been there since the beginning of the twentieth century, when some of the buildings on this side of campus had been built. I grabbed the knob and twisted it, then rushed through the doorway, hoping to disappear from these happy onlookers and be alone for a few minutes.

It was dark in the hall on the other side, and a bit musty, as if no fresh air had circulated in it for years. There was no light switch, or none that I could find, as I carefully ran my fingers along the wall. Not wanting to go back through the crowd, I crept forward into the dark, seeing a thin light up ahead. Maybe the passageway would open into a less congested area, if not directly to the outside. Walking with my hands outstretched to avoid running into anything, I kept my eyes on the sliver of light. I put one foot almost directly in front of the other as I got closer and closer to what I hoped was a door. Why had I left my cell phone and its trusty flashlight in the car?

Finally, I saw a diamond-shaped window in a door up ahead, with sunlight streaming through it. Just before I reached it, a reflection caught my eye. I squatted down. It was a key, like the ones we used to have to our dorm rooms, on a ring with a tiny metal sculpture—some famous mathematical shape, although I couldn't remember the name. I grabbed it and put it in my purse, then straightened up.

When I got to the door, I found the knob and exited the hallway. The air outside smelled so clean. The warm sun shining on my arms felt fantastic. Birds were singing, and I could hear conversation and laughter all around me. It was a glorious day, and my heart felt lighter almost instantly. This was a courtyard I remembered from my time here. A few students were playing Frisbee on the grass, and others were chatting in groups. One guy was sitting on our old bench under the tree—the one where Will and I had shared countless lunches and conversations. With a book balanced on his knee and one arm thrown over the backrest, he kept scanning the courtyard, as if looking for someone. When I saw his face, I was astonished to see that he looked just like Will. I couldn't help gawking. We had lost Will soon after graduation, just over nineteen years ago, and this guy didn't just have Will's coloring and features; he had the same familiar way of absently shoving his hair out of his eyes and the same easygoing but confident posture.

"Hey, Lauren." The guy put his book down with a smile. "I'm so glad you came out. I was afraid you'd get stuck inside the dorm all day."

I was stunned. Maybe I was dreaming. Maybe it was one of those dreams where you know it's not real, but you're still very much involved in it. Somehow, it didn't have to make sense.

"Yeah, it's too pretty to stay in, but luckily I'm off duty now," I agreed, thoroughly confused on one level but somehow not missing a beat. I was young, and I was wearing shorts and a tank top. If this was a dream, I sure didn't want to wake up anytime soon.

I sat down beside Will, and he said, "I got a little break between getting the freshmen set up and was about to eat my lunch, but I brought some extra stuff, hoping you'd show up. Join me?"

There were two sandwiches and two cans of soda in an insulated bag in his backpack. Will dug around theatrically, then with a flourish produced a Pez dispenser. He set it upright on the bench like a trophy, the plastic head wobbling in the breeze. "And look—food of the gods for dessert."

I had to laugh. Will and I, along with our other friends, were big *Seinfeld* fans and loved to watch the reruns whenever we could.

"Oh, I shouldn't. I certainly don't need to eat anything," I said, feeling self-conscious. Eric often reminded me I wasn't thin enough. Thin was "perfect" in his eyes, and he told me that as frequently as possible.

"What are you talking about?" Will said. "Even beautiful geniuses need nourishment. Or are you able to run on sunlight alone these days?"

I felt a big smile breaking across my face. "You're too kind."

He handed me a drink and a ham-and-Swiss. I popped the top on my soda. It was cold and fizzy. It was real. Whatever this was—daydream or hallucination—I was going to enjoy it and try my best not to wake up. I wanted to stay right here on this bench with Will. Forever.

"So, how's your week been?" I asked. Somehow, I knew exactly where we were and what was going on. The new freshmen had moved in, and we were both doing a little paid work helping set up social activities for them. Our classes were starting in a few days.

"Oh, it's been good," he said. "After the freshman thing is over, I'm hoping to get in a little camping trip before the semester gets going. How about you?"

"Same, except for me it's going to be the quickest beach trip in the world. Amy and I are leaving later today." I watched a guy make a spectacular Frisbee catch. "You'll start interviewing this semester, right? Got any idea which company would be your dream job?"

"Not yet," he said. "I want to see who's recruiting this fall and where I might want to go. Wouldn't it be beyond cool to find a position at a startup in California or something?" He turned to face me, his elbow on the backrest. "And what about you? Do you know where you'll apply for grad school?"

By this point, I was deep in the experience, or the dream, or whatever was going on, and I was enjoying sitting here with Will. Everything had always been so effortless with us, and there weren't many people I could say that about. He was always full of life, smiles, and fun ideas, and he never failed to make me feel happy and energized.

Soon I heard the whistle begin to blow. How had it been almost an hour since I'd sat down? I was looking right at Will, about to respond to something he had just said, when I found myself standing in that dorm hallway again, with parents and students all around me. I scanned my surroundings. Everything was just as it had been. It was all so ordinary again. What had just happened? Had I been lost in a daydream, standing here this whole time? Or had I been in a janitor's closet? And where was that door I'd opened?

I was terribly disappointed to be back in reality but felt a lot better than I had when I first left Sean's room. My mind was whirling with questions, but not knowing what else to do, I started making my way toward the exit. I found my car and backed out of my parking spot, managing to avoid running over any oblivious pedestrians, then drove the short distance to the interstate. As I traveled up I-75, I realized I had a silly little smile on my lips.

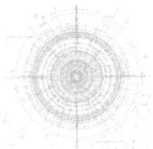

COLLEGE – First Light

SEPTEMBER 2002

I t was a Friday night in mid-September of my junior year, and I found myself at a party. My freshman-year roommate, Marily, had invited me, and she'd said everyone could bring friends. The house was in a suburb in the northeastern part of Atlanta and belonged to her parents, who were away for the weekend. I'd ridden to the party with Savannah, a friend I'd had chemistry classes and labs with my first two years at Tech.

There was a good mix of people I knew and ones I'd never seen before, so the evening was a lot of fun at first, but after a while it got crowded and a little too warm inside. It was time for some fresh air and another beer. The kitchen door opened onto a wooden deck at ground level, surrounded by a large fenced-in backyard. There were about fifteen people out there near the keg, and occasionally someone would reach down to pet a black dog. She appeared to be a lab and border collie mix, with a sleek coat and a sweet face.

Once I'd filled my cup, I sat down on the edge of the platform with my feet in the grass. I reached out my hand and spoke to the dog, and she came over. After I'd played with her for a moment, she sat down beside me. I loved college life, but I'd grown up with pets and missed being around animals. Sitting outside with a beer and this adorable creature was a real treat for me.

I was looking out at what I could see of the yard in the glow from the lights behind me when I noticed a hand reaching down to pet my new friend. A tall, lean guy sat down on the other side of her, giving me a friendly look.

"How's it going?" he said.

"Pretty good." I smiled. "Even better now that I've found this cute baby."

"Her name's Bella," he told me. "And I'm Will."

He had tousled light brown hair, clear grayish-green eyes, and a nice tan. He had been attractive enough at first glance, but when he smiled and revealed his beautiful white teeth, he was gorgeous.

"Hi Will, I'm Lauren."

"Nice to meet you, Lauren. How do you know Marily?"

"She was my roommate when we were freshmen," I said. "We still get together now and then. And you?" I rubbed Bella's head. It was as soft as it looked.

"I just came with some friends, so I don't really know her. But she seems great, and I'm always down for a party. It was a bonus to see this pup. I love dogs."

"Me too. And cats, and any other pets I can get my hands on."

He nodded. "I haven't had a pet in forever. Wish I could have a dog, but my landlord won't allow it. That's definitely a goal for a couple of years from now." Bella was lying on her back, paws in the air, so he scratched her chest. "It's awesome to be outside, right?"

"Oh yeah. There's nothing like a summer night." I angled my body toward Bella and Will. "Couple of years before you can get a dog, huh? Do you go to Tech too?"

"Yep. I'm a co-op—an ME." So, he was a mechanical engineering major working in industry every other semester to pay the bills and gain work experience. "I think I should get out in a couple more years. How about you?"

"Just starting my junior year—biology," I replied, playing with one of Bella's ears.

"And I'm guessing you're a native Georgian?"

"Yeah, from an awful little town I thought I'd never escape," I admitted.

He laughed. "Well, you made it. Glad you're here now."

"Me too. So where's home for you?"

"Oh man." He ran a hand through his hair. "I grew up in a bunch of different places—some in the Northeast, a couple out west, and now here for school. My dad was always changing jobs, and finally . . . The important part is, I've been renting a house near campus with a few buddies for the last couple of years, and now I consider that home." He petted Bella's head, and she tried to lick his hand. "It's great. I run with some guys a few days a week, and there's always a crew hanging out. We do fun stuff, especially on weekends. You should join us sometime."

That sounded nice. It would be great to have a new group to hang out with. The last two years, I'd gone to football games and hung out with some people who shared a house on Estelle Avenue, just northeast of campus, but somehow—despite their constant partying—they had all managed to graduate the year before.

"So, what do you do for fun besides pet strange dogs and chat with strange guys?" Will asked.

I laughed. "That takes up more time than you'd think. But I also like to draw and get out in nature, especially if there's a nice trail to explore." I looked down to give Bella a scratch, then back up at Will. "And you? What do you do when there aren't any strange dogs around?"

"Anything outdoors, for sure. I love camping, rafting—all that good stuff. Right now, I'm trying to get in shape for a mountain bike race in north Georgia. But hey, tell me about your drawing. What do you like to draw?"

"Lauren, time to go," Savannah called me from right outside the back door. "Remember, I have to get up tomorrow morning."

This had to be the first time in my life a friend wanted to leave a party before I did. "Sorry, that's my ride," I said, standing up and brushing off my shorts.

Will got to his feet too and said, "It's been so great to meet you. Hope to see you again soon."

"Very nice to meet you too." I gave him a smile and started turning away. I felt him touch my elbow.

"Lauren?" he said. "What's your last name?"

"My—Oh, it's Mahan," I told him, wondering why he wanted to know. "And, um, have a great night. See ya." I gave Bella a last pat and followed Savannah through the house.

◇ ◇ ◇

Sunday morning, my phone rang.

"Hi Lauren, this is Will. We met at the party Friday night?"

Wow, he must have looked me up in the student directory. Holy shit. Who'd seen that coming?

"Oh sure, how are ya?"

"Real good, thanks. So, a bunch of us decided to go tubing down the river, and I wondered if you'd like to come?"

My mind started racing immediately. Did I want to do that—spend the afternoon with a group of strangers? I had wanted a little more excitement this year, so why not.

"Sure. What time?"

"Well . . . right now, as a matter of fact. Sorry for the late notice. We came up with the idea last night around midnight, and I didn't think I should call you then." I could tell from his tone he was smiling.

I looked around the room wildly, as if I'd find a hint there about what I should say next. Why the hell couldn't I think faster?

"We have plenty of tubes, and one guy, Josh, will take those up in his truck. Some people are already at the house getting things together, but I know you'll need time to change, so how about I swing by and get you in a few minutes, then we'll ride up to the put-in point together?" he said.

"Okay." I looked in my drawer. Thank God I'd brought my cute new black swimsuit to campus. "I'm in east campus—Grant dorm."

"Got it. See you soon."

Wow. Well, at least I didn't have time to get nervous or shy or anything. I needed to move. Fast.

◇ ◇ ◇

Will and I headed north in his Jeep, an indie playlist providing the soundtrack for our adventure. Every now and then when we weren't talking, he'd hum or softly sing a few bars. Pretty soon, I surprised myself by singing along with him on a song I knew well. He shot me a quick grin, and we kept it up for a few more minutes.

As we got closer to our destination, we swapped stories about our previous adventures floating down the Chattahoochee, and he filled me in on his friends and what to expect from the day.

"They're really great people," he said, giving me a quick glance. "Super welcoming and easy to be around. Josh is one of the nicest guys you'll ever meet, and his girlfriend Melissa has this friendly energy you'll love."

He adjusted the volume of the music a little. "Let's see ... Jason and Rob live a couple houses down from me, and they're lots of fun. Oh, and my roommates Dave and Nick, along with Nick's girlfriend Hannah, are always cracking jokes and keeping things light. Nobody gets uptight about schedules or anything. We're all just there to relax and have a good time together. I think you'll fit right in."

I appreciated hearing about them all in advance, and maybe Will sensed that. Being around him was so easy that I'd forgotten any trace of shyness I'd felt when I first decided to go.

At the take-out point—where we'd exit the river later—we picked up Dave, Nick, and Hannah, who had parked their car there. Jason and Rob had done the same and hitched a ride to the put-in location with Josh and Melissa. With everyone accounted for, we made the short drive upriver.

Once we were all gathered and ready to go, we pushed our tubes in, seating ourselves as we floated away from the bank. The water was freezing, and it was sort of brown, but with the delicious sunshine on my skin and the mingled scents of sunscreen and the river itself, I knew this was going to be just the little break from the city and studying I needed.

The group seemed nice and friendly, and I'd seen some of them around campus over the previous couple of years. A few of the guys had brought coolers in tubes they'd attached to their own. We couldn't bring glass on the river, but cans were fine.

Josh, who was floating closest to me, offered me a drink, but I knew we'd be away from the nearest ladies' room for two to three hours, so I thanked him but declined. Then I noticed that Melissa, who had one foot propped on Josh's tube, seemed to be drinking with no worries at all, and figured maybe I should just relax for once.

Our group drifted down the river in a cluster for quite a while. We all went around a bend under a large overhanging branch, and I closed my eyes and lay back, just basking in the sun as we floated. This was the life. Then the motion of my tube changed, and it moved backward just a little. When I opened my eyes, there was Will, lying back on his inner tube, his arm extended so he could hold the side of mine. He was smiling at me, and once again I couldn't take my eyes off those beautiful teeth. We were both wearing sunglasses, and I could barely see his eyes. Could he see mine, or would it be all right for me to sneak a glance at that runner's body of his, with the amazing sun-bronzed skin?

"Having fun?"

"Yes. This is sheer heaven," I told him. Sun and water and not a care in the world.

"Want a beer? You twenty-one? I don't want you getting busted out here on our first adventure."

"Yep, turned twenty-one last Saturday, so no worries," I said. "And I'd love one, thanks."

Will twisted around, getting two cans from his inflatable cooler, and gave me one. We popped the tops and sipped our drinks as we floated along.

"You guys do this a lot?" I asked him.

"We try to. Of course, it's a lot more fun to go whitewater rafting in North Carolina or Tennessee when we have time to drive up there, but when it's hot outside and we just have a few hours, we make it a point to come here. Unless it's a football day." He took a swig. "We go to all the home games together. You should come with us."

"I'd love to. I love our team, but this year I'm without my football buddies—they all graduated." I shifted in my tube, the shock of the cold water brushing my skin, and added, "The people I hang out with now either don't like football or grew up following some other team."

"Well, Lauren, this is great timing. You're with us from now on."

A happy grin broke over my face. Will's easy sociability was incredibly relaxing, and his friends were just as fun and welcoming as he'd promised. This year was starting out great.

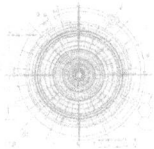

CURRENT – Same Old Reality

August 2023

As I got off the interstate and took the winding, tree-lined suburban roads to the house I shared with Eric, I basked in the memory of that summer, when Will and I spent so many golden hours together. With my daydreaming in full gear, I pulled into the driveway and activated the garage door.

Once inside, my feelings started coming down to earth, with the realities of our home crowding out the more fantastic ideas I'd been entertaining. Unlike during the years when Sean had been here, the house was now quiet, and it felt empty and dead. In the past, he and his friends had been responsible for much of the laughter and life in this space, and I'd have to get used to the newly empty atmosphere.

Before I could think about it, my phone was in my hand and I was dialing Emily. I wanted to hear her voice, to make the afternoon feel a little more normal. And I had to admit, I was dying to tell her what had happened. My call went directly to voicemail. My sister was an attorney who handled civil issues, so sometimes she was quite reachable at her desk, but she would set her phone on silent or turn it off if she was in court.

I left her a quick message so she'd know there was nothing urgent. "Just saying hi. Maybe we can get together this weekend."

In my home office, I opened Facebook and typed in Will's name, but there were no results. Well, of course not. What was I thinking? He was already gone by the time Facebook became popular. Still, I couldn't help but put his name into the search bar on Google, hoping maybe some story from his youth, some scrap of text about him would give me a little echo of the thrill I'd had this afternoon.

There was nothing there, no trace of him. It was so strange and so sad—he was really gone. All these years, I had done my best not to think about him, avoiding the grief, but now that I'd seen him, if only in my mind, I wanted the happy illusion to continue.

Just as I was about to give up, I realized there was one more thing I could try, an electronic journal I had written on my student computer all those years ago. Today wasn't going to be the day, though; I was afraid the details were too raw and too real. Although I wanted to prolong my happy reminiscence about Will, the sad reality was rapidly returning. I felt the guilt and grief approaching like a cold, gray fog.

It was time to mentally shift gears, to get away from the computer and do some more active things, starting with a run around the neighborhood. Later, I'd see if I could prepare some food that Eric would actually like.

◊ ◊ ◊

Since I had been off all day for Sean's move-in, I cooked dinner. It was just about ready when Eric returned from work. I had marinated a couple of mahi-mahi filets, and I was planning to serve them grilled, with a kale and quinoa salad. As soon as he had changed into shorts and a T-shirt, he came into the kitchen and began examining the food I had prepared.

"You didn't toast the quinoa in oil before cooking it, did you?"

"No oil. Just toasted it dry," I replied. "Why?"

"I just wondered. Did you massage the kale before mixing it in?"

"Sure did. I also talked to it and bought it a glass of wine," I joked.

Eric looked at me for a moment. It reminded me of the way he had looked at the furnace once when it was making a strange sound. Finally, he turned away from the counter, which told me the inspection was over and I had passed, maybe with a B minus.

I dispensed some ice and water into tall glasses, adding a lemon wedge to mine. This kitchen had never felt like it really belonged to me. It was all stainless steel, quartzite, and glass, plus a stone tile floor—Eric's choices. But that Sub-Zero kept my lemons and other goodies nice and cold, so I couldn't complain.

Once we were sitting at the table eating, he said, "I assume Sean got moved in?"

"Yes, he and Zach are all settled. I hope he loves it there."

"You know, he would have been just fine if he had driven down on his own." The corners of Eric's lips turned up in a closed-mouth smirk as he continued to chew.

"Yes." I tried not to clench my teeth. "Of course he would have been fine on his own. He wanted both of us to come, just for fun, and to help him and Zach haul their stuff there." I stabbed some kale with my fork. "Since this was a day for parents and freshmen, I thought it would be good to give them a hand and show him we're interested."

Eric leaned forward a fraction of an inch, spine perfectly straight as always, and persisted. "I drove all my own stuff almost four hundred miles to campus when I was his age, and no one helped me. It's not that hard." With Eric, every conversation had a winner and a loser, and he always wanted to walk away on top.

"Yes, of course he could have done it alone. But he didn't have to. He wanted his family to help, and all he had to do was ask."

Pivoting away from that exhausting exchange, I asked Eric how his day had been, and he told me a couple of general stories from his office. He was trying to make a transition to a concierge practice, privately paid for by the patients. He saw it as a way to make big money as fast as possible. He'd made it clear that he wanted to live in a huge, lavish house someday and drive the most expensive sports car he could find. After the sweet hour I had enjoyed earlier, it was all I could do to even halfway listen to him and respond.

After dinner, Eric retreated to his home office to read financial news and manage his investment accounts. I poured myself a glass of wine and curled up in the den. The house felt like a mausoleum without Sean and his friends, and my mind kept drifting back to the afternoon at Tech, as impossible to grasp as a dream. I let myself enjoy the feeling a little longer, then opened my iPad and bought a legal thriller to read.

Around ten o'clock, I got a text from Sean.

We bought books, went to freshman cookout, met some nice people

The message made me smile. Typical, thoughtful Sean. He knew his old mom would like to hear something about his day. College could be some of the best and most important years of a person's life. I only wished my experience, or one particular minute of it, had gone a bit differently.

I was in bed with the lights out and my eyes closed when Eric came in, but I wasn't asleep. I kept replaying what had happened—or what I had imagined—or whatever it was. In some ways, that brief interlude was the most exciting and meaningful thing—other than being Sean's mom—that had happened to me in almost twenty years. Whatever had taken place in that courtyard, it had felt completely real. Will's laugh, his smile, the way he'd looked at me with such warmth—it was exactly as I remembered from all those years ago. For one precious hour, I'd felt young again.

My college self had been the real me. I had worked hard, certain I was going to go to grad school and do research some-day. I had been thrilled to be at Tech, making progress toward what I assumed would be a bright future, and I had enjoyed my leisure time too. Most of my best memories were of things I had done with Will and the people I knew through him. When we met, he had brought me into his world of friends and fun, and it had transformed my life.

But in the end, as wonderful as Will was and as much happiness as he had given me, I had hurt him and pushed him away. He and I had always been able to discuss anything in the world, but the last time I had seen him, not long before he was killed, I had been so full of anxiety that I had abruptly shut him down when he tried to talk to me. That was something I could hardly bear to live with.

All my hopes and dreams had died in the warm, sunny days after our graduation. Instead of conducting research in a cut-ting-edge lab, I was now writing routine reports for a mediocre little company. And instead of having a marriage full of love and joy, I had a grudging pairing with Eric, focused strictly on giving Sean a two-parent home. Still, those disappointments were nothing compared to Will's death.

As I became drowsy, I kept thinking of Will and his smile. My mind began to drift toward sleep when something nagged at the edge of my consciousness—something I was supposed to remember. Just as I was dropping off, it came to me with a jolt of panic: I had a guest article for a huge website due tomorrow at five, and I hadn't even picked the topic yet. They had offered me the opportunity weeks ago, and I'd assumed I would have all the information in my head and be able to write the post after taking Sean to campus, but by now it was past time to go to sleep. The article could be about anything I wanted that had to do with personality types, and if I hadn't put it off, it would have been so easy.

My stomach sank with dread. I couldn't throw away this chance. If my article was good, I'd get more invitations to write for other websites, and every time I did that, it would gain me many new readers for my own site. Maybe I'd be able to quit my miserable little job at Doralabs someday.

As tired and anxious as I was, I knew it was better not to try to write it now. I could hardly think. I'd try to get a good night's sleep and do it tomorrow. Something would come to me in the morning, probably while I took my shower, and I'd simply write it up during my lunch hour. Maybe I'd wake up with a million ideas. My whole life seemed to be a study of personality types, so there was no shortage of stories to tell.

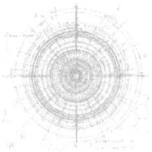

COLLEGE – Game Day

September 2002

S aturday a few days after our river trip, we had a home game, and it was so much fun. It was unseasonably warm even for Atlanta, with the bright sun feeling almost hot in the student section. It had been a perfect day. We won, and I was grinning as I walked with Will, Josh, Melissa, and Drew, one of their other friends, to Pie High for a little celebratory pizza afterward.

We were drinking cold beer and eating, having a lively conversation about the game, when some girl with expensive clothes and perfect makeup and hair stopped by our booth.

"Lisa. How's it going?" Will greeted her. The others said quick hellos, but Lisa's eyes were on me where I was sitting between Will and the wall. "Have you met Lauren?" he continued.

"Hi," I started to say, but she interrupted me.

"I wouldn't remember if I had." She looked me up and down.

Wow. I couldn't have heard that correctly, could I? It must have been the rudest thing anyone had ever said to me. I looked across at Melissa, hoping to catch her eye, but she was staring into her beer.

Will's expression changed, just for a second. "Well, now you have," he said. "Lauren's great."

Lisa looked a little surprised but continued talking to Will as if the rest of us weren't there. "A couple of girls and I just came to have a quick salad before we get ready for our party tonight. I saw you and just wanted to stop by." She used her hand to sweep some of her full, beautiful hair off her shoulder. "I'll see you around," she added, and off she pranced in her designer shoes.

As Will turned to me, I asked, "Is that your girlfriend?" I was curious. He seemed too nice to be with someone like that.

It had been just over a week since I'd met him, but I had spent hours talking to him since then, and this was the first time he seemed to have trouble finding his words. After a few seconds, he said, "We used to go out, but that's ancient history now." His expression relaxed to his usual easygoing look. "Where would you get that idea anyway—you psychic or something?"

"Mmm, yeah, I have a special antenna," I told him. We ordered another round and launched back into our postgame analysis.

After we'd finished our beer and pizza, I reluctantly excused myself and trudged back across campus to my room, because I had some serious studying to do. Will gave me some crap about being no fun, but I had a test that Monday, and physics didn't come naturally to me the way it did to him. The few beers I'd had hadn't totally killed my concentration for the night, and I could at least do my laundry and some of the easier problems, then hit the books hard the next day.

Just as I was punching holes in some handouts to put in my binder, my phone rang. It was my friend Pam. "Whatcha doing?" she asked.

"Oh, just procrastinating, really. Got a test Monday I need to get ready for."

"I wanted to let you know that Eric Whitman saw me in the lab yesterday, and he came up and asked about you."

"Asked about me?"

"He asked for your number."

"Holy shit. Eric Whitman *asked* about me?"

Pam and I had been enjoying dollar beers at Finn's Tavern back in April when a ridiculously handsome guy came up to say hi to her. She introduced us, but only by our first names. We talked for a few minutes, and during that short time, I developed a massive crush on him. I'd only learned his last name and major, chemical engineering, because I had grilled her relentlessly after he left. I was a little surprised he remembered the occasion.

"Yep. Thought I'd give you a heads up. Guess he's going to call you."

A giddy thrill passed through me, followed by a slight panic. I had enjoyed dreaming and talking about him for months, but now I felt sort of like a puppy who had been chasing a car and somehow managed to catch it. Out of sheer nervous energy, I stood up and paced for a minute as we finished our call.

Although my mind wanted to wander off into delicious daydreams, somehow I was able to settle back down, and I began doing some physics problems. I started with the easier ones, hoping it would get me into the zone, and I was making good progress when the phone rang again. It took every bit of willpower I had to let it ring twice before I answered. I tried not to let my nervousness show.

"Hi, this is Eric. I assume Pam told you I might call." His voice sounded super confident. "What're you up to tonight?"

"Uh, I'm studying physics. Got a test Monday."

"Oh. Do you think you'd like to take a break later and grab a beer?"

"Umm . . . sure. Sounds like fun."

"How about I pick you up at nine?"

"Great."

I couldn't believe it. I was really going out with the handsome Eric Whitman in just a couple of hours. I fussed with my hair and makeup until I was satisfied, then grabbed my phone to call Emily.

"What?" she said when I told her. "You're going on a *date* with the guy you've been talking about all this time? The one you only met for a minute?"

"Yes. I don't know exactly how this happened. But it's not a big deal. Really, I'd forgotten all about him, but this will be fun, you know." I was walking around my room while I talked.

"Yeah sure, I know."

"Really, it will. It's good to have friends. Especially good-looking friends with black hair and eyes the color of the sea," I said.

"Exactly what sea are you thinking of?"

"Never mind." I wanted to get off the phone and go back to the mirror. "I'll call you tomorrow."

At five minutes before nine, I started to get nervous. I brushed my hair again and put on the tiniest bit of tinted lip gloss, then sat down, trying to strike a casual pose so I could convince my brain that I was relaxed and confident.

At exactly 9 p.m., I heard a knock on my door. Someone must have let Eric in the building. He was perfection in human form, so why wouldn't they? I grabbed my purse and swung the door open, and there he was.

"Ready?" He was smiling.

"Sure." I was smiling too. How could I not? He was just so handsome and perfect.

◇ ◇ ◇

From campus, we went up Peachtree Road to a place called Brews. One look inside told us we'd be better off at the outdoor tables at the front of the building. The dimly lit bar was crowded, loud, and smoky, while the patio was quiet and mostly unoccupied. There was no lighting or canned music out there, just the ambient glow from other businesses and headlights along Peachtree.

We sat down at a black wrought iron table for two, and Eric ordered us a pitcher of beer. Once it arrived, along with two frosted mugs, we fell into relaxed conversation. It was incredible; I'd been infatuated with Eric since April, simply because of his face, his body, and the way he walked. I hadn't known anything else about him, after all. But now I was talking to him—about school and other normal stuff—and I could hardly believe it. Apparently on top of looking like a god from a mythology book, he was a regular guy from the Research Triangle area of North Carolina who had to study and wanted to go to med school someday.

Eventually, we decided we'd had enough to drink, so we climbed back into Eric's car, but before we got anywhere near campus, he pulled into the parking lot of an apartment complex in Midtown. He turned to me with a grin and asked if I'd like to come in and listen to some music. That was fine by me. I was enjoying this magical evening and asking myself how this could be real.

Eric shared a two-bedroom with another guy who was also pre-med, so once we were inside, he led me to his room and closed the door. After he put on a Norah Jones CD, we sat down side by side on the couch, which had a lofted bed above it. He turned and put his arms around me and kissed me.

Somehow, although it was all thrilling and perfect, I wasn't nervous at all. I was just happy, and I hoped that after all these years of dealing with a number of Mr. Wrongs, I was finally with Mr. Right. Surely this was meant to be.

We continued our kissing, and I could tell he was about to try to take my sweater off. I stammered suddenly, "Oh, it's getting so late, and my roommate is expecting me back before one o'clock." I was lying; no one was waiting for me. My roommate lived with her boyfriend, keeping the dorm room only to hide that arrangement from her parents.

I wondered what the hell was wrong with me, breaking up this incredible evening. But Eric wasn't upset. He slowed down, still kissing me a little as he told me not to worry, that he'd have me back on time. We stood up, smoothing out our clothes, and left the apartment. This time, he took me all the way to campus and parked in a loading zone near my dorm. At the door, he pulled me close once more. Oh, he smelled so good. Soon our hug was over, and he said, "I'll call you soon."

"Thanks Eric. I had a great time."

◇ ◇ ◇

The next morning, I could hardly contain myself. I decided ten o'clock should be late enough for anyone to sleep when there was good news to be shared, so at exactly ten I called Amy. She had been my lab partner in many biology and chemistry classes since freshman year, and we had been close friends for that long, too. She had heard more than she wanted to about Eric since I'd met him in the spring.

She barely had time to answer before I said, "Amy, I went out with Eric. He is so perfect. I can't imagine going out with anyone else now."

I told her about our date. Although last-minute and oh so casual, it had been perfect in my eyes. It was totally real and human, unlike the intoxicating daydreams I'd always had about him, the ones that had been short on details and overly feminine and dramatic.

"So, do you have plans to go out again?"

"Not yet, but he said he'd call." I couldn't allow myself to think past this moment, or I'd start getting anxious and really screw things up. That was my special gift.

"Do you think you should have told him you were busy and made him try again instead of jumping to go out with him the same night he called?"

"No. This was two people going for beer, not a date for the spring formal," I said. "I'm not going to play games with him—that's high school crap." I knew he'd call soon; he had to. I wondered why I'd even told Amy about this. Her practical advice was eroding some of my elation. "Ugh . . . let's talk about something else."

We agreed that we'd get together for a quick dinner the next night and hung up.

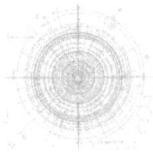

COLLEGE – Natural Forces

September 2002

Although I attempted to dive into physics after Amy and I hung up, there were a couple of things I just didn't get. I was lying across my bed rereading the textbook when Will called.

"Hey, how's the studying going?"

"Funny you should ask. There are a couple of types of problems I just can't figure out," I said. "We're allowed to bring in a formula sheet tomorrow, but my problem is knowing which ones to use."

"Easy," Will told me. "How 'bout I show you how it all really works, and you'll never have to worry about memorizing stuff again?"

"Really?" Did he realize I only had today to learn this secret of the universe he apparently had?

"Yep. Where can we get together? I just want to show you some basics in a real commonsense way. Then you'll always know how to tackle any problem you come across."

"I'll come to your house. Is that okay?" I was already gathering my book and papers.

"See ya," he said.

◦ ◦ ◦

I did great on my test the next day, and I must admit, a lot of that was due to the easy understanding I now had of the subject, thanks to Will. Understanding physics meant no more blind memorization and a more intuitive way of doing things. It hadn't taken long for him to cover the material I'd asked about, and it saved me a ton of time. I couldn't believe the boring textbook went on and on for an entire chapter when just explaining the damned concepts in clear English was more than sufficient.

As I left the physics building, I couldn't wait to tell him, and there he was coming toward me on the sidewalk.

"Hey Will, I got a ninety on my test! Thanks so much. I owe you one—wish there was something I could help *you* with."

"Way to go." He looked at me for a minute. "Actually, there is something you can do that would really help me."

"Name it." Since he was so nice, I knew he wouldn't ask me to do something horrible, like scrub the bathrooms in that old house of his.

"All right, mystery task. If you have a few hours, be ready Saturday morning around nine. Wear jeans and some sneakers that you don't mind getting just a little dirty. I'll pick you up, okay?"

I realized there might be some manual labor in my future after all. Oh well. Will was a great guy, so if he needed help with a project, I'd do it. Usually on Saturdays we'd gather at his house with food and drink to get ready to go to the afternoon football game, but this weekend we had a night game, so there was no conflict.

◇ ◇ ◇

Saturday morning, I took my pill, drank my SlimFast, showered and dried my hair, and put on just a little mascara and lip gloss. Will was cute, and I wanted to at least try to look decent.

At nine, he pulled his Jeep up in front of the building, and I hopped in.

"So, where are we going? Not your house?" I asked him. Surely, I could have walked up there if he needed a hand with some yard work or something.

"No, I've picked up a little weekend job I could use your help with," he said. "It'll save me a lot of time and be way more fun with you around. I think you'll really enjoy it."

I was a little surprised when we got onto the interstate and headed up I-75/85, but I was a lot more surprised when we kept going past the perimeter and out of the city. Where was this job—would we be building a barn? And he thought I'd enjoy it?

Once we got off the highway, we took a long road into a semirural area, and finally Will turned into a long dirt-and-gravel driveway. There was a wooden fence around the property, and a sign near the entrance said "Double L Farm." It turned out that the "farm" was just a house and a small barn, but I was still a bit concerned about what I was going to be asked to do.

Will drove past the house, straight toward the barn. Getting out of the Jeep, we walked on the hard-packed clay toward the open doors at the end of the building. Pleasant notes of cedar shavings, leather, and horses were on the morning breeze. Inside were four stalls, and brown horse heads stuck out over the half doors of two of them. One horse nickered at Will.

"Hello there, Sam. How are you today, buddy?"

Will laid his arm along the animal's neck and scratched his ears, causing Sam to tilt his head to the side in appreciation. He had a small white spot in the middle of his forehead, right above his eyes.

The other horse had a white strip running down the length of his face. Will told me his name was Copper, and that he was nice; I could rub his face. At first I petted him tentatively, ready to jump back if he tried to bite me, but he seemed placid.

"I have some friends who are out of town," Will told me. "They have a neighbor kid coming to feed the horses every morning and night, but I told them I'd come up and make sure everything's really in good shape and take them out for a little ride today and tomorrow, to give them some exercise and something interesting to do."

"Why can't you just let them out into the pen there and let them run around on their own?" I asked.

"Aw now, don't be chicken. An easy trail ride will be a lot more fun for the horses, and for us, too. They need to see something besides this barn, and seeing a few trees will do wonders for our own state of mind, I promise."

He opened a stall I had thought was empty and started pulling out equipment. "I'm going to put a bridle on each horse, and we'll take them outside and saddle them up."

Will went into Sam's stall and put the horse's bridle on gently, avoiding hitting his teeth with the metal bit. He led him out and asked me to hold the reins. He put a saddle pad and then a saddle on Sam, who stood nice and relaxed through the whole procedure. I petted his face, looking into his large, intelligent eyes. Then Will repeated the procedure with Copper, the reins just hanging to the ground for a minute while he put the saddle onto his back.

The horses were now ready for us to ride. They looked so tall. This always looked so easy on TV.

Will caught my eye. "For today, I think I'll let you ride Sam, if that's cool with you. He's a follower, so he'll stick close to Copper no matter what. Copper walks faster, so he prefers to be right up front. Are you okay with being behind us today?"

"Sure," I said, as brightly as I could. I wondered how the hell I was supposed to get up there.

"Usually, you'll want to get on the horse's left side and turn the stirrup like this." Will twisted the stirrup clockwise so it faced me. "That'll make it easier to get your left foot in. Then reach up, grab the saddle, and up you go—just swing your right leg over. But I'm going to give you a leg up since it's your first day."

He told me where to stand, then, stepping closer, placed his hand gently on my left shin to help boost me up onto Sam's back. Will showed me how to hold the reins and gave me a quick lesson on using them to turn the horse and to signal him gently to stop.

Once I was seated, Will swung himself up onto Copper's back and turned him toward the trail. Sam didn't need me to tell him where to go; he automatically followed them. Despite my earlier fear, I found myself smiling as we entered the trail beneath the canopy of leaves.

Will looked over his shoulder at me. "You told me you were into nature and animals, so I was hoping you'd love this," he said.

"I do—it's perfect," I said. I looked around at the trees and the well-worn path ahead of us. "You said the people who own this are your friends?"

"Yeah, I consider them friends by now, since I've been doing this for a while. They hire me to check on Sam and Copper and exercise them any time they go out of town. It's a lot of fun, and I'd do it for free, but they said if I won't let them pay me, they can't ask me to do it anymore. Really, if it weren't for the distance from home, I'd love to start every day like this."

"Wouldn't that be great?" I said as I patted Sam's neck with my free hand. "I'm adding it to my growing list of fun-to-think-about but unrealistic goals for life after Tech."

Hearing the horses' hooves as they walked, plus the occasional relaxed snort from one of them, added to the fun. After about a quarter mile, the trail became wide enough for us to ride side by side. I looked up at the sunlight filtering down through the leafy branches.

"Been meaning to ask you—I remember you're a mechanical engineering major. I know that can go in a lot of directions. What kind of stuff are you into?"

"Yeah, when I first got to Tech, I picked ME because I've been tinkering with things and creating gadgets ever since I was a kid, so I knew I'd love it. But once I started to co-op at a company that makes medical devices, it changed everything for me," Will said. He raked his fingers through his hair. "Solving problems, and dreaming up new possibilities, gives me the hope that I can make a real difference and even help save some lives. Kind of makes all the hours of class and homework a lot more meaningful." He caught my eye. "How about you? What are you hoping to do with your biology?"

"Wow, I sure wish I had gone first, because there's nothing at all noble about my dreams." I laughed. "I love microbiology and work part time as a research assistant at school, but since I got into molecular biology class, I'm hooked. Every day is like getting a little farther into a thriller book that doesn't have to end. So, I'm just a science geek hoping to get a PhD and work in an awesome lab someday."

"The world needs passionate scientists too," he said.

"I may embroider that on a pillow," I told him. Not that I knew how to embroider anything, but I could just see it. Maybe I'd make a little sign to put over my desk.

We were descending a slope, about to cross a small creek. The water was clear and only a few inches deep. Copper kept moving at his normal pace, but Sam stopped to put his nose in the water and paw at the surface with one of his front feet. It startled me at first, but it was cute once I realized I wasn't going to fall off.

"He's just playing," Will said. He and Copper were waiting on the other side. "He's been on this trail a million times, so he knows it's fine to cross here. He'll follow Copper once I get him going again."

After a couple more splashes, Sam and I crossed to the other bank. Once we were side by side again, Will looked at me. "I've been forgetting to ask: At Marily's party, right before you had to leave, you told me you like to draw. What kinds of things do you usually do?"

"Oh, mostly animals, sometimes an outdoor scene, and *very* occasionally a portrait of a friend. For people and pets especially, I work from a reference photo, because it takes hours, and I want to capture what they really look like, not the distorted 'cartoon' in my head."

"That sounds amazing. Would you show me some of your work sometime? I'd love to see it," Will said.

I met his gaze and nodded. I'd only known him a couple of weeks, but I already trusted him with my feelings, my authentic self. He would be kind.

We continued on the trail for another fifteen minutes or so, just making idle remarks when we saw something of interest.

The end of the path came into view, and we rode to the barn, where Will dismounted, then came around to make sure I got down without disaster. He showed me what to do, and we removed the saddles from the horses and gave them some water, brushing their coats well before Will gently removed their bridles and turned them loose in the corral. He showed me that from there they could get to an area with shelter and water if they needed it before the kid showed up at dinnertime to feed them and put them back in the barn.

Driving back toward campus, he asked, "Would you mind if we make one more quick stop? I need to drop off some notes at a buddy's house."

I couldn't think of any reason why not, and the morning had been so enjoyable I was in no hurry for it to end.

Pretty soon we got off the interstate and got in line at the Taco Bell drive-through.

"Free lunch today," Will said. "Carl can't get enough Taco Bell. What would you like?"

"Oh. How about a chicken burrito and a Mountain Dew, then?"

"You got it."

He ordered what sounded like a ton of stuff, with three drinks, so they gave us a little tray for those. The food smelled wonderful; I couldn't wait to get to his friend's house so I could dive in. We soon pulled up in front of an old house just a mile or so northeast of campus.

"Carl has an apartment in the basement here. He's a developer, and we have a little software business. A *tiny* little software venture."

"What, really?" I asked. "How do you have time for that?"

He smiled. "I do the fun part. I just dream up new applications and deal with the customers, but Carl has to work all alone, doing the coding."

We got out with the food. The guy who answered the door was a few inches taller than I was and had dark hair and soft brown eyes behind wire-framed glasses.

"Hey man, how's it goin'?" Will greeted him. "Lauren, this is Carl. Carl, Lauren. We brought lunch."

Carl greeted us politely but didn't say much. Will made up for that, of course, as we went inside and sat down.

"Sorry if we smell like horses. We've been riding this morning and decided to stop by on the way back. Hope that's okay." He got out a little notebook. "Okay, so I met with Anderssen a couple of days ago, and I have some notes on mods he wants made. Nothing major—I think we're getting real close to what they want . . ."

The two of them talked about the software as they ate, and I hungrily tore into my burrito. Looking around, I realized the only light in the room came from the sun streaming through a single window and the glow of Carl's computer setup. Apparently, he preferred to work in near darkness—or dimness, rather. A large desk dominated one side of the room, with what looked like a custom-built computer tower on the floor beneath it and two monitors perched on top. Both screens displayed lines of brightly colored code. A keyboard and mouse rested in front of them, and there was a laptop perched on a loveseat adjacent to the desk. I wished I knew more about programming. Carl's role in his little software company seemed like good, nerdy fun to me.

◇ ◇ ◇

Once Will and I were on the road again, I said, "I don't think your friend liked me too much."

"Sure, he liked you just fine. He's a super great guy, just shy around women. The only creatures he ever sees that look even remotely like you are in his comic books."

I laughed. "I'll assume you're not talking about succubi or harpies."

"Got something against succubi?"

We talked and laughed the rest of the quick trip to campus. When we pulled up in front of my dorm, Will shot me a playful look. "So, you didn't mind helping me too much today?"

"I guess it was all right," I said, but I knew he could see the happiness on my face. "But didn't you give Josh some all-out tutoring last week? Why didn't he 'help' you?"

"Now why would I want to go on a trail ride with Josh?"

I was still smiling when I let myself into my room.

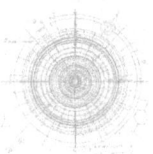

COLLEGE – Deep End

SEPTEMBER 2002

Today had been a fun day after all. I'd loved the horses and talking to Will. As I took off my sneakers and socks, my phone rang. It was Eric.

"What're you doing?" he asked.

"Um, I just got home from horseback riding. It was a lot of fun."

"Wow, all right, I wasn't expecting that. Want to get some dinner tonight?"

"Sure." It was something I had dreamed of many times, but I would have liked about a week to prepare for it.

"Okay, I'll pick you up at seven."

So, I had mere hours in which to transform myself from a horsey-smelling girl with barely any makeup on to a creature who would interest Eric Whitman. I fought a wild urge to call him back and say I couldn't make it. I didn't know what to wear or what we would talk about.

I knew why I was so much more nervous than I had been the previous week. Last time, I had stopped him at kissing, although I'd been pretty half-hearted about it. This time, I felt as if I was in way over my head and didn't know how to swim.

I decided on an outfit for the date. After getting out clean towels and my shower stuff, I headed to the bathroom.

◇ ◇ ◇

When I came back to my room, the phone was ringing again. Maybe Eric was postponing the date for a week. I would have been relieved. In fact, I'd have nothing but salads and water for the next seven days, if possible.

"Hey Lauren." It was Will. "Earlier, when I dropped you off, I forgot to mention the game tonight. Of course, a bunch of us will be going down together as always, but I wondered if you'd like to grab something to eat beforehand?"

"Thanks, but I won't be able to go tonight. I already made other plans."

"Oh, okay," he said. "I'm sorry I didn't ask sooner. I just assumed, you know."

He sounded disappointed, and I kind of was too. I loved the games, and I loved every minute I spent with him and his friends. The only way I'd ever miss that was if I was going on a date with Eric Whitman. And that was what I was about to do.

"Raincheck," I said, "all right?"

"Of course. Well, you have a great evening," Will said, and we hung up.

I dried my hair carefully and did what I could with my makeup. No one was going to mistake me for a supermodel, but I gave it my best shot. Then it was time to pace back and forth again and try not to be nervous. I had wanted to be with Eric for months, and now I had my big chance.

At exactly seven o'clock, he knocked on my door. I managed to say hi in a friendly voice when I saw him.

"Hi there. You look great," he told me.

I relaxed a little. His opinion was all I cared about.

Once we were in his car, he asked, "I assume you like Italian?"

I sure did. Soon we were parking in a lot near a brick building, which had a lime-washed finish and a curved copper shelter over the door. We got one of the last spots, and I could see the crowd of people outside waiting to get in. A sign with graceful scroll lettering above the door said "Giorgia's Ristorante & Bar."

Delicious aromas floated in the air, and Eric took my hand as we walked toward the entrance. My nervous feeling started to give way to sheer, heady pleasure. This was everything I had dreamed of.

He held the door for me, then stepped up to the host stand and told her we had a reservation. As she led us to our table, Eric pulled out a chair slightly—but I couldn't tell if it was for me or for himself, so I awkwardly took the seat across from him and thanked the hostess as she left.

Our server, Richard, appeared. Looking at the wine list, Eric asked some questions about a couple of reds. All of the names were new to me. Finally, he started to order a glass, but then looked at me. "Or should we get a bottle?"

"Yes," I said. I knew I'd be more than happy to drink whatever Eric Whitman thought was good. "That sounds great."

Once Richard had gone to get our wine, I picked up my menu.

Eric said, "So you went riding today? Did you rent a horse somewhere?"

"No. I was helping a friend with a little side job." I took a quick sip of water and added, "It was amazing how relaxing it was to get out of the city and see some animals and big trees."

Once Eric and I got started on our wine, I grew less nervous, but it was still tough to keep the conversation going. When our food arrived, I tried a trick Amy always used on me when we went to dinner together, which made me do most of the talking while she got to eat: I asked him an open-ended question.

"Pre-med, huh? What specialty are you aiming for?"

"I dunno. Something with no emergencies. Something where I can do interesting work and get paid very well for it." Eric forked some veal into his mouth.

"No emergencies—so something like dermatology?" I persisted, hoping I was being a good and interesting date.

"Nope. I hate sick people. Who knows. Got a lot of school left before I worry about that."

I smiled uncertainly. Simultaneously, we lifted our glasses to drink some more wine. I tried to think of something—anything—to say.

◦ ◦ ◦

After dinner, Eric opened the car door for me, and we started driving back toward campus. We talked a little about upcoming events, both on campus and off, and I was surprised and a little disappointed when he passed the turnoff to his apartment and instead drove directly to my dorm. I wondered if he thought I was too boring to even try to sleep with. He wasn't the easiest guy to talk to, but I sure had tried.

Eric parked in the loading zone and got out to walk me to my door.

"Thanks for dinner," I said.

"We'll have to do it again soon." Leaning toward me, he planted an unforgettable kiss on my mouth. He straightened back up, holding my hands, and said, "I've never dated a woman who's my intellectual equal before."

So many questions were overloading the pathways in my mind that all I could do was smile and squeeze his hands slightly. He was so far out of my league.

"Well, see ya soon." He started walking back to his car.

I hurried to my room, hoping Emily and Amy were available for some debriefing time.

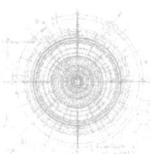

CURRENT – Writing for Freedom

AUGUST 2023

T he night after I helped Sean move to Tech, I had a lot
of confusing dreams. Nothing made sense, but I knew
that if I could do . . . something, everything would work out.
I couldn't quite figure out what that something was, but I felt
placid. I knew it was going to be just fine as soon as I could
figure it out, or—

The shrill beep jolted me awake. Groggy, still half searching for the answer I'd been seeking a few minutes ago, I stumbled into the bathroom for my shower. Time to get back to
mundane, mediocre work stuff. Except it hit me again: I had
that piece due for the huge personality website, and I had not
yet written it. If today was quiet enough, I'd do it at lunchtime,
stretching out that period as much as I could. My procrasti-
nation had been stupid; I was counting on opportunities like
this, and they didn't come along every day.

Although I'd never been great at literature or composition
when I was younger, writing about subjects that interested

me was fun, and I saw it as a path toward being able to set my own schedule and work in any location I wanted. Now that I was living in northwest Georgia, over eighty miles from Atlanta, and had been out of college for almost twenty years, the most I could hope for was the freedom to write blog posts from my little home office instead of having to commute to my soul-sucking job. That would be so enjoyable, if I could get there.

As I drove the five miles east to Doralabs, I sipped my coffee and let my mind wander, trying to come up with a topic. I hoped to do my work on autopilot and compose a killer article in my head, then somehow type it up before five o'clock.

When I got to our office suite, I took one look at my space and already felt overwhelmed. Nothing like being gone for even one day to make the tedious workload more unbearable. There was a messy heap of lab reports on my desk, and the red light on my phone was blinking. Hoping to at least read my email and get a mental handle on things before I had to deal with anyone, I powered up my computer.

"There she is." I jumped. Dan's booming voice had come from right behind me. "Get Ashley and Joe, and let's meet in my office in ten minutes to do some brainstorming."

I groaned and cursed to myself, then hoped I hadn't done so out loud. I sure wished this could wait till later. Like tomorrow, or even better, next month sometime.

I smiled as brightly as I could and said, "Sounds good." This was the only job even halfway related to science in this little area, so I had to stay in my boss's good graces until I could earn at least a partial living writing online. He continued past my desk, and I went to find my coworkers.

With the four of us sitting in plastic chairs at the round table in Dan's office, I shifted between trying to be concise with my own answers to keep the meeting moving along and completely zoning out when the others went down long, pointless paths of nonsense. I found myself tracing absent-minded circles in the margins of my notebook, my pen moving in lazy spirals. Each time my coworkers started beating the proverbial dead horse, my thoughts were irresistibly drawn back to Will and that courtyard. I felt a renewed ache of sadness that he was gone, despite the many years that had passed.

That summer after it happened, I'd avoided everyone but my sister and Amy, because life had been painful enough without having to listen to platitudes or having people who hadn't been close to Will indulge in speculation or casual talk about the tragedy. My withdrawal from the world was necessary to protect myself from the searing pain. But my friends and acquaintances didn't seem inclined to give me a pass, and many people stopped calling after a few weeks. They apparently found it insulting that I didn't want to go over the tragedy again and again with anyone who wanted to talk about it.

Suddenly I had an idea for my article: "Grief and the introvert." That was one thing I could write an in-depth piece about before the looming deadline with no research at all. No one knew more than I did about how we "quiet types" could be when it came to dealing with awful feelings. Immediately my mind was engaged, thinking of examples, thinking of how to introduce the topic.

"Lauren? Has that been your experience, too?" Dan was asking me about something he and the others had been droning on about. What was it? I had been vaguely aware of them discussing the usual problem we had, customers requesting "rush" lab reports, which guaranteed disappointment for them and stress for our group most of the time. I hoped that was what they were talking about, anyway.

"Um, yes," I could feel my face burning. I looked at Joe for a hint, but he seemed absorbed in writing in his Moleskine notebook. Ashley met my gaze, looking like she was stifling a small laugh.

Dan said, "I was asking about the regulations, what we were just talking about. Making sure all workers have a copy of them and really know the regs and aren't just operating on their memory or assumptions as far as what's required. Do you see similar problems to the ones Joe and Ashley mentioned?"

"Right. Sometimes, especially when someone has worked somewhere else, they assume they know all the regs, but . . . um . . . we need to make sure everyone's trained." I had no idea what he wanted but hoped the inane crap I had just said would do it.

Dan's phone timer sounded, and he silenced it. "Guys, I'm sorry. I have another meeting I need to get ready for."

I almost let out a big sigh of relief. It looked like I could finally go back to my desk.

"I'm booked most of the day. Hmm . . ." He made an especially annoying clucking sound with his tongue. "How about we go to Louie's for lunch at noon and knock out the rest of these bullet points?"

No. No! Lunch was sacred. He couldn't trample on my lunchtime. I needed it to write my article. Inside my head, I was screaming.

"And you're buyin'? Sure." Joe was happy, and Ashley agreed. I tried to look pleased and said that sounded great. There went my hopes of ever becoming an independent writer. If today continued like this, I could look forward to many years of these dreary meetings rehashing boring bullshit at Dan's round table.

◦ ◦ ◦

Somehow, in between handling lab reports, I managed to type up a draft and flesh it out by four thirty. Writing the article turned out to be as easy as writing an email to a close friend. I proofread it one last time and started on my author bio.

"Ah, almost that time." Ashley plopped herself down in a chair across from my desk and gave me an expectant smile. Usually, we'd spend these last few minutes of the afternoon in friendly conversation, but today the timing couldn't have been worse.

"Yeah," I agreed, looking up from my screen. "It kind of sneaked up on me. I'm trying to hurry to write a few more paragraphs so I can get out of here." She had no idea that I was freelancing, so I let her assume I was talking about a lab report.

She got to her feet. "I won't keep you then. Have a good one." She was off, probably to talk to someone else until quitting time.

Now I felt anxiety creeping up again, but I finished the bio and emailed it, along with my article and photo, to my contact at the website. The deadline was still minutes away. Now all I had to do was wait for the book offers to come rolling in. I laughed to myself. My hopes for this writing thing were almost certainly too high. Even if I wrote eight hours a day, I probably wouldn't make enough to buy my coffee. Better not piss off the people at my day job.

I shut down my computer, grabbed my purse, and got ready for the drive home.

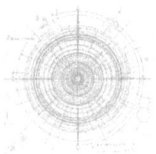

COLLEGE – Finding Balance

OCTOBER 2002

Two days after my second date with Eric, when the whistle blew and my last class was over, I headed downstairs to the microbiology lab, where I was a research assistant.

The first thing I had to do upon arrival was to prepare more culture medium for the organisms I'd be growing and working with in the next few days. I went to the prep bench and mixed some dehydrated medium with deionized water in a large flask. I got it started on the magnetic stirrer, then wrote in my notebook and went over the steps I needed to do this week.

"Lauren, do you have a minute?" It was Dr. Campbell, the head of the lab. He was wearing his battered white coat, his name stitched on the breast pocket.

"Of course." I stood up.

"Do you have any extra time in the next few weeks?"

No, I sure didn't. Definitely not. I was carrying a full load, including biochemistry, physics, microbiology, and a psych class. And I really wanted to have a good social life too, somehow. So of course I said, "Sure. What's going on?"

"I've been awarded a one-year grant from a private biotech company, and I could use your help with some of the prep work. It would mean about ten extra hours a week for you for a while, paid at your usual rate, of course."

Well, just as I valued getting good grades and enough sleep, I wanted this man to think I was the perfect assistant. He'd be writing letters of recommendation for me later, or at least I hoped so. "That sounds exciting. What's the new study going to be?"

I wondered where I was going to find ten more hours a week, but if Will could run a company and do little jobs on the side, surely I could manage more time at a job that was in the same building as some of my classes.

After Dr. Campbell had returned to his office, I removed the stir bar from the liquid medium and took the flask to the autoclave to sterilize it. As I went through the familiar motions, my thoughts turned to Eric. I wondered when I would run into him again and if he would call soon. I hoped the wait wouldn't be long.

◇ ◇ ◇

The rest of the week went by in a blur. Biochemistry was interesting but included a lot of memorization, which I'd never liked doing. At least physics was going well, thanks to the new way I viewed it, courtesy of Will.

Wednesday, I had lunch with Amy and confessed my anxiety over Eric and what might come next. Would he call soon and ask me on a third date? And what would happen then? Amy had her own drama going on with Bobby, her crush since freshman year. She had always gone hiking and done other fun things with him, but now some new girl named Alex had started hanging around, and he seemed interested in her.

"Why is this happening to us?" I asked. I was using my finger to doodle in the condensate on the side of my glass. "We're too smart for stupid stuff like this."

"If we really were, we wouldn't be waiting around for these guys," Amy said.

"Here's a thought—I'm going to do all the homework I can before dinnertime tomorrow and then grab some food and go to Will's and watch *Seinfeld* reruns. It's a fun group of people, and being there helps me relax for a little while. You want to come?"

"I don't know," she said, with a slight shake of her head, "I usually grab something to eat with Bobby on Thursday nights after my last lab."

I raised an eyebrow. "Guess what, Bobby? Tomorrow Amy's not available."

"It's really not a bad idea." She gave a half shrug. "I've been meaning to broaden my horizons. Okay, give me a call when you're headed over there."

"It's potluck and my turn to bring meat, so I'll probably bring some roasted chicken from the Kroger deli or something like that. If you want, we can kind of coordinate and get chicken and a large side."

We now had a plan to conquer the world.

◦ ◦ ◦

Forty-five minutes before the show started, Amy picked me up, and we went to Kroger, then to Will's. Parking spaces were precious in his neighborhood because the homes, originally designed in the 1950s for single families, now all housed multiple students, and everyone needed to park. Since it was relatively early evening, we found a spot just one house over from Will's. Carrying two large bags loaded with chicken and warm, fragrant yeast rolls, we gave a quick knock on the door before letting ourselves in.

"Hi guys," I said, pointing out Will, Josh, Melissa, and Drew to Amy as we came in. "This is Amy."

Most everyone smiled and said hi from where they were sitting—everyone except Drew, who stood up and came toward us, his eyes on Amy's face.

"Nice to meet you, Amy," he said. "Here, let me take that bag." He grabbed it and began walking with her to the kitchen. "Can I get you a beer or soda?"

Still standing by the door with my own bag, I was kind of surprised at how suddenly Drew had come to life, and I stood there staring, forgetting that I had the chicken everyone was waiting for.

Will finally called my name and asked in a teasing voice, "Do I need to take that bag for you, or do you remember how to get to the kitchen?" He laughed and tilted his head toward Amy and Drew, just visible inside the kitchen doorway, talking to each other as if everyone else was forgotten.

"It might make *me* feel a little more special if someone came and got it, and maybe opened a beer for me too." Even as I was saying it, I was taking the chicken to the kitchen and opening the bag, getting ready to set it out for the others.

"Everybody hurry and fix your plates. Don't want to miss the opening monologue." Melissa began helping us open the containers.

As we brought our dinner into the living room, I claimed the end of the sofa, Amy beside me and Drew on the other end. Will grabbed his food and slid down to sit on the floor at my feet, leaning back against the sofa and resting his plate on his knee. He opened his beer and flicked the cap toward the trash can. It hit the rim with a metallic ping and skittered under the armchair.

"Oh, I didn't see the potato wedges," I said, reaching down to steal one from Will's plate.

"Please help yourself, Ms. Mahan," he said, glancing up at me with a grin.

We ate and laughed with Seinfeld, then cleaned up and went our separate ways. Amy and I had been there for a couple of hours, just the break from studying and lab work I needed.

On our way back to my dorm, I asked Amy what she thought of the group. I was pleased when she asked, "So, that guy Drew. Is he pretty nice? Seemed like he is."

I assured her that as far as I could tell, he was exceptionally nice, except I'd never seen him quite as *animated* as he had been tonight.

She laughed softly and said, "Can you believe it? Just before we left, he asked if I wanted to go for a bike ride and have a casual dinner on Saturday."

Excellent.

Once I was back in my room and deeply into some biochem study, my phone rang, and my own Saturday evening plans were made.

◇ ◇ ◇

Saturday, we had a one o'clock game, and I went with Melissa, Josh, Will, Nick, Hannah, and Dave. It was a lot of fun as usual, but when halftime came, I started saying my goodbyes and making my exit.

"You're leaving?" Will asked.

"Yeah, I'm going out in a bit, so I have to go get ready."

He looked like he was about to ask another question, but he didn't. As I turned to go, he said, "Have fun, Lauren. See you later."

I thanked him and began finding my way through the crowd.

◇ ◇ ◇

Eric would be picking me up at four for our third date. We were going to the art festival at the park, then to dinner. But first, I had to talk to my team.

Amy answered my call on the second ring.

"Third date. What do I do? What if he wants me to stay over?" I was pacing my room.

"Go for it," Amy decided.

"Really?"

"Lauren, you've been analyzing this guy for weeks. Just see what happens." She was about to leave to get together with Drew, but it was just their first date, so she didn't have to be nervous like I did.

"I'll let you know how it goes," I said. "Hope you and Drew have fun."

◇ ◇ ◇

Every time I had dealings with Eric, I was a bundle of nerves, with my stomach in knots. But by now I was happily addicted, and I couldn't go back to a bland life with no highs and lows.

When four o'clock arrived, so did Eric. He greeted me with a big smile when I opened the door and put his arm around my shoulders as we walked to his car. Soon, we were on our way to the park.

The art festival was fun. We walked through the crowds of people, looking at paintings and pottery made by local artists. Occasionally, Eric would pick up an object and examine it in great detail, but he never said anything about whether or not he liked what he saw. I loved everything about the festival and marveled at how creative and talented the artists were, but eventually we had seen all there was to see.

"Where do you want to eat?" he asked me.

I decided to hide behind Amy in case he didn't like what I suggested. "I hear there's a new Mexican place a few blocks away. My friend said it's good."

"Then Mexican it is." He squeezed my hand. My stomach did a complete flip inside my body—I was sure of it.

I told him which way to go, and soon we were seated on the outdoor patio of the colorfully decorated restaurant, with the aroma of fajitas—and of course fried tortilla chips—wafting through the air. The background music was just loud enough to be festive, but we could hear each other talk. I was well into a top-shelf margarita, and I was feeling just fine. It was turning out to be a perfect evening, and Eric and I had finally spent enough time together for conversation to come a little more comfortably to us.

"Talked to my dad today," he said.

I had never heard him mention his family before. "Oh. And how's he doing?" It was all I could think to ask with what little I knew.

"Pretty good. Dad doesn't talk on the phone much. He and Mom just wanted to make sure I'm still alive down here." Eric grinned.

"Did you assure them that, on the whole, you're still alive?"

"Yep. I told them life has become a lot nicer in the past few weeks."

Did he mean me? I was fumbling, but finally smiled. "Well, here's to a nice life." I raised my glass and took a big drink of my margarita.

◇ ◇ ◇

As we were driving back after dinner, we approached the area where Eric's apartment was, and he asked me in what sounded to me like a meaningful tone, "Do you need to get home early tonight?"

"No," I said, full of bravado powered by tequila. "I can do whatever tonight."

He smiled, and without another word, drove straight to his apartment. I didn't allow myself to think ahead. I didn't know what the hell I was doing, but nothing was going to stop me now.

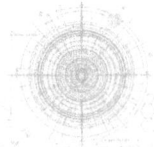

CURRENT – Ripples of Memory

AUGUST 2023

The Sunday morning after Sean moved to Tech, Eric left the house at seven, because he and his friend Ed were planning to ride their bikes almost a hundred miles. They'd follow the Silver Comet Trail westward all the way to the state line, then pick up the Chief Ladiga Trail and continue into Alabama. Usually, they would have left home even earlier than that, but we'd gone to a party at the home of a prospective investor in Eric's clinic the night before, so he had delayed it an extra hour in order to get enough sleep.

I straightened up the house and did a little light yard work. Emily and I had agreed via text yesterday that I'd come to her house this afternoon, so after an early lunch, I headed that way.

My sister was married to a human resources exec for a large manufacturing company. Richard was an affable man, and I always enjoyed seeing him, but today I was hoping for a good stretch of time to talk to Emily alone. They had two kids—Olivia, who was at the University of Virginia now, and Ryan, who was a sophomore in high school.

When I arrived, Emily said Richard and Ryan were off on some sort of Boy Scout project for the afternoon, so we had a chance to catch up. "Do you want to go shopping or see a chick flick, or what?" she asked.

Any other time, I'd have jumped at the chance to do either of those things with her, but today I wanted to fill her in on my strange episode. She hadn't known Will personally, but she'd known almost everything that went on in my college days, so this was a real chance to have a second pair of eyes on the problem.

"I'd just like to have some girl talk, if that's all right."

"Sure."

She poured us some lemonade, and we walked out onto her partially covered deck, where we could sit among all the beautiful flowers she had there. Her golden retriever Bailey followed us, his fanlike tail waving back and forth as he padded to a suitable spot to lie down in the shade. I made a minor detour to rub his head and baby talk to him a little before joining Emily at a dark bronze bistro table.

As we sat down, she looked at me and said, "All right, what did he do?"

"Hmmm?" I'd been thinking so hard about how to start my story that I had no idea what she was talking about.

"You look like something has really rocked your little world, and that makes me suspect Eric has done something thoughtless, tactless, or just plain asshole-ish. Please correct me if I'm wrong."

I laughed. "No, this is something entirely new. Something weird I have managed to get into on my own. Leave it to me."

She smiled. Yes, if anyone was going to stumble into the kind of situation that wouldn't happen to most people, it was me. I seemed to be lucky that way.

I told her that being back at Tech with Sean had really hit me hard. She nodded sympathetically. Emily had been my rock when the tragedy happened.

I described seeing the door and following the hall to the scene from the past, and her expression changed. Now she was wearing a little smile, her eyebrows slightly raised, keeping eye contact with me as she listened. I knew that face. I'd made that face. It was a tolerant "I'm trying to be encouraging, but I really don't get it" kind of expression.

"I know it sounds crazy," I said as I finished my story, "but I swear to you it was totally real. I wasn't asleep; it was daytime, and I was on my feet."

"Sure, I believe you remember that scene, but maybe that's because it really happened. A couple of decades ago. Could that be it? Do you remember sitting on the bench and sharing Will's lunch and having that conversation?"

It was funny—the memory was so fresh I felt like it had only been a few days since it happened, but I supposed it could have been exactly that way twenty years ago. Once again, I thought about the computer files I had from back then.

"I can check. Believe it or not, I have an old electronic journal I kept during college. But what about my recent experience?"

"Do you suppose it's like déjà vu? What is it they say—your brain has one or two similar things happen in sequence, so it makes a connection. It thinks, 'Hey, I've been here before.' Something like that?" She jiggled her glass to set the last few drops of lemonade free from the ice, then put it to her mouth and drained it.

"As I understand it, the feeling of déjà vu is caused by little mismatches and errors the brain makes, making us think or feel something is coming from our long-term memory when it's really happening right this minute. Wonder if the reverse happens too," I said.

My sister looked at me for a few seconds. "Well, I don't know what happened there, girl, but I do know it's midafternoon now, and we could officially switch to cold beer, if you'd like."

"Definitely." A hot Atlanta weekend afternoon called for an icy brew. "I'll get 'em, then let's hear what you've been up to this week."

I headed in to fetch the drinks. Bailey raised his head as I passed by, and I gave him a scratch, but he decided he didn't need to be polite and get up. I was family, after all.

◇ ◇ ◇

When I got home from Emily's, Eric wasn't back yet, so I just had the house to greet me. This time I didn't experience that empty-nest pang. I was feeling a bit obsessed about the campus visit and my college years and craved another sweet taste of those happy times. But was Emily right? Could this have been a reverse case of déjà vu? Could I have possibly just stood in that hall, vividly remembering something from twenty years ago but feeling like it was happening right then?

The brain is a funny thing, and I had learned about many disorders and symptoms of various kinds of damage in my abnormal psychology class. Still, it was one thing to read about something in a textbook, but quite another to entertain the idea that I couldn't trust my own mind. Suddenly I had a flash of understanding of the hell that must accompany severe mental illness.

Dying to find out more, I decided I'd at least see if what I'd experienced had really happened in the past. No one knew about my college journal except me—and now Emily. Somehow, I had never been able to delete the files, even though I hadn't been able to stomach looking at them again before today. Each one contained one month of entries, and I had simply appended to it each day.

In college, I'd had routines I almost never strayed from. I took my birth control pill every morning and typed my journal entry before going to sleep each night. If I ever slept somewhere else, I'd simply write it the next morning, while my memory was still fresh. That meant I now had a good way to go back to any month and year and read what I had written.

I had thought diaries were for middle schoolers, but at the beginning of my freshman year, my composition professor had urged us all to get a spiral notebook and write a page each day. I kept the required notebook that first semester, but I always had the professor in mind when I wrote. I filled it with reports about how much I studied for my classes, my wide-eyed wonder at the great diversity of knowledge, opportunities, and opinions I was finding on campus, and other matters that wouldn't cause anyone to look at me twice. Parallel to that, I started my electronic file, my real journal.

Long after that class was over, I continued my daily writing. I enjoyed the routine, and I also enjoyed being able to reread what I'd written. Sometimes the file would give me perspective, because if a problem hadn't lasted more than a few days, maybe I didn't need to get so anxious about a similar issue next time.

A few years earlier, I'd updated the journal files to modern formats and password protected them. They now resided in an encrypted area on my hard drive, which I had labeled "Women's Fiction" to make it even less alluring. Eric didn't care about computers and mysteries, though, so my little files were safe.

Feeling a twinge starting in my gut, I took a deep breath. The conversation with Will must have happened right before the fall semester began. We'd been talking about helping with freshman move-in week activities, so the timing shouldn't be hard to narrow down. Could I stand to revisit these memories again? I believed I had to. I could at least find out if the episode had actually happened or if I'd completely dreamed it up.

I found the entry I was looking for, from right before my senior year started. With my heart beating a little faster, I started to read.

As much as I love summer, I'm beyond excited about the fall semester. My senior year is going to be packed with great science and great friends, plus I'll finally apply to grad schools. This morning, I had to work a few hours helping with an event for the freshmen, but it made me a little money for a quick beach trip.

At lunchtime, I went out to the courtyard to get some sun and fresh air. I swore to myself I'd stick with SlimFast all day long, with no solid food to get me off into a snacking binge, but of all things, Will was out there with enough lunch for two, and he urged me to eat with him. He doesn't seem to have a clue about the fact that we women need to try to keep our body fat as low as we can manage.

I asked him where he's going to apply to work after he graduates. A lot of seniors will be signing up for interviews soon, and I wonder if he'll be among those camping out for the ones with the big-name companies that are thousands of miles from here. We have to go where the job or grad program takes us. I really can't imagine life without him, but I guess that happens with most college friends. I don't think I ever really laugh when he's not around.

I didn't see Eric today, but I'm still stressed out about where he will get into med school next year. Since I interrogated him and found out he's applying to Duke, Emory, UNC, Wake Forest, Virginia, and MCG, I keep wondering, what is his plan?

Starting next week, I need to get serious about picking a specialty and applying to grad schools myself. Just a bachelor's in biology will not get me where I want to be. I'm going to go deep into my field and join a team doing interesting research. All I have to do now is decide exactly what that field is. Ugh.

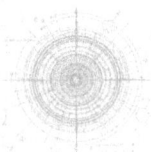

COLLEGE – Caught in the Moment

OCTOBER 2002

The weeks after my third date with Eric were so good I almost couldn't believe they were real. He called me every day, even if just to talk for a few minutes. I had to go to class and work in the lab and do homework, but every couple of days, he and I took a few hours to grab lunch or dinner and have some time alone. He was even better looking without his clothes, but strangely, although I was seeing a lot of him, I still found it almost impossible to talk to him about anything other than superficial topics, like crazy news stories and our classes.

"How is it possible to have seen someone naked so much and still feel as if you don't know them at all?" I was painting my nails Exquisite Scarlet while I held the phone between my ear and left shoulder and talked to Amy.

"What do you mean?"

"It's hard to describe. It's like, I can touch his skin all I want, but I'll never know what's going on in his mind, his heart."

"There's probably nothing going on in there, at least not while you're touching him and he's naked."

I laughed and accidentally painted the side of my thumb. "Ugh, I've made a mess. I'll let you go. Lunch tomorrow around noon? And I promise, it'll be your turn—we can analyze your date with Drew."

"Sure," Amy agreed, and we hung up.

I wondered what to do next. I had what Dr. Chen called "a little quiz" the next morning in biochem, and I had only worked three hours in Dr. Campbell's lab so far this week, thanks to my new delicious habit of spending so much time with Eric. I decided I'd better go there for a while, because bacteria grew at their own rate without regard to my social life, and I really needed to make and record my observations and continue the experiment. Then I'd have the fastest dinner in the world and study biochem until I could no longer keep my eyes open.

◇ ◇ ◇

Walking across campus to the biology building, I started mentally going over what I'd do in the lab. I had some agar plates in the incubator that needed to have their bacterial colonies counted. That had to be done soon, according to the protocol I was following for the study we were doing. I'd start with that. Then there was instrumentation I needed to use, and finally, I had to write summaries in my research notes. If no one else was in there, I could get it done in a couple of hours or less. Until it was finished, I wouldn't allow myself to worry or even feel stressed about tomorrow's test, because I could only do one thing at a time. I was only human.

As I turned a corner a couple of blocks from my destination, I was surprised to see Eric coming toward me, apparently from the chemical engineering building. He looked happy to see me and stopped to talk.

"What're you doing?"

"I'm headed up to the lab for a while."

"I think you need to come to my place first."

"Um . . . I really need to go to work." I lifted a hand to point vaguely in that direction with a regretful smile.

"Come on," he said. "I'll make it worth your while."

How could I resist? Did I want to give up everything and everyone around me for the slim chance of someday becoming a famous researcher who lived alone with her fifteen cats, or should I take a chance on trying to have a life with this stunning man? Hadn't someone once said you never regret the things you do, only the things you don't do?

"Well, maybe for a little while. I have a biochem test tomorrow though, so I'll need to study later. By the way, why are you so carefree?"

"I had three tests today, so I'm giving myself the night off. So, it's settled—let's go celebrate."

I had to go with him, just like the moon must stick close to the earth. With only the slightest twinge of stress, I turned my back on the biology building and followed Eric to the commuter lot where his car was parked.

◇ ◇ ◇

Thursday, I went to Will's for *Seinfeld* as usual. It was just Josh and Melissa curled up on the loveseat, Will and I on the sofa, and we were getting to the end of an episode when Will's phone rang. He walked to his room and answered it. I heard him talking for a minute or two, followed by the usual tones people use to wrap up a call.

A second later, I heard a loud bang followed by an, "Ugh!"

I stood up.

"No, no, you don't want to go in there," Josh warned me.

"Why not? He wouldn't bite my head off, would he?"

"Worse." Melissa laughed. "He'll make his problem your problem too. I'll bet you a beer he's overscheduled himself again, and now he'll be looking for a crew of 'volunteers' to make everything happen the way he promised someone."

"Yeah, we may have seen this happen a few times," Josh agreed.

Whatever it was, I had to help Will if I could. I stood up.

"So, you're taking that bet?" Melissa asked me.

I walked into Will's room and saw him sitting sideways at his desk, elbows on his knees, running his fingers through his hair.

"Hey, sorry," he said, straightening and letting his hands drop.

"What's going on?" I sat down on the edge of his bed.

"Oh, I'm supposed to have this huge project meeting Monday night, but now this kid I've been trying to reach—He finally called and asked if I'd help him with his math. Monday night. I'm the group leader for the project, but I can't change the date on all those other people."

"What kid?"

"He goes to the high school a few blocks away. I've told one of my friends who's a teacher there I'm available to anyone that wants study help, but this one kid has always been . . . aloof? Hard to reach. I really think he could do great if someone would take an interest, but now he needs it at the worst possible time."

"Well, what about Tuesday?"

"He has a review session Monday at school, then his test is Tuesday morning, so he was hoping we could go over some stuff Monday night. It's all right." Will gave a little shake of his head. "At least he called—I'll get him next time."

"What kind of math is it?"

Will's eyes locked on mine, and his expression changed from unhappy to hopeful.

Oh boy, he has me.

"It's just algebra, very basic stuff. And he seems like a bright kid, just kind of quiet." Will gave me a second, but when I didn't protest or interrupt, he continued. "His brother would bring him over here and get him back home after. You could work with him in my room."

I shook my head and snickered. "Go ahead and call him."

He lost no time in doing just that. "Brandon?" he said into his phone. "Today's your lucky day. For your first study session, I found someone who's a lot prettier than me. Oh yeah, she's wicked smart, I promise."

When I returned to the living room, I stopped by the loveseat and rested my hand on its arm. "What kind of beer would you like?"

She grinned. "Oh, we're going out. Girls' night soon!"

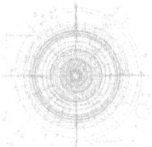

CURRENT – Seeking Understanding

AUGUST 2023

M onday, the day after I visited Emily, I got up an hour and a half early. I had a lot of work to do on the blog, and there were many reader comments that needed replies, which I'd put off for the past few days while helping Sean get his things organized and packed. I had several thousand subscribers by now, and I often got questions sent to me by email. I published some of them along with my answers, and readers would add their comments. Everyone knew I didn't have a PhD, but they appreciated the way I analyzed their situations and gave them insight into new ways they could approach their work and personal relationships.

I sat at my desk facing the window in my office, my favorite spot in the house. I could hear muted bird song and other pleasant morning sounds from our relatively quiet street. While I worked, I alternated between focusing and totally spacing out, as bits and pieces of the past came floating back to me. I didn't think I'd ever felt as close to another human being as I had to Will, before or after. I had my sister and some girlfriends, sure, but he and I really got and complemented each other on an intuitive level that defied description, even though he was as fearless and outgoing as I was careful and introspective. We never had to explain what we meant or how we felt to each other, and although we had wildly different reactions to a lot of things, we appreciated and respected those differences. He had been like a part of me, a part I'd lost forever but had been lucky enough to get one more glimpse of a few days ago.

Today I would get to share my little story at lunch with my friend Heather. We hadn't seen each other in over a week. Even if she didn't understand what had happened to me that day, she would empathize and appreciate its impact. I always felt better after talking with her. Hearing her thoughts and getting her perspective often helped me see things more clearly or deal with them better.

I finished an article about ten ways for detail-oriented people to be effective in meetings with impatient "big picture" folks and scheduled it to be posted at two o'clock, along with posts to my Instagram and Facebook page linking to the new material. I figured that would buy me time to get some work done at the office after a nice, relaxing lunch. Later, I could sneak in a little online engagement with my readers, replying to their comments during my afternoon soda break. I knew Heather, a paralegal, would similarly dump lots of information on her firm's clients right before noon so she'd be free for lunch while they read the documents and responded.

I hurried to get dressed and leave for work.

◇ ◇ ◇

My morning was uneventful, and that was fine with me. I was just getting ready to send off a lab report when I got a text from Heather.

Rosie's ok?

That sounded great to me, and I answered without delay. Mexican food and talking with her should be a pleasant escape from my empty-nest sadness and the confusion I'd felt the last few days.

At noon, I drove to Rosie's and parked in the lot. I saw Heather's navy-blue Hyundai pulling in at the same time. She looked great as always in a suit and heels, her blonde hair in a stylish cut.

It was all I could do not to start spilling my story as soon as I saw her. I told myself that ten more minutes of waiting wouldn't hurt. In fact, I deliberately delayed until we had ordered our food and made a little small talk, asking about each other's weeks. When it was my turn, I tried my best to describe my experience.

"I was feeling emotional enough leaving Sean on campus—I'm going to miss him so much and probably have to get about five cats. But then something really weird happened."

"What?" she asked, sipping her Coke and scooping up a generous helping of queso with her chip.

I described the whole thing to her as best I could remember it. She had not known Will, but I'd mentioned him to her once after a few glasses of wine. I told her about his kindness and what a lot of fun he was, although I'd never told her about the horrible day not long before he died. As much as possible, I had tried not to allow that memory to surface.

Heather listened to my story with a slight smile, looking me in the eye while I spoke. Maybe the smile was a little too sympathetic. "Wait, so do you think you were kind of asleep on your feet and dreaming?"

"I don't know. It felt totally real, but the guy I was talking to was Will. And I was young too. So of course it wasn't physically real." I took a quick drink of Coke as I searched for words. "But it felt as real as anything else I've ever done."

"Do you think the combination of Sean's moving out plus being on campus again made you go into a kind of . . . some sort of temporary crazy? The stress and emotions just made you escape to a happy place for just a little while?"

I admitted that had occurred to me, too. It had been such a loaded day. Maybe my little mind had simply snapped for a few minutes?

"Could be. But whatever happened, I think I wish it would happen again," I told her. "I used to take for granted all the fun I had talking and doing things with Will, but this time, I really savored it. I think I'd forgotten what it feels like to feel simple happiness."

"Well," Heather ventured, "I hope you can find new ways to be happy now, whatever happened a few days ago."

"Yeah," I said.

"I'll bet in a few days you'll be deep in a new routine and maybe a new hobby or two and will have forgotten all about this. And by the way, since you don't have Sean at home for a while, want to come to exercise class with me tonight? Mondays are core and upper body. I can bring you as my guest three times, I think, and you'll feel *great* when you walk out of there. I know I always do."

"Maybe so. You still like the classes?"

Now it was her turn to share what she'd been doing the past few days.

◇ ◇ ◇

Sharing my story with Emily and Heather had been comforting, but it hadn't done much to help me figure out what had happened to me. I appreciated their listening to my crazy tale, though. It would be hard to imagine telling it to most people and not getting ridiculed. I didn't know what else I could do or who to talk to next, and it was time to get back to work.

When I returned to the office, Dan pulled us into a meeting. Luckily, it was pointless and added little to my to-do list for the afternoon. After two o'clock, I sneaked online several times. I enjoyed seeing people's reactions to my newest post and replied to a lot of their comments. My readers and I were a community, representing all ages and nationalities, and I always looked forward to interacting with them. Because so many were in time zones well ahead of mine, I often posted before bed so I'd have their reactions the next morning when I woke up. Since I hadn't managed to do that today, I would simply keep an eye out for the next set of comments and questions, which was likely to pick up late this evening. Thank God for the internet. I couldn't have stood my life without it.

Now that Sean was gone, I planned to immerse myself even deeper in my online world. Or maybe it was time to sign up for some tough exercise boot camp or yoga. Just trying to keep up with the experienced and graceful people in those classes should give me something to concentrate on and get me out of my head for a bit.

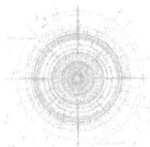

CURRENT – Ember of Hope

AUGUST 2023

T he next morning when I woke up, I thought of someone I should have contacted when I first got back from
campus. I texted my friend Janie to ask if she'd like to meet for
coffee, and we made plans to go to our usual place.

I showered and dressed and headed to Raven & Roast,
the newest cafe in our area. In the lot, luxury cars filled many
of the spaces. They most likely belonged to the young people
inside who were wearing expensive faded and torn jeans, but
fortunately the place was not too crowded yet and could ac-
commodate a couple of old ladies like Janie and me.

Janie was a few years my senior, but you'd never have
known it by looking at her. A professional artist who had
designed beautiful murals, she also did amazing commission
work, including painting fantasy-type pieces for clients. If
someone wanted a picture of themselves with realistic feathery
angel wings and perhaps a purple-and-aqua scaled tail, Janie
was the best person to turn to. She wore little makeup, but

her beautiful face was framed by wavy platinum hair that gave her an eternally youthful look. This morning, she was sporting a flowing indigo dress with leather sandals and lots of bangle bracelets.

Once we got our drinks, we claimed a round high-top table near the window. We hadn't seen each other in about a month, just one of those things where the calendar kept marching on despite our best intentions. She told me she had some painting commissions to do—a lot of them—and had been busy. She sketched and painted the subjects first, then added the magic parts.

Of all my friends, Janie was the most mystical. Well, Eric always said she was "witchy." Over the years, she had often spoken about her new age beliefs and other things I otherwise heard little about in our community. Her artwork sometimes included concepts and symbols that appealed to me in an "oh that's cool" way, but I must confess I didn't understand them or feel any motivation to find out more. Until a few days ago, I'd only been interested in the conventional natural sciences, nothing that could be considered woo-woo, unless I was suspending my disbelief temporarily to enjoy a novel or movie.

I threw my story at Janie to see what she would make of it, and she didn't disappoint.

"You feel you have to reject the fact that you really saw Will just because he's crossed over?"

Crossed over. That was pure Janie, but I already liked how it sounded compared to the horrible ways I had thought of it all these years. I nodded.

"We humans are so limited in how we're able to think about time and understand it. I hope you'll try not to let that keep you from recognizing that something important happened," she said.

"It was important to me, sure, in how it made me feel. But what do you think it was?" I found myself leaning forward to hear her answer.

"I think your spirit traveled to meet him. The soul knows no boundaries of time or space. Maybe you and he have some unfinished business. Do you think so?"

For some reason, even though I knew Janie didn't limit her ideas to those entertained by the average person, her comment struck a nerve. All those years ago, hearing that Will was gone had meant the end of his time on earth. It meant I could no longer talk to him, no longer see him. Ever again. But at the suggestion that we might have unfinished business, I felt a flicker of something exciting. Just the tiniest spark I was afraid to acknowledge, because I didn't dare to hope. I knew Janie was just a visual artist, not some sort of spiritual medium, but something about her statement rang true.

Was it possible that Will was out there somehow? Was it even a millionth of a percent possible that my thoughts or spirit had communicated with his in some form? Maybe my confused mind had transformed the contact to a little scene it could understand, the same way our brains will try to make sense of those optic puzzles and tricks? On some level, I could almost intuitively believe it without understanding it at all, the same way I could try to imagine infinity. I wanted to believe it, that's for sure.

I played with my mug for a few seconds, then managed to say, "We do, but I've always thought it was too late." I whispered those last two words, and the enormous lump in my throat forced me to stop talking.

Janie remained serene, as always. She folded her hands beside her cup, displaying a jumble of colorful bracelets. "We think of time in the only way we can observe and understand it with our limited physical senses. We usually think of it as linear, a sequence of events, with cause in the past and effect in the future, but maybe it's not that simple."

"Not that simple?" I said, desperately trying to remember anything I had learned about time and the universe in college twenty years earlier.

"Don't you think it could be true that you managed to travel and talk to him again, and you went to a time when he was physically there with you?"

Oh, how I wanted to think so. I felt another stir of excitement but was still reluctant to acknowledge it, afraid of the plunge of disappointment that was sure to come.

"Did you feel or hear anything strange?" Janie pressed. Seeing my blank look, she continued, "Did you have a feeling of leaving your body and traveling?"

"No, not at all." I laughed a little, although nothing was funny. "I just walked down a hall and opened a door, and there he was. And I wasn't me, like I am now." I waved my hand to indicate my face and body. "It was really a day in the past, because I was young too. By the time I'd been there a few minutes, I'd almost forgotten that it wasn't just a normal day a couple of decades ago."

"Keep listening for him. He put that door there for you to come to him," Janie said. She reached across the table and touched my hand. "The veil between worlds isn't as solid as we think, Lauren. Sometimes love creates doorways where none existed before."

She touched one of her rings and seemed to be thinking. "You know, in many traditions, they say love is a force that can transcend time itself. Maybe that's what's happening here."

I was touched by her words, a tiny ember springing to life inside me despite my rational mind's protests. Did I dare to entertain the hope that Will was reaching out to me?

I nodded and mumbled something affirmative. I finally remembered to observe normal social convention and asked my friend about her own life.

We soon turned our conversation to our usual topics, like gardening and Janie's pets. I always wanted to hear every word about her dogs and cats, because Eric said we absolutely couldn't have any at our house. He really meant it—he promised me that any pet I brought home against his will would be taken to the pound without delay. Beyond not wanting hair on the furniture or floors, he didn't want to be bothered with creatures that made messes and couldn't care for themselves.

From what I could see, Janie and her husband relaxed and enjoyed their lives. I knew they had dogs and cats and a large vegetable garden, and I usually loved enjoying those things vicariously through her stories. This time, on the surface I was talking with Janie, but my head was still buzzing from the tiny pinprick of hope she had given me. Maybe I had really been with Will. It had been that real. Telling myself I hadn't really seen or talked to him would be like telling myself I wasn't sitting at this table with Janie right now. I was feeling happier than I'd been in quite a while, letting a lively hope spread across my mind.

As we got up to leave, Janie hugged me goodbye. "Lauren, the next time you find that door, remember—love doesn't just transcend time. Sometimes it can change it."

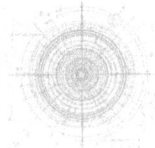

COLLEGE – Paths Not Taken

OCTOBER 2002

It was late October, and since we all rotated bringing various things to Will's for our potlucks on Thursdays, I didn't skip this one, despite Eric keeping me so busy. I had arrived a few minutes earlier and was in the kitchen alone, looking for a big spoon to put into the mac and cheese I had brought. Will came in and walked up to me, talking a little more quietly than his usual enthusiastic tone.

"I mentioned I'm doing a mountain bike race in north Georgia pretty soon, right?" he said.

"Yeah, I remember you were getting in shape for that. How's it going?"

"Great. I've put in plenty of hours on the bike and hit some real technical trails, and this Saturday I'm heading up to preride the course to check out the terrain," he said. "The leaves are beautiful up there now, and if you'd like to go with me, you could enjoy a little hike in nature while I check things out. They have a separate path just for walkers and horses, so you wouldn't get run over by idiots like me." His smile was adorable. "I wouldn't leave you on your own for too long, I promise. Afterward, I can clean up and we can grab dinner somewhere in the area, if that sounds good."

"Thank you for thinking of me," I said. "But I have plans for Saturday night and part of Sunday too, so I'd better just stay local and maybe do my homework that afternoon until it's time to get ready to go out." I'd found a spoon and was now doing a quick stir before setting the bowl out for serving.

Will leaned against the counter, looking at me. "Sorry, it was a stupid idea to ask you to walk alone. I was just thinking you'd enjoy the escape into nature. What if we do the main trail together? I can check the course features another day."

I left the spoon in the dish and met his gaze. "Thank you—it sounds wonderful, and normally I would be thrilled to walk in all that beauty and daydream while you ride your bike, but I really do have plans, and I have to start getting ready late Saturday afternoon."

The expression in his eyes was so gentle. "Is it okay if I keep asking you to come on foolish ventures with me?"

"Of course." I rested my hand on his forearm for a moment. "That's my favorite kind."

"Great," he said. "And meanwhile, if you ever want to do something, just call me and I'm there."

Before I could reply, Josh came barreling in. "What smells so good in here? And—hi guys; sorry if we're a little late." He grabbed the spoon, already fishing in the bowl.

Will laughed, his voice rising back to its normal exuberance. "Mac and cheese, your favorite. Hold on buddy; let me get you a plate." He opened the cabinet and pulled out a stack of plates, handing one to Josh and putting the others on the end of the counter.

Melissa walked in, carrying a large paper bag which smelled fantastic. "Hi Lauren, Will. We brought wings. We had to wait for them, but they should be nice and hot."

Will's eyes met mine for just a second—a quiet acknowledgment of what we'd been talking about before Josh and Melissa had come in. I returned his smile. The day he had proposed had sounded incredibly fun. I only wished I could have been in two places at once.

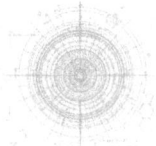

COLLEGE – Fault Lines

OCTOBER 2002

F riday morning, I finally made it to the research lab. Dr. Campbell was in his office on the phone, so I tried to sneak in and get started without drawing attention to myself. I put my backpack under the area of the counter that served as my desk and put on my lab coat. I walked to the incubator and opened it, but my agar plates were gone. My stomach lurched. What had I done? Had I plated out these bacteria and forgotten to incubate them? Had I left them on the counter at room temperature, where the organisms never would have multiplied, or had I simply thrown them away while drifting along in a daydream? All the horrible possibilities came to me in vivid images.

After one last desperate look in the incubator, I closed it and started looking in the cabinets under the lab benches.

Dr. Campbell came out of his office. "I was beginning to wonder if you were ill," he said. He didn't sound angry, but he wasn't smiling.

"No, um . . ." I couldn't think of what to say. "I'm so sorry. I had a test."

"Lauren, when you applied for this opportunity, you knew it would be a challenge to find the hours for it, especially since so many of our studies are time sensitive. It's not like doing research on inanimate objects that will wait for the next time it's convenient to work on them."

I nodded, feeling terrible, but didn't have time to respond before he went on.

"Also, the graduate students rely on you to have certain tasks performed so that they can continue their experiments in a timely manner."

"Yes," I began.

"I trust you will get your priorities in order."

"Yes," I said, in a voice that even I could barely hear.

◦ ◦ ◦

As luck would have it, a few days later, my problem of Eric demanding too much of my time was over, and I didn't know why. I had sacrificed so many things for the chance to be with him every time he wanted me around. I had ditched work. I had made some bad test grades, because instead of cramming in lots of extra details the nights before, I had rushed to wherever he wanted me to be. The sudden end to his calls and invitations had me feeling desperate and needy. So, I started obsessively analyzing my situation with Amy and Emily whenever they'd let me.

"Maybe he's just studying. He wants to apply to med school next year, right?" my practical sister reminded me on the phone.

"But that didn't stop him for the past few weeks. He wanted to be with me constantly. It has to be something I did the last time we were together." I looked out my window at the people walking by and wondered how many of them were worried about relationship stuff.

"What could you have possibly done to make him stop calling?" I heard what sounded like dishes rattling and water running in the background, so I guessed Emily was cleaning up after dinner.

"I don't know," I practically wailed. "There are two possibilities, and both are bad. One, he realized I wasn't getting any better in bed and he's done. Two, he's found someone else. He's so drop-dead handsome—how could he not have two hundred women on this campus alone?"

"You should ask him."

"I can't ask him anything. I'm stuck in this limbo hell forever. I always just wait for him to see me when he wants to." By now, I was up and back to my usual pacing.

"I have an idea," Emily said. "Why don't you use this time to study for your classes and catch up on the work you're supposed to have been doing all this time?"

Disappointed, I said, "Not helping, Em."

"I wasn't kidding. He may start calling again in a few days, so why not take this opportunity to accomplish the things you've probably wished you had time to do?"

I had to admit, if I knew for sure he was crazy about me but *couldn't* call me, I'd be happy enough. But could I really stand it if I didn't hear from him for several days? I didn't think so.

"Thank you. That does sound like a plan," I said, trying to lighten up. "But seriously, how will I ever know if he has someone else?"

"You've slept together. Wouldn't he have the decency to break up with you and not simply disappear?" she said.

Decency. I didn't know. I didn't really know Eric well at all, except how his muscles looked, how his eyes . . . I just didn't know.

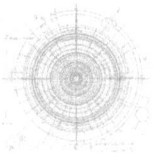

COLLEGE – Under the String Lights

November 2002

The first Thursday night in November, *Seinfeld* was over and everyone except me and the guys who lived at the house had left. I loved to hang out at Will's, so I was usually the last to leave.

We were finishing cleaning up when he said, "Know what? We have an away game this week. I think it's time for a party."

Dave said, "Let's do it. How'd we get this far into the semester without it?"

Nick agreed. "Hell yeah. I had a terrible electromag test today, and the days of studying leading up to it were even worse."

"You want to have a party Saturday, and it's Thursday night already?" I asked. I couldn't imagine taking on something like that at the last minute.

"Absolutely. We'll grab a keg and some chips and stuff. Easy. Dave's right—this is the first party we've had this semester, so we've got some serious catching up to do," Will said.

I supposed I should have been glad he'd thought of it tonight instead of Saturday afternoon. "Okay, what would you like for me to do?"

"First, I should see who has a keg available. In the meantime, could you start a list of people, so we don't forget anyone?" Will said.

"That sounds an awful lot like planning, coming from you," I teased.

He grinned. "Don't get used to it."

I still hadn't heard from Eric, and with my luck, he'd probably ask me out for Saturday night after not calling for so many days. But I'd worry about that if it happened.

◇ ◇ ◇

By early Saturday afternoon, the keg was in place in its metal tub, with ice all around it. Will and Dave were setting up a long folding table in the backyard and stringing some lights from tree to tree. Nick and Hannah were doing some house cleaning, and I could hear their laughter as they squabbled about what was "good enough" for each room. I had brought a lot of raw vegetables and ingredients for several kinds of dip and was preparing them on the kitchen counter. A huge supply of Solo cups as well as bags of several kinds of chips were piled nearby. I didn't know why I had thought we needed more time than this.

Once the dips and cut veggies were in the refrigerator, I went to find Will outside. "Is there anything else we need to do right now?" I asked. "I was thinking I'd go home and freshen up—maybe change out of this queso-stained T-shirt."

"You always look great, even with a little queso on you." He flashed me that charming smile of his. "But yeah, go home and take a break. You'll need your energy for an epic party."

He seemed to think for a minute. "Would you like me to pick you up later? Street parking will be tough to find close by, plus I could get you safely back to your door later if it's like two in the morning or something."

"Aww, that's so sweet, but no thanks. I'll be fine," I said. "I'll be back early to help set up."

"If you change your mind, just call."

◇ ◇ ◇

Everyone started arriving soon after dark, and the house and yard began to fill with friendly people and lively conversation. The backyard had been transformed by the network of white lights that crisscrossed overhead, casting a warm, magical glow across the space. Music from Will's extensive playlist was pouring from speakers in the living room, kitchen, and yard.

Amy and Drew were there, of course. She and I hadn't seen each other as much as usual outside of class lately, but we got together when we could. We enjoyed our usual companionship, but we no longer shared and analyzed details about our dating lives the way we had in the past, since I knew Drew and several of his friends. I was content to know that they were getting along great and spending lots of their spare time together.

I'd already gotten to know some of the rest of the crowd over the past few weeks. The new ones seemed to be really nice too, and several of them said they were glad to "finally" meet me. Maybe some of the people I already knew had mentioned a new face hanging around; I had no idea. It was a pleasure to talk to them all and feel so comfortable.

◇ ◇ ◇

I was in the yard by the long table, setting out some more raw veggies and refilling one of the bowls of dip, when Will came over, standing very close to me. The soft glow of the lights accentuated the warmth in his eyes and the curve of his smile. "You seem to be happy and relaxed tonight. I'm so glad, because I didn't have any luck finding a rental dog for you to play with," he said.

"Yeah, well, no wonder." I looked up at him. "You waited till the last minute."

"Totally my fault. Next time, I promise, it will be the first thing on the list."

"If there's always such a great group of people, maybe I can wean myself off of party dogs."

"I'll make it happen," he said.

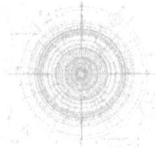

CURRENT – Life as It Is

September 2023

L abor Day weekend was the quietest I'd experienced in a
long time, and it started out a bit depressing. Eric was
content to do his projects and chores alone, and of course, I
appreciated the fact that he was capable and productive. However, until a few weeks ago I had never considered how much
we'd relied on Sean to make us a real family who spent lively
weekends together. I had some good friends, but I usually just
saw them for dinner or happy hour after work, with occasional
girls' trips.

Eric didn't care for the husbands of most of my female
friends, so he and I didn't socialize as a couple except for oc-
casions that would advance his career. He never said anything
bad about these men, but when he spoke to them, his tone was
patronizing, as if he found them dim-witted or not worth his
time.

I decided not to mope around hoping for an exciting holiday weekend I would not get. My friends would be spending it

with their own families, but the online world was open 24/7. Some of the most heartfelt emails and questions I received from readers came on holiday weekends, when people had time to let their problems catch up with them.

I had a question in the queue now that was really going to be a judgment call for the asker, but I threw out some helpful ideas to get her started. People could pay me for my time and have me focus on their situation and coach them, but I also answered and posted at least one email from the site's "mailbag" each week just to keep the web traffic up and to build my audience. The letter I was about to answer could almost have been written by me twenty years before. As I read it, an ache bloomed in my chest. This woman's letter made me see my own past in a new light—not because our situations were the same. She was consciously weighing her choices between two men, while I had been completely blind to having any choice at all. Reading her words, I saw something even more clearly than before. Back then, in those early days of our friendship, Will had tried. He had invited me to do things with him several times—casual dinners, little adventures—just the two of us. But I had been so infatuated with Eric, caught up in that whirlwind of attraction, that I hadn't recognized Will's intentions. Either I had turned him down because I had plans with Eric, or I had missed the significance of his invitations altogether, assuming he meant group activities.

I had never told Will about Eric, but he was perceptive. He must have sensed I was preoccupied with someone else, or perhaps he had simply assumed I wasn't interested in him romantically.

By the time football season was over that junior year, Will had stopped asking. He transitioned gracefully into the role of my best friend and confidant, still there, still Will, but never pushing.

Dear Lauren,

I'm a senior in college, and there are two guys I've been dating, but both would like to take things to the next level. It sounds crazy, but I could see myself being happy with either of them for the long haul. It's just that I can't imagine life if I didn't have both.

One guy, Chris, is very sensible, smart, and responsible. That sounds boring, I know, but we do have some laughs together. I love the fact that he has his act together. If we're going somewhere, he makes reservations, or if it's an outdoor pursuit, he has every supply we could possibly need. He even brings dental floss to picnics. On the other hand, he can be rigid, to the point where I feel criticized. He thinks he's always right, and I don't feel that he respects my thoughts on any subject.

The other guy, Ron, excels in just about everything he tries, but he often gets excited about new ideas and abandons old ones. He's an extrovert with a huge pack of friends. I never feel like I have an evening of Ron's time all to myself, but he keeps asking me out, and he's very relaxing and lots of fun. He never criticizes me or anyone else. If a disaster were coming, I think he'd be the one having fun until the last minute, insisting it wasn't that bad. Me, I'm an INFJ—introverted but very empathetic, and probably too sensitive for my own good, as you know from our personality type. Chris hurts my feelings sometimes, but it scares me that Ron isn't quite "grown up." What do you suggest?

Between a Rock and a Totally Different Rock in Denver (she/her)

As I prepared my response, I felt as if I were writing an email to a friend about Will and Eric. The reader's friend Chris understood facts and figures, no doubt, but Ron, with his fun energy, surely had almost irresistible chemistry with her, along with their deeper emotional connection. Will and I had had that—something almost magical. We dreamed together, told wild stories, and shared a connection I'd never found with Eric. I didn't think Eric had enough imagination to even have crazy ideas, and if he did, he'd never have mentioned them, because to him that sort of thing was a total waste of time.

My gut reaction was to urge the woman to go with Ron. Sure, life might be a little more unpredictable than she would like, and he might always have people around, which she might grow tired of sometimes, but if she wanted to feel 100 percent alive . . .

I realized my own mistakes and prejudices were getting in the way, creating a dirty lens through which I was looking at the situation. This woman's decision couldn't be as simple as that. I started writing a detailed response, pointing out to her the pros and cons of each choice. If security and predictability meant more to her, then could she let go of the fact that Chris was always calm and rational and not particularly fun or passionate? Or if she wanted someone who could share her emotional highs and lows and bring more excitement and laughter into her life, could she see herself enjoying being with Ron even if he had lots of friends over every week—or even every night? Would it be all right if she often found herself winging it with him instead of having the security of reservations and a plan? I urged her to take her time getting to know each guy better, seeing how they could fit into her life. To try not to take Chris's suggestions and observations personally. To step back and let Ron do some of the thinking and planning. And to see where all that led her.

As I finished the second page of suggestions, Eric stuck his head in my office. "I just went to Mr. V's and got us a couple of filets. Why don't you make us some drinks while I start marinating them?"

"That sounds great," I said, brightening.

I saved my work and scheduled the letter to post to the blog later in the evening, then walked into the bar area of the kitchen to make cucumber martinis. It was going to be a decent night. We could sit outside and have drinks and grill the filets and learn to have fun again, just like other empty nesters. I'd take my own advice and not expect my husband to appreciate my dreamy side, but just accept him for who he was.

I sampled my drink, automatically relaxing a little as I felt a tiny, pleasant buzz beginning. My thoughts about college would soon recede, no doubt, and the strange and compelling experience from a couple of weeks ago would surely fade.

◇ ◇ ◇

A few days later, it was my birthday, so I had taken the day off from work. Eric was already gone when I woke. He had mentioned no reason for it, but he also liked to work out early sometimes, then shower at the gym before going to the office, so I assumed he had done that. Still, as I got up and went to the kitchen, I couldn't help checking and hoping there would be a note or a card, but found nothing. Oh well. I was going to enjoy today no matter what.

I made some coffee and sat down with my iPad to read my Facebook messages. That cheered me for a bit—people I never talked to otherwise wishing me a happy birthday. I realized it was meaningless and automatic for many of them, but I still enjoyed the greetings. At eight, I got a text from Emily.

Happy birthday. Still coming for dinner and cake tomorrow?

I replied that I wouldn't miss it. I was a lucky woman to have my wonderful family.

By ten, I'd gotten another message, this one from Sean.

Happy birthday Mom

I replied:

Thanks. Having dinner at Aunt Em tomorrow if you care to join

After a minute, he responded:

Thanks but no time

Of course I understood. He was already well into the fall semester, and the drive to Emily's and back alone would have taken a couple of hours.

I almost rushed off to start doing something productive, but decided to dawdle with my coffee. It was my damned birthday, wasn't it?

◇ ◇ ◇

When I got back from running errands late that afternoon, Eric was already home, bent over a project at his little workbench in the garage. Did he remember what day it was?

When I got out of the car, he said, "Happy birthday. Guess we want to go to dinner tonight."

"Sure."

"Okay, anywhere you want. You're the birthday girl." He went back to examining the piece of equipment he was working on.

I stood there for a minute until I realized he wasn't going to say anything further. Without another word, I went into the house to find my iPad so I could start looking at restaurants and menus.

◇ ◇ ◇

For my birthday dinner with Eric, I chose to go to Sarah, a relatively new restaurant in our area. I'd been once before, with Heather. It had elegant décor and great food, but it was comfortable and not too fancy. Luckily, they had a table available when we arrived, since we didn't have reservations.

Eric ordered a nice bottle of wine, then we settled in with our menus.

He asked, "What did you do today? I thought you'd gone to work, until you got home with those bags."

"Yeah, I took the day off. Something about being in excruciating meetings on my birthday just doesn't sit well with me." I tried to say it in a lighthearted way, but I'd never been more serious. There was no way I was going anywhere near Doralabs on my birthday.

Our wine arrived, and he approved it. I was glad to get my glass, and it was heavenly.

"Why do you work there if it makes you miserable?" he said.

It was strange—I had been married to Eric for nineteen years now, yet I couldn't or wouldn't use my words to ask what he meant by that. Did he mean there were other places to work in our area? Or did he mean that now that Sean was out of the house, I didn't need to live in Green Valley at all? My crazy mind often took things from A to B and then all the way to Z, and that had served me well on standardized college entrance exams, but not so much with men. I didn't press him; I decided I didn't want to know.

"It's not that bad," I said. "I just wanted to be queen for a day, I guess. And how about you? I noticed you were home early."

"Yep, the last patient of the day canceled, so I threw all the files on Trudy's desk and told her they were her problem. Then I got the hell out of there."

Trudy at his office always took care of transcribing paper notes and results into the patient portal, but I hoped he hadn't really said that to her. Or maybe he'd been joking. Who cared. I went back to enjoying some more of the delicious wine.

◦ ◦ ◦

When we got home, Eric had a present for me. It was from a trendy boutique near his office, and it was gift-wrapped. Inside the package was a narrow belt made from very soft leather.

"Thank you. It's beautiful," I told him.

"Glad you like it. I hope it goes with some of your clothes. I told the girl in the store I thought you were about her size."

I laughed, although I knew he was probably telling me exactly what had happened. I was happy to hear he hadn't sent Trudy. I knew she had done a lot of his errands in the past, and she'd told me she didn't mind a chance to get out of the office, but I was glad he had cared enough to go himself.

"It's going to go great with lots of my stuff. Thank you."

Eric looked pleased. He wandered off toward his laptop, and I went in search of my iPad.

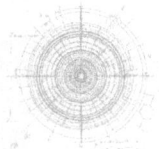

COLLEGE – Rocky Trail

NOVEMBER 2002

The Saturday after Will's party found me with Eric again. He had called two days earlier, asking me to come hiking with him in northern Georgia. He had given me a detailed list of things to wear and bring, and one of them was hiking boots. We'd be walking about eight miles—four in and four out. Although I'd never hiked that far in a mountainous area, I figured anyone could put one foot in front of the other. How bad could it be? I certainly walked all over campus every day. I had boots I had bought the year before, but I'd only worn them enough to break them in, and boy were they heavy. They were supposed to be good for crossing creeks, protecting ankles, and just about anything that could happen.

Unfortunately, now that we were on the trail, I was getting exhausted from walking with them on my feet. I hated to admit it to myself, but this hike was starting to be not so fun. As we wound our way up the trail, it became a little steeper, cutting through a young forest. The leaves were flaming red, orange, and yellow, and occasionally I could hear the rush of water nearby. Oh, how I would have loved to take my boots off and look at the water and those beautiful trees while I soaked my feet. I kept trudging along, though. I had wanted to be with Eric for months, and I wanted to show that I was someone he could have fun with.

A couple of times when he'd gotten a little ahead of me, he'd looked back and asked, "Are you okay?"

I said I sure was, and that I was having a great time. But after about an hour of that, I felt as if I couldn't pick my feet up much longer.

"How's it going? You gonna make it?" he asked, looking back to see why I was going so slow.

I tried to smile. "I'm not used to this. How about a little rest next time we find a rock big enough to sit on?"

"Do what you want," he said. "I want to make it to the peak before lunchtime."

Without another word, he kept walking at the same pace, not looking back at me again. I was stunned and wondered what I had done wrong. I was just so damned tired, and my feet felt like they each weighed about fifty pounds.

I made it to a clearing and stopped walking, leaning against an enormous oak tree as I looked around. Thank goodness I had my own water bottle. I drank a little and tried my best not to cry, although I was angry and full of self-pity.

A few minutes later, I heard people talking, getting closer. Two women, a man, and a black dog were coming around the curve toward me. One of the women, who had curly brown hair and large, kind blue eyes, looked at me with concern. "Everything all right?"

"Yeah. Thanks. I'm just tired," I assured her, putting on my brave-girl smile. I still couldn't believe Eric had left me like that. Was I supposed to wait here until he returned from the summit? And he had all the food.

"We're going to go a little farther up the trail, then we'll stop for a snack. Would you like to walk with us? We have plenty of cheese and crackers—and wine."

These people must be angels. I straightened up and took a few steps toward them, grateful that they had stopped for me. "Sounds like heaven. Thanks."

The black dog came rushing forward, panting happily and sniffing the hand I offered him.

"That's Russ. He's never met a stranger. I'm Rachel, and this is Mary, and this is Ben."

We all exchanged smiles and hellos as I continued up the trail with my new friends, looking forward to getting off my feet and enjoying some wine and cheese. To hell with Eric.

⋄ ⋄ ⋄

Later, as our little group neared the top of the mountain and the most spectacular view I'd ever seen, Eric appeared, nimbly making his way down the rocky trail. "There she is," he said in a hearty voice. "Thanks for taking care of her," he told the group. He put his arm around my shoulders. "Someone needs to get in better shape before she tries hiking again."

"It's not only that." I wanted to justify my failure. "It was my feet. These boots are too heavy."

Eric didn't say a word, but he pointedly held out one foot so that I could see his own leather hikers. "You've made it this far. Let's let you see the view before we go back to the car."

I was so angry I didn't speak. Angry at him, angry at myself—totally furious. I stalked beside him as best I could, although my feet were once again getting heavy. At the top, he took my shoulders and turned me around to face the vista.

"There. Isn't it great?"

I was so furious and exhausted I was afraid I'd cry and ruin the whole day. So I nodded silently, keeping my back to him, pretending I was just looking around and examining every angle of the beautiful view.

He turned me back toward him and kissed me on the lips. "You still mad at me?" He looked as if he were holding back laughter. The bastard.

"I'm not angry. But I want a hot bath and about a gallon of something cold to drink."

With a grin, he took my hand and started us walking back. *If I ever make it to that car,* I thought, *I'm going to get these boots off my feet even if I have to cut them off myself.*

◇ ◇ ◇

When we got back to Eric's and I finally got my boots off, I noticed him staring at my forearm. There was a cut I hadn't even felt, probably from brushing against something in the woods. It wasn't a big deal, hardly worth mentioning, but of course he'd noticed.

"You should wash that," he said. He disappeared into the bathroom for a moment, then came back with some antiseptic and antibiotic ointment. "We'll need to make sure it doesn't scar. Looks like it's deeper on that end."

I looked at the tiny cut again. "I'm pretty lucky," I said, shrugging. "My scars usually heal eventually."

He raised an eyebrow. "Then they're not scars, are they?"

I suppressed a sigh, knowing that whatever I said next would also be wrong.

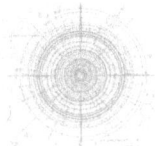

COLLEGE – Kitchen Music

November 2002

The next Saturday was a game day, but it would be a night event, so that morning I went to Kroger to grab some beer and snacks to restock the supplies at Will's house. Everyone who hung out there brought extra food and drinks periodically, and this was an easy time for me to do it. I grabbed a couple of bags of tortilla chips, a box of crackers, smoked Gouda, aged white cheddar, salsa, and four mix-and-match six-packs of craft beers that I knew Will and the others liked.

When I got to Will's, his Jeep was in the driveway, so I loaded the bags into my arms as best I could and knocked on the door with my elbow. Will seemed surprised to see me. He let me in with a big smile and grabbed the heaviest things from me.

In the kitchen, as we put the supplies away, he said, "I was gonna call you in a little while. You know our game is at 7:30. I assume you want to go?"

"Oh yeah, wouldn't miss it," I said as I put the bottles in the refrigerator. "This has been the most fun football season, thanks to you guys."

"Glad to hear it! Yeah, it's been great." He leaned back to face me, putting one hand on the counter behind him. "So, I know gameday traffic will be gridlocked around here during dinnertime, and we probably don't want to go out, but how about I pick you up before all that starts, and I'll make you my famous burritos before the game?"

"Sounds great. Want me to bring something? How many people will there be?"

Will hesitated for just a second. "Well, you're actually the first one I asked," he said. "Figured I'd see if you were in before inviting anyone else. But I have everything we need. We can cook here together, if you're up for it."

"I'd love it. But I'll walk up here. Don't move your Jeep, or we might come back to find someone's big-ass Excursion parked diagonally in the driveway."

He laughed. "Always the planner, but you're right, as usual."

◇ ◇ ◇

Cooking with Will was a blast. He had music going, and soon we were chatting and laughing while we sipped cold beer and chopped vegetables, chiles, and cilantro. He had grilled some chicken right before I got there, because he knew I liked it better than beef in my burritos. What a sweetie.

Once we had everything cut, Will combined diced tomatoes, onions, jalapeños, and cilantro in a bowl and squeezed lime juice over it. After adding a pinch of salt and pepper, he gave it a quick stir.

"Okay, taste test time," he announced. He broke off a bite-sized piece of tortilla chip and scooped up some of the pico de gallo, then held it near my mouth. Being hand-fed by a cute, playful guy was definitely a first for me, but I leaned in. The flavors were incredible—bright and fresh, with just the right amount of heat.

"Absolutely perfect," I said.

Will fixed another bite for himself. "Yep, perfect!"

Next, I shredded the chicken while he roasted peppers and onions in a sizzling cast-iron skillet. As their edges caramelized, the kitchen filled with a delicious aroma. This little home tailgate was coming together.

We started on the guacamole. I diced more onions and jalapeños and tore up some cilantro, and Will mashed avocados and mixed it all up according to his "secret" recipe—which apparently involved a pinch of cumin and an extra splash of lime. He hummed along with the music, occasionally singing a line or two in my direction, making me laugh. As we finished, I was feeling bold and festive, so I tore off a section of a tortilla and wrapped some guac in it, then held it out for Will to try. He moved closer, and I popped it into his mouth.

His face brightened in approval as he chewed. "Damn, Mahan! I think we got it."

Just then, the front door opened, and our friends piled in. Will and I hurried to arrange the last of the fillings and toppings as everyone grabbed plates and the kitchen came alive with conversation and laughter.

"Will, you had to go and raise the bar for pregame food, huh?" Dave teased.

"Burritos with those amazing-smelling vegetables would be impressive enough, but *grilled chicken*?" Hannah said as she spooned some pico de gallo over her burrito. "Is this a special occasion we didn't know about? Maybe we should have dressed a little better." She laughed.

"Hey, when you've got the perfect sous chef, you gotta show off a little," Will said, draping an arm around my shoulders.

Josh loaded his tortilla with chicken and roasted vegetables. "Well, whatever inspired this feast, I'm not complaining."

"Seriously though," Melissa said, swiping a piece of chicken from Josh's plate, "this sure beats our usual chips and beer."

Will looked at me. "Lauren's the one who suggested we actually make something. Would have been the same old stuff otherwise."

I smiled and shook my head. "Nope. He's the one who thought of it and made it happen. I just helped with prep work and a little quality control."

"Quality control?" Nick raised an eyebrow. "Is that what you guys are calling it these days?"

Will laughed. "We had to make sure it all tasted good!" He glanced at me, his eyes happy, then turned back to the group. "All right, dig in everybody. And check the fridge—Lauren brought some amazing craft beer."

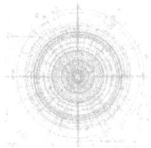

COLLEGE – Expectations

JANUARY 2003

It was early January, and "spring" semester of our junior year had started. I had left campus on a rare free afternoon to get a haircut and look for a new outfit, and my brake light came on. As I signaled and pulled into the nearest parking lot, I tried to figure out what to do. I knew nothing about cars, aside from that you had to keep the gas tank full and get the oil changed every five thousand miles. So I did what I would have done to my PC: I turned the engine off and started it again, hoping that would reset it. But as I drove slowly from my parking spot, the damned light was still on. I cautiously applied the brake, and it seemed to work. So, what was wrong? I got out my phone and called the landline at Will's house, hoping someone would pick up.

Will answered. I was so glad to hear his voice.

"Hey, it's me. I'm in Midtown and my brake light just came on, and I'm kind of scared to drive in traffic. Should I get the car towed? Or would it be safe to drive it to a mechanic?"

"Does it stop like usual?"

I drove a few feet, and it felt okay—no strange sounds or anything. "Yeah, it stops just fine."

"Why don't you take it real easy and drive to my house? I'd be glad to take a look at it this weekend, okay?"

I hadn't realized how tense I felt, but now I relaxed. I wouldn't need the car again until next weekend, anyway. I eased out of the lot and started driving toward Will's house, staying well behind the vehicles in front of me. By the time I got to Will's, I had almost forgotten about the stupid light. He was going to take care of it. And I had made it.

Dave let me in, telling me Will had left.

"That's okay. I'm going to leave my key on his bed. I'm having a little car problem, but he's going to fix it."

"Need a lift anywhere?"

"No thanks. I think the walk will be kind of nice."

And off I went. I was lucky to have a mechanical engineer for a close friend.

◇ ◇ ◇

The weekend came and went without Will mentioning the car, and I didn't want to bring it up either. I was at his house Saturday morning to grab a book I'd left there, and I assumed he was planning to work on the car that day. But shortly after I arrived, someone called him, and he left. I didn't hear from him the rest of the weekend, so I knew my car was still at his house, needing repair. By Sunday night, I realized I had no idea how long I'd be without it.

All week, I was anxious, but I still didn't mention anything to Will. Clearly, he had forgotten about the car. I certainly hadn't expected him to fix it when I called him that day; I had been scared and just wanted him to tell me what to do.

Friday afternoon, I did something I had never done before. I called Eric. Whether or not he was serious about me, I desperately needed his help. He listened to my description of the problem and said that the fix would be simple.

In contrast to my usual adoring manner, I was a bit impatient and demanding. I couldn't let someone else make empty promises and leave me with no way to do my errands. I said, "Please just do it. Whatever it needs, do it tomorrow."

Saturday morning, Eric picked me up, because I'd told him I didn't want to drive my car until it was fixed. He was wearing an old sweatshirt and faded jeans. No matter how he dressed, he looked incredible, but I was so anxious it hardly affected me.

Will wasn't home, but Nick let me in. I went to Will's room and found my key on his dresser. Grabbing it, I went outside, where Eric was waiting.

We left Eric's car on the street and took my car to Eric's apartment complex, where he could work on it in the lot. While I waited outside, he trotted upstairs and came back out with an immaculate toolbox. Of course. He worked both inside the passenger compartment and under the hood for about thirty minutes, and it looked to my inexperienced eye like he was checking and cleaning some connections.

"So, what was the problem?" I asked.

"You don't need to know," he said, smirking as he strode past me, carrying his tools back to his place. Properly silenced, I was angry at him, but I was also grateful. He might be an ass, but he was a reliable and capable one.

When Eric and I got back to Will's neighborhood to pick up his car, he said, "There wasn't anything mechanically wrong with your car or any danger, but I knew you'd never stop worrying if that light stayed on." He had his little smile on and reached over and tousled my hair a little.

"No doubt. And thank you for fixing it. Dinner's on me tonight if you're free."

◇ ◇ ◇

Will called just before five. "Where's your car? And your key isn't here, so I assume you got it?"

"Yeah, someone else fixed it. But thanks."

"But I was going to fix it. I was planning to do it right now, because there's still plenty of daylight left."

"No problem. Thanks for the offer. I'm all good now."

The guy was wonderful, but time meant nothing to him. Who could live like that?

◇ ◇ ◇

That night after dinner, Eric and I went to a comedy club. The show was great, and we had a lot of laughs and some great drinks. As always, he held my hand as we walked to and from the car. He was always physically affectionate, even though he'd never once told me about any emotion he'd ever had, even annoyance or anger.

When we got back to his place, he pulled two beers from the fridge and decided to show me some of his photos. I had never been near his computer when it wasn't locked, so this was new. Was I finally going to get to know the guy I'd been going out with since last semester? His images weren't a big, disorganized mess like mine were though; he already had the folder he wanted to show me ready.

"This is my sister. She's at Penn now," he said. The picture was of a smiling woman standing next to a large rose bush in what looked like a park. "I don't think she eats—she stays so skinny."

"Oh no, she's not skinny," I said. "She looks great." And she did. She was as beautiful as he was, with the same almost-black hair and azure eyes.

"Right," he said. "Skinny is . . . perfect."

I had walked right into that one. I didn't comment. I also got to see a few pictures of family vacations at fancy-looking resorts, as well as a few of old girlfriends, all the way back to when he'd been in ninth grade. They were all striking and slim, and most had blonde hair. My own hair was light brown, and although I wasn't overweight, no one would ever have called me skinny.

"What about your pets? That's what I want to see," I said.

"My mom had a little dog a long time ago, but after that, no pets. Too much trouble."

Just when I began to wonder what else we'd find to say to each other for the rest of the night, Eric opened another folder. It turned out he had some good pictures from organized bike rides he'd done over the past couple of years. He apparently liked to do the hundred-mile "century" ones on the roads of Georgia and neighboring states pretty often. He was in a lot of the pictures, so I supposed someone else must have taken them and emailed them to the group. I'd known he had a bicycle in his room, but he'd never mentioned it to me. I would have enjoyed hearing about the rides when they occurred, but maybe I'd ask from now on. At least now I knew a little more about Eric's world.

I stayed over, and the next morning he asked if I wanted to join him for grocery shopping before he took me home. I figured it would save me a trip, so I tagged along with him and put lots of fruits, vegetables, and whole grains in my cart. I'd get my Doritos, Oreos, and Mountain Dew another day.

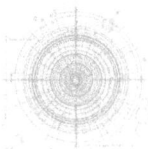

COLLEGE – Dreams and Dumplings

JANUARY 2003

It was the third Tuesday in January of our junior year, and our books and notebooks were spread across Will's coffee table, along with empty cans of Mountain Dew and a half-empty bag of Doritos. I was deep in my biostatistics homework when Will snapped his dynamics book shut.

"That's it. How about some real food? Chinese—our usual?" He was already reaching for his phone.

I nodded. "Sounds great. My brain is completely gone."

Thirty minutes later, we were sitting side by side on the sofa, sharing fried dumplings, garlic pork, and chicken lo mein.

"How's dynamics going?" I asked.

"Good! It's amazing how much I can accomplish when my favorite study buddy is here. When it's just me, I don't get much done before I end up deciding I need to make a few phone calls or even run an errand or two. Tonight, I've been killing it."

"Wonderful," I said. "It all does seem more tolerable when there's another poor soul in the room doing the same thing."

Will gave me a quick smile, then looked down at his food again. "Got another email from Mr. Dukes today."

"Your high school physics teacher?"

"Yeah. He sent me all these job listings to encourage me about the future I could have. Boeing, GE, Lockheed Martin, places like that." Will set down his chopsticks.

"What is it?"

He met my gaze. "Mr. Dukes spent so much time with me junior year, staying after school, showing me how pure math could connect to the real world. He introduced me to topology—got me obsessed with these wild mathematical shapes that totally defy our usual ideas about what's possible." A trace of his usual playful grin returned. "You'd love it, by the way."

"I'm sure I would. He sounds like a great mentor," I said.

"He is. Instead of just being the class clown, I started learning about all these amazing patterns and possibilities. He really believed in me." Will's voice grew quieter. "And now I feel like I'm letting him down."

"Why do you say that?"

"He invested so much of his own time in me, and if not for him, I probably wouldn't be here at Tech. I know he wants the best for me, but when I think about spending my life chasing management positions and bonuses . . ." Will shook his head. "I want to work on things that directly change or even save lives. Is that crazy?"

"Not at all," I said. "But remember, Mr. Dukes is a smart guy. He could be making a lot more money if he weren't teaching high school physics and mentoring lively guys who could be engineers if they'd just sit still for a minute, right? So, I'm pretty sure he doesn't think money is the top priority in life."

I folded one leg under me as I turned toward Will, my knee resting comfortably against his thigh. "He probably just sends you those articles because he thinks of you when he sees them, or maybe he thinks they will keep you motivated. I'll bet he was just proud and excited that you came to Tech and he wants to encourage you."

Will gave me a warm look. "That does sound like him."

"Have you ever told Mr. Dukes about the things you've been working on? The ideas you're passionate about?"

Will shook his head. "Nah. When he sends those job things, I just try to steer the conversation somewhere else, asking him about his family and what's going on at the school and anything else I can think of to fill an email."

"I bet he'd be super interested in the cool stuff you're doing and learning here. And he's one person you could tell the real technical stuff to. He'll be proud of you no matter what, but probably proudest of all of the way you want to use your talents to help make the world better for everyone."

"Mahan, how'd you get so damn smart?"

"Must be all the Mountain Dew." I gestured to the empty cans. "Actually—I'm sort of in the same boat. My dad keeps sending me MCAT prep books, saying I'll never make enough for a 'good life' if I go into research," I said, adding air quotes. "Apparently, getting a PhD is even worse because there are fewer jobs at that level. He thinks if I don't go to med school, I'm wasting my chance at the big bucks and prestige.

"That's ridiculous," Will said. "You don't want to be a doctor. Where would he even get that? You've been excited about research since long before I knew you, looking forward to investigating all those interesting questions that no one else has answered yet." He picked up a chopstick and pointed it at me. "Know what?"

"What?"

"I think we both need to stop worrying about what other people think is right for us. Even people who care about us."

"Deal," I said. "If you find yourself questioning your dreams and wondering if you should be chasing promotions and bonuses, come to me and I'll set you straight."

"Same here. I'll remind you of why you came to Tech," he said, snagging the last dumpling and placing it on my plate. "I'm going to email Mr. Dukes this week and tell him about the project I'm working on. He might have some great insights. I bet he'd love to see how the time he invested in me might make a real difference out there."

I squeezed his arm. "I think that's an awesome idea. He'll be thrilled to hear it."

Will's eyes were full of warmth. "Thanks. Glad you saw what I totally missed."

"Same here," I said. "You seem to be pretty damn smart too. I'm gonna use the MCAT books to keep our napkins from blowing away when we eat lunch outside. Let me know if you need any to prop doors open or anything; I got plenty."

Will laughed, and I couldn't help but join him, feeling the last of my stress dissolve. Any future heavy hints or packages from my dad wouldn't bother me at all.

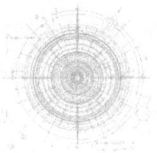

COLLEGE – Winter Refuge

FEBRUARY 2003

A couple of weeks later, the talking heads on the news were going on about how we'd have the coldest night we'd had in many years next week. Meteorologists could already tell that the air from Canada was coming straight for us and that the temperature would drop into the single digits for an overnight low by Tuesday night.

"Brrrr," the red-haired anchor, Janet Fuller, said with a giggle.

I despised winter, and I was in no mood to hear anyone being silly about it. To us in Atlanta, a night below ten degrees was bone-chilling. We had people living on the streets, poorly insulated pipes in our houses, and all kinds of situations that didn't mix well with frigid temperatures.

I hoped and prayed that the warming shelters would take care of the people who wanted to get into them, but one thing that was right in front of me was a little colony of three feral cats that hung around Will's house. I had asked him about them when I first started going over there, and he confirmed they refused to come inside but said that he and a neighbor took turns feeding them, and he had done the trap/neuter thing so they wouldn't produce more kittens.

I remembered that he wasn't supposed to have pets in that house anyway, or he would have had a dog. He enjoyed having the cats around as casual semi-pets, and they seemed to appreciate having a porch to crawl under and a reliable source of food and clean water. But in their lifetimes, it had never gotten as cold as it was about to get.

"What can we do about those feral cats?" I asked Will when I was at his place to help him tutor some students in algebra one night. He was still volunteering to help local kids who were eager to learn but needed extra guidance, and sometimes he got more takers than he could help one-on-one, so I was starting to fill in more and more. They hadn't yet arrived, so I decided this would be a good time to nag—or rather, *ask*—him about the animals.

"Well, they won't come in. I can get my hands on one or two of them, but they're terrified of being in here," he reminded me. "Maybe I could build them a little insulated house."

"Oh, that's perfect." I grabbed his arm, excited he had offered a solution. "You're the best. When can you do it?" I wouldn't shut up about it until the students arrived and I had to change gears.

◇ ◇ ◇

I didn't hear from Will that whole weekend, and as far as I knew, he hadn't done anything about the cats. I even tried to call his landline a couple of times on Saturday, but the one time someone answered, they said he wasn't in.

I told my tale of woe to Eric over dinner that night. Eric could fix things. Eric could take care of anything if he wanted to. Would he help me with the cats?

"Let the fittest survive," he said with finality, then calmly cut another piece of his steak and took a bite.

Since he only dealt with chemistry and calculations, I understood why he didn't know anything about evolution, but he used his ignorance to justify not helping any living being except for himself. I felt a loathing deep down, scared that this was an ugly red flag. Was I really sleeping with someone who would rather see these animals freeze to death than to expend a little effort? I tried to smother the horror so I could try to forget it. This was the type of thing I'd seen other lovesick people do—dismiss their partner's awful trait rather than face it. And now I was one of them.

Anyway, it was time to hit Will up about this again. It was his house, after all, and he was always helping everyone and anyone who asked. Couldn't he drop something else this week to save some innocent creatures?

I ran into him on the sidewalk Monday morning, and I immediately asked about the cats.

"Oh yeah, I need to do that," he said.

"Yes. It's going to be awful. We can't let those babies suffer or freeze."

I felt as if I were trying to push a pile of sand. He seemed to have no sense of urgency. That day after my last class, I drove past his house slowly. There were the cats, lying on the driveway in the last of the weak winter sunshine, but there was no sign of any little house being built for them. I was getting angry. Of course, it wasn't as if I had done anything myself, but why the hell had he volunteered if he didn't intend to follow through?

At the door, Nick told me, "Will's not here. I think he's at Carl's."

Oh yeah. Carl, his brilliant programmer friend he still worked with in that little partnership. But why couldn't he leave that until tomorrow and stay home for one day to help me? I wondered if this was just another time he had said yes to too many of us, living in the moment. This particular task had a hard deadline though, and if we missed it, those poor cats would freeze right there in Will's front yard.

Tuesday, the day that was supposed to be followed by a night in single-digit-temperature hell, I still couldn't reach Will. It was already unpleasantly cold, so it wasn't as if I was going to see him out playing Frisbee, but I would have felt so much more reassured if I could have spoken to him, asked him what the plan was, or reminded him again. It looked like it was all going to be left up to me, and I was pissed off.

As soon as I could get away from the lab that afternoon, I ran to Kroger and bought a dozen cans of cat food plus a large ceramic water bowl. I knew the water would freeze quickly, but I intended to change it right before I went home that night, so the little animals would at least have some for a little while, and if they ate some of the wet food before it froze, the moisture and calories would also keep them going. There were plenty of people and other creatures out there who needed help too, but these animals were right there in my territory, and I felt responsible as the only person who seemed to give a damn.

I asked the store manager if I could have some cardboard boxes, and he gave me several. I had some old towels and sweaters I was planning to stuff into them to make beds for the cats to lie on, assuming no dogs or other beasts scared them away.

I loaded my car with the supplies and started back toward Will's neighborhood. When I got to the house, I saw he was out front, bundled up in a parka and gloves, and it looked as if he was installing a wooden cat house right next to his, with a large extension cord running from it to an outlet on his porch.

I jumped from the car as soon as it stopped and ran up to see what he was doing.

"Hi Lauren. Made this thing yesterday at Carl's, wanted to get him away from his computer for a while. I think it will do what we want." Will opened the top of the house by raising it on its hinges. "Not pretty, but it will get the kitties through this cold snap. The top is covered with lightweight shingles for waterproofing, and there's a ceramic emitter that will heat the interior. It's better than rope lights, because the cats won't want the lights on all night. I mean, would you?" He smiled.

"The real key, though, is this double-wall design. I used foam insulation to create a dead air space. Same principle as a thermos—it minimizes conductive heat loss. With single-digit temperatures, even a small source like this can keep the inside above freezing if you limit heat transfer."

"This is amazing. Will the emitter stay on the whole time?"

"It might tonight, but it won't need to on milder frosty nights. There's a thermostat I've set to turn it off once it's warm enough inside to keep them safe. I also tested it last night to make sure there aren't any hot spots. We don't want it too warm or unsafe for the little guys."

I could see that he had installed a double layer of flaps for the doors to keep the wind out.

"There are two different door holes," he explained, "so the cats won't get trapped if a raccoon enters or if a predator sticks its nose in.

"Wow. Now what? How do we tell them it's here?" I asked.

"While the top's open, I'll put some food inside, plus a towel from their usual sleeping spot so it will smell like them. Catnip may work, too. I've already lined the inside with a thick layer of straw—best thing for insulation and keeping them warm without trapping moisture. Then I'll lift in any cat who will let me. Even if he runs right back out through one of those doors, he'll know it's here if he needs it. I hope the more skittish ones will want to check out the catnip or see their friend inside having a feast later and decide to join him."

I felt grateful to Will and so ashamed of my anger and lack of faith in him, even though I hadn't voiced them. I threw my arms around him and said, "I'm sorry for all the nagging and all the stupid reminder phone messages. I really thought you'd gotten spread too thin this week and forgotten about me."

He wrapped an arm around my shoulders while I hugged him. "Never," he said. "I promise I'll never let you down again."

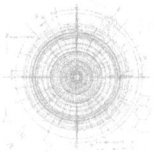

COLLEGE – Cookies and Concerns

MARCH 2003

It was a Wednesday in early March of our junior year, and I took my lunch out to the courtyard near my dorm during the midday gap I had between classes. I was sitting on a bench with a ham-and-Swiss on rye on a napkin on my lap, a can of Mountain Dew beside me. Will had asked a couple of days before what I usually did for lunch, and I'd told him I liked to come out here to enjoy the sunshine when the weather was decent. I told him he should join me sometime and we could solve all the problems of the world in an hour, but I knew it was probably too far out of his way.

I was on my second bite when I heard my name. It was Will. I knew he was between his classes, which were on the other side of campus.

He set his backpack on the ground and sat down beside me.

"Hi Will, glad to see you. Would you like me to run to my room to grab some food and a soda for you?"

He smiled and shook his head. "No need, thanks. Got it right here." He had a sandwich and a can of Coke in an insulated bag in his backpack.

I asked, "How's your morning been?"

"Oh, class was interesting, but I got tired of being confined in there, as usual. How about yours?"

"Can't complain," I said.

We chatted about our classes and upcoming projects while we ate our sandwiches. When we were finished, I asked, "Is it okay if I run inside for a second?"

I wanted to grab a little surprise I had for him. A few months earlier, I'd discovered his love of cookies when I'd made some for the group. I'd found time to bake some more last night, intending to take them to him later, but this was even better.

"Of course," he said. "Take your time."

I dashed to my room and was back within a minute or two. Will saw the paper sack in my hand and sat up a little straighter.

"Is that what I hope it is?" he asked.

"Yep, dessert."

"You baked yesterday? When?"

"Ah, I took a page from your book and made the time last night," I said.

"What kind?"

"Chocolate chip."

"My favorite."

I handed him the bag, and he opened it and inhaled appreciatively. He held them out for me to take one.

"Oh, none for me, thanks," I said. I felt my happy expression fade a little when I remembered that Eric had seen me eating a cookie a couple of weeks ago and had asked if I knew how many calories were in it. Although his comment had filled me with shame and resentment, I'd tried to look unaffected when I told him that yes, of course I knew the number.

Will paused, looking at me for a second, then his friendly expression returned. "You like these too, don't you?" He tilted them toward me again. "C'mon, I can't eat alone. Don't be cruel and make me wait."

"Okay, just to be sociable," I said, taking one.

He bit into a cookie, looking at me as he did. "Have I ever told you how perfect and beautiful you are?"

His words made me smile. "Not sure, but it never gets old," I said. "Might make me more likely to do this again soon." Yeah, I was sure my cute friend knew that.

I took another look at him. "Hey, I can tell something's up. Is everything okay?"

"You do have a special antenna. Just something that bothers me once in a while when I think about it." He took a moment. "You know I've been working at MED-ATL during my work semesters, right?"

"Yeah, I remember you said you worked for a company that makes medical devices, and that you found it inspiring."

"Absolutely. The innovations out there are amazing. Some allow for less invasive surgeries, some monitor patients' health, and some even work automatically to correct issues. It's incredible. But I can't help thinking about those who won't benefit from them, especially in parts of the world where access is limited. Aside from the price tags of the devices themselves, there are so many other barriers. The medical infrastructure often isn't there, nor are there enough trained professionals. And sometimes, it's because they don't even have something as basic as a stable power grid to keep the equipment running. It's a lot to process." He looked out at the courtyard scene for a couple of seconds, then back at me. "I've known that, of course. I mean, it's true of so many of the things we take for granted every day."

I turned to face him. "I know you're going to do something to help. What are you thinking?"

"Oh yeah, right here at Tech there are tons of amazing people in organizations working to improve access and care around the world. I'm glad to be part of that. But it's discouraging, you know? No matter what I do, I feel like it won't be enough. This is my field—I feel this strong urge, almost a responsibility, to fix it. But even with all the work I will put in, I know I'll never make a *real* difference, not fast enough, not in the ways I want to," he said.

"I'm so sorry, Will. It's hard when you care that much. But people like you—people working on these issues—are the best hope those folks have. You're making a difference, even if it doesn't feel like it."

"I'll keep doing whatever I can, even if it's one small step at a time." He turned toward me, his arm on the backrest. "Thanks for letting me unload. This might sound crazy, but sometimes I have to let myself really feel the weight of something that seems impossible, feel frustrated and even like I'm hitting a wall. Then, if I'm lucky . . ." He brushed his hair away from his eyes. "My mind starts seeing new angles, finding ways around the barriers."

"I'm always glad to listen, and I sure wish I could help you work a miracle right now," I said. "Obviously, I don't know *anything* about this stuff. But I do know you, and I know you're going to figure out how to make a difference." I paused for a moment, thinking about all the things that made him special. "In the months we've been friends, I've seen how good you are at bringing people together. You get them to pull in the same direction, and somehow it doesn't just feel like work—it's like everyone actually enjoys being a part of it. And on top of all that, you're the smartest, most innovative person I've ever met. I mean, I'm sitting on the Tech campus when I say that. So, who knows what kind of changes you—and your future team—are going to make possible."

He flashed me that beautiful smile of his. "Wow, that's so nice. Thank you, it means a lot." He glanced away for a second, then met my gaze again. "Okay, then. If I end up at some cool company and start making breakthroughs, you'd better remind me of my goals if I get obsessed with fancy sports cars or something."

"Count on it."

After a beat, he said, "Oh, and let's keep this between us, okay? I'm not looking for attention or trying to be a 'savior' or anything. I just want to help."

"Of course. In fact, I'm proposing that anything we talk about out here stays just for us. 'In the vault,' as our *Seinfeld* friends would say. I think both of us will need that sometimes. Sound good?"

"Agreed. And just so you know, no subject is off the table for me. Whatever you want to talk about, I'm in."

"Same here. Anything you want," I said. After a few seconds, I made a show of looking at my watch. "We still have a couple of minutes. Want to play truth or dare?"

Will laughed. He crushed his Coke can and lobbed it into the trash bin. "That's why I love you so much, Mahan."

He looked more relaxed now, like himself again.

The whistle blew, and we stood, brushing the crumbs off our clothes, ready to head our separate ways.

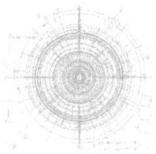

CURRENT – Coming Home

OCTOBER 2023

One Monday evening in late October, I was half watching a new sitcom on TV while texting with Emily and a couple of girlfriends and looking at various articles on my tablet. Eric was doing a combination of work and news reading on his laptop at a little table at the back of the den.

I looked up from my iPad. "Ryan's going to be in an orchestra concert next week."

Eric turned to me and asked, "Why are you telling me that?"

Stifling an eye roll and a sigh, I said, "I dunno. Just thought you might like to come with me."

I thought he would bury his face in his laptop again, but instead he said, "I bought homecoming game tickets. I think we should go this year and spend the weekend. Can you take Friday off?"

Wow. All these years, I'd been getting emails from my department about the various tours and reunion opportunities available during homecoming. I always deleted them. And even if I hadn't been avoiding going back to Tech and had wanted to go to an activity there, Eric had never shown any interest, so I would have had to go alone. He wouldn't even attend football games with me when we were students. Something must be up.

It was a good thing I'd had a little wine to lend me hope and courage, because I was still nervous about returning to campus. I believed I was ready to do it, though, especially because I wanted so much to see Sean and enjoy his sweet, lively company for a while.

"Sure," I told him. "I'll ask for the day off. Just curious—why do you want to go, after all this time? Is it because Sean's there?"

"Nope. There are a couple of classmates I'd like to talk to. What better place and time than when everyone's feeling all warm and fuzzy about their college days?"

"You mean you want them to help fund your clinic?"

"I'm always glad to have investors." He had his smug grin on.

That made sense. Why would Eric have wanted anything to do with our alma mater that wasn't about dollars and cents?

◊ ◊ ◊

Friday morning, we put our bags in the car, along with a large one for Sean. By now he wanted some of his fall clothes and other odds and ends he hadn't thought about in August. We also brought a small bag for Zach, which his mom had dropped off the night before.

We made good time getting to Atlanta. We parked in the deck at our hotel and left our things in the trunk until it was time to check in. Eric rolled Sean's bag behind him, and I took

Zach's as we walked the few blocks to get to the east side of campus and the dorm. On the way, I sent Sean a text message.

Just parked, there in 10

We got there before noon, and Sean was waiting to let us in the exterior door. He looked tired, but who knows whether that was from studying, drinking all night, or just having rolled out of bed. He gave us both a big smile and hugged me. I had forgotten how tall he was. It was so good to see him.

"This way," he told us. Taking the handle of Zach's bag from me, he led us to his room. "I just need to get my shoes."

We went in with him, and I could see that the room had quite a "lived in" look now. His desk was covered with papers and folders, plus his laptop and an attached monitor, which gave him dual screens. There was a mechanical pencil sitting on an open lab notebook, and it looked like he'd just gotten up from studying.

Sean closed the computer to put it to sleep and put on his sneakers. "It's so great to see you guys. Where do you want to go to lunch?"

"Want us to take you somewhere really off campus? Do you ever take time to explore the city?" I asked him. Eric frowned at me, no doubt thinking about the fact that he had just parked the car and walked several blocks to get here.

"Ah, I wish I could. I have class this afternoon and don't have much time. So I was thinking either some kind of fast food near here or pizza, something like that."

"Sounds fine," I said. "You show us what's good. What about Zach?"

"He's in class. Poor bas—poor guy has back-to-back classes from eleven to two every Monday-Wednesday-Friday."

The three of us walked a few blocks to The Varsity, a place famous for its delicious burgers, hot dogs, onion rings, and shakes. Eric was silent on the way over, his lips pressed together in a disapproving expression, probably because he was being forced to eat "unhealthy" food, but I was happier than I'd been in a long time.

Sean seemed happy too. He talked about his classes and projects almost the whole way. From what he said, he was loaded up with hard and engaging work, but he wasn't stressed out. He was thriving.

We entered the restaurant and got into one of many lines at the long counter. It went fast, and soon we were carrying plastic trays loaded with burgers, sodas, and fried onion rings to the nearest available table and sitting down together.

"Hope you're not studying all the time you're not in class." I smiled at Sean. "You have any time for fun?"

"Yeah. I'm having fun with some new friends, and we've done a few outdoor adventures, but the thing I like best might sound boring." He popped an onion ring into his mouth. "See, some of the in-state students who come here from rural areas or the inner city don't have the same math background as me. They're smart, but their schools didn't have as many advanced classes, especially in calculus. So, I started a study group to help out." He took a quick sip of his Coke. "Tech has tutoring and all that, but sometimes when a freshman just needs a quick answer, they'd rather ask a friendly classmate than call a random number or go to the tutoring center."

I nodded, and he continued. "It's fun—everyone works together on problems, and we have potluck dinners too. The group's growing every week, with more people volunteering and more people coming for help."

I could tell from the way he was talking that he was genuinely enjoying himself. "That's awesome, honey. You're not just making friends, but helping others too. I'm really proud of you," I told him.

Eric finally spoke up. "What's really in it for you?" Sean and I looked over at him, and he added, "I see what the others are getting from *you*, but how is this going to help your own grades, or anything else? Seems to me you're wasting your time."

I was kind of shocked at his bluntness and the ugly sentiment, but Sean gave him a big smile. "I just love seeing the light bulb go off when someone finally gets it. These people are really smart—they just get stuck sometimes and need someone to explain things in a different way. It's great getting to know everyone, and it's so satisfying to help them out, you know?"

I nodded, reassuring him that we knew. He was happy, and that made me happy too.

We finished our food all too soon and started walking back to campus. Once we got to the sidewalk outside his dorm, Sean said, "Gotta go to class now. Mom, Dad, thanks for lunch. Have fun this weekend. I'll be in the student section at the game tomorrow. Hope we win!"

"Wait, Sean." I put my hand on his arm. "If you want to fill those bags with stuff for us to take back home, I can come back and get them later and bring them to the hotel."

"Great," he said. "I'll be back in the room by three thirty, so any time after that."

With another flash of his beautiful smile, he separated from us and sprinted into his dorm to get the things he needed for class.

◊ ◊ ◊

Once we'd left Sean, Eric attended a gathering at his own department, while I took part in a lab tour and mixer at mine. I was impressed by all the changes they had made over the years. Of course, anything science-related would keep changing and improving, and instrumentation and other equipment had to be kept modern, but still, the things I saw and the work they were doing blew me away. Seeing what was going on there also gave me a brief pang of envy, because I was supposed to be part of this. I had studied so much and given up many social opportunities to keep my grades high so I could someday devote my life to investigating fascinating questions in science.

Of course, I knew I'd gotten something much, much better instead: Sean. If I hadn't had him when I did, well, he wouldn't be Sean, of course. He was the best thing that had ever happened to me, and I loved him with all my heart.

As the tour came to its last stop and our guide started taking individual questions, people began breaking up into pairs and small groups. A sudden feeling of loneliness hit me. I usually enjoyed being alone at home, or especially on a long walk, but there was something bleak about loneliness in a crowd of couples and happy families. Being among these strangers, all of whom had at least one other familiar person with them, I felt like I was on my own in the world. It didn't seem to matter that I was married; I still never had a partner to do things with when I wanted one. I blew out a sharp breath, willing myself to relax, and decided to take a walk around campus.

As I started down the hall, searching for an exit, I saw a friendly-looking woman walking toward me, smiling. I was stunned to realize it was Amy. I had kept up with her by email, about one per year, but this was the first time in a long time that I'd seen her in person. She had moved to Texas for grad school and was still out there, teaching physiology at a private university.

"Hey Lauren." She threw her arms around me and hugged me tightly.

"It's so good to see you," I told her, returning the hug. As always, my words were inadequate, but it didn't matter. The years slipped away as we stepped back and took each other in.

Her eyes looked exactly as they had in our college days, when we'd been so young. Suddenly, I was my old self again, the person who'd been Amy's friend and who'd had such high hopes for the future. It was probably because I was now face-to-face with someone who really knew me, the genuine me I had been before the tragedy and the years had added a protective shell around my tender soul. As I opened my mouth to tell Amy she looked great, a familiar deep voice behind me spoke.

"There you are." It was Drew. He and Amy had dated almost from the night they met, and they'd gotten married the year after we graduated. I was glad one relationship from our group had turned out good, anyway.

Now he gave me a hug. "Lauren. Wow, how many years has it been?"

"Too many," I said. Just being with the two of them again felt so comfortable. I almost expected Will to walk up to us next.

"What have you been up to, Drew?" I asked him.

"I have my own electric company. Not designing anything really cool like I used to dream about here. No, I just create systems for industry, and I have electricians on staff to do the installations. But it helps pay the bills."

"How are the girls?" I knew Amy and Drew had two daughters, and I believed they were in high school, but I couldn't remember exactly how old they were.

"They're doing great, spending this weekend with Drew's parents," Amy told me. "Grandma and Grandpa only live about twenty minutes from us, so we get to see them a lot, and the kids feel right at home there." She suddenly looked at her watch. "We both have to go to seminars now, but do you want to have dinner tonight?"

"I'll have to check with Eric," I began, then changed my mind. I hadn't seen these people in so many years—why would I let him decide if I got to spend a fun evening with them?

"Um, yes. Yes, that sounds perfect. I don't know if Eric will be available, but hey, who cares? I'd love to."

"Okay, why don't you give me your number and we'll text you in a couple of hours so we can make plans to meet back up," Amy said.

I rattled it off, and she put it into her phone. I also added both of their numbers to mine, because I only had their email addresses.

"Enjoy your seminars," I told them. "I'm going to go pick up Sean's summer stuff to take to the hotel and just wander around campus some. Talk to you in a couple of hours."

Before I left the building, I took one last detour down the main hall. The chair of the department was standing in his doorway greeting visitors. He had been one of my microbiology professors, so as he turned and said hello to me, I stopped and introduced myself.

"I'm Lauren Whitman, formerly Lauren Mahan. It's been a long time," I said with a smile. I sort of dreaded having Dr. Jackson ask me what I was doing now. Everyone else had moved on to great things. Some, like Amy, were university professors, some were physicians, and some had their own businesses. And here I was, a little person with a mundane job and a side blog, whose husband treated her like an idiot.

When he asked, I said, trying to be vague, "I'm a writer, although right now my writing is more oriented toward psychology than biology. I mean, it's a blog, but I have a lot of readers and am hoping it will get big soon."

Dr. Jackson's expression didn't change much, but I was sure he must be wondering why I was doing that after the years of relentless lab work and studying I had put in as a student.

I babbled on. "See, I had a baby right after college and stayed home with him a few years, so I let my skills get out of date. And we live up in Green Valley, so there's really no good place to work." I finally made myself shut up. I could feel my face getting hot, and I realized that a few more people had joined us, waiting to say hello to Dr. Jackson. Why had I gone through that whole explanation?

He turned to one of the newcomers, a guy I remembered from some classes but hadn't known very well. "Michael, good to see you again. I was just having a conversation with Lauren Mahan. She lives in the Green Valley area. Aren't you guys starting a new biotech company out that way?"

"Yeah," Michael, who I now remembered a little more, confirmed. "Biolution. We're officially open, at least some of the labs. We have polymer chemists already on board, and a couple of textile engineers coming next week, but the microbiology lab won't be ready until after the first of the year."

I was riveted. Microbiology lab. "Wh-what will the micro lab be like?"

"Oh, it'll be really cool. Twenty thousand square feet of brand-new lab, and we'll have all state-of-the-art equipment. A few sterile rooms, huge incubators, anaerobic chambers. The space is being designed, and the instrumentation is being ordered right now." Michael looked proud and seemed to enjoy talking about his new venture.

My mind was full of happy visions, but I didn't know what to ask. What a dream it would be to work in that lab. To get my hands on cool, modern equipment and do real experiments to find answers to questions and new ideas. It was what I'd wanted for so many years.

I said, "That sounds great."

Michael pulled his wallet out of his pocket and thumbed a business card out of one of the slots. "Here's my card. Why don't you call me next week? We don't mind out-of-date skills when we know you have the work ethic and brains to graduate with good grades from this place. From what I've heard, most bacteria still operate about the same way they did a couple of decades ago." He smiled. So, he must have overheard my sad speech to Dr. Jackson.

Finally, I said, "I will, thanks," and took the card. I felt as if I was holding my future between my fingers as I slid it into my purse. One thing was certain—I was going to read all about modern microbiology equipment and lab techniques on the internet as soon as I got back home. If there was a place for me at that new lab, I'd bust my ass making sure I was the best employee they could hope to have.

I left the building and started walking through campus, enjoying the familiar atmosphere. Now that I had dinner plans and even some hope of getting a real job, I wasn't lonely at all and was free to enjoy all the sights and sounds around me. I loved seeing everyone walking around, some with young people Sean's age, some just older couples or singles. Although many huge new research and teaching facilities had gone up in the past two decades, the old familiar buildings were still there too.

Now, at least temporarily, I could see with a clear, new perspective. After Will's accident, I had been careful to compartmentalize my life. Since I'd been far from Atlanta with a new husband—and, months later, a new baby—to take all my attention, it hadn't been that difficult. But it made me a little brittle and artificial, a woman with no history. Living like that had been simultaneously exhausting and boring, and I hadn't even seen it at the time. I was too busy trying to keep going. I had tried to erase the fine years I'd enjoyed being a student at Tech and hanging out with Will, but today I felt like the young woman I had been before I graduated. I knew I needed to stay in better touch with that person and vowed to keep this door open from now on, to visit campus more often and get together with old friends as much as possible.

What should have been obvious to me all along was breaking through: I wasn't helping Will or his memory in any way by avoiding all the good times we'd had here. Instead, I was wasting those wonderful recollections by not enjoying them as much as I could. He was the best friend I'd ever had, and it was crazy for me to bury that just because my guilt and grief were painful.

Was this why my mind had taken me back to the past when I'd been here in August? Were those memories simply bubbling up to the surface, too powerful to stay suppressed? Or, if I wanted a really "out there" explanation, like Janie had suggested, maybe Will had given me that happy little scene to bring me back to my old self and tell me it was all right to live and enjoy my life. There was a thrill and a lot of comfort in that crazy thought. And today I was open to anything.

Before I got to Sean's dorm, I summoned the courage to cut through the little courtyard where Will and I had shared lunches and sat and talked sometimes. "Thank you," I whispered as I walked past our old bench. "You know I loved you. It was just . . ." I had a lump in my throat. If he was listening, he surely knew what I meant, even if I didn't know how to say it.

I got to the dorm at a quarter to four, so I assumed Sean was back from class. A group of parents and students were going through the door, and I followed them in.

I stopped to use the ladies' room in the lobby. I washed my hands and brushed my hair, looking at my reflection. Yep, I had a few extra miles on me, but I was the same person I'd been when I was a student here. And that gave me an irresistible idea.

I left the restroom, but this time, to avoid getting caught by Sean or possibly even Eric, I took the stairs to the third floor before starting down the hall, past where Sean's room was on the floor below. Walking back down to the second floor, I started looking at every inch of the walls, but I didn't see the door I was sure I had opened during freshman move-in day. Well, damn, I must have imagined it. I figured I should probably go on and grab Sean's summer stuff.

Yep, there was the whistle, about to blow, so it was five minutes to four. It sounded just as I turned toward Sean's room. Then there it was—my ancient door. I hurried and grabbed the knob and opened it, slipping into the hallway.

The passage was dark, but this time I had my iPhone with me. I turned on its flashlight, but there really was nothing to see except old wooden walls on both sides. I walked as rapidly as I could without stumbling until I finally saw daylight shining through the window of the door up ahead.

When I got to the exit, I pretty much exploded into the courtyard and the fresh air. The day was sunny, and there were students walking around, some alone, some in pairs or small groups. Everything was real. This was no dream. Had I walked into this real outdoor space, and maybe the conversation with Will was all that I had dreamed or imagined last time? I couldn't exactly ask someone what year it was.

I looked down. Wow, no, this wasn't just another day. Instead of my forty-two-year-old body in my business casual outfit, I saw a smaller waist, young-looking arms, and a pair of faded jeans. I scanned the area to see if anyone I knew was here. What I wouldn't have given to talk to Will again. Sitting and laughing with him, hell, even going through bad times with him, made me feel . . . Well, complete felt too corny. But connected, happy, understood, content. As a student, I had enjoyed it, but because it had been so easy and natural, it hadn't occurred to me it might end. Unfortunately, it looked like he wasn't around today.

With every second that ticked by, I felt more and more like part of the current scene, as if the fortyish me would fade away completely if I stayed here long enough.

It was time for midterms, and I had an awful lot to do. I opened my backpack to get out my molecular biology book. I wanted to fill in some gaps in my notes and enjoy the October sunshine as long as I could, but I had to meet my study group at five, so I kept checking my watch as I worked.

At ten minutes before the hour, I finally gathered my stuff and stood up, ready to walk the few blocks to the library, but the whistle blew. It must be five minutes later than I'd thought. I'd better hurry.

◇ ◇ ◇

I found myself back in the hall of the dorm, looking at the wall like I had been earlier. But I had just been on my way to the library.

I looked around to see if anyone was staring at me, but everyone seemed to be minding their own business. I looked at my watch. It was now almost five. It had been an hour since I entered the old passage, and the door was no longer there. Still reeling, I turned and strode on autopilot to Sean's room. I was wrapped in the sweetness of my experience, but it was tinged with sharp disappointment that Will had not been there. I would do almost anything to have another chance to live through those years again and do things differently this time.

◇ ◇ ◇

The rest of the weekend was nice, but my mind stayed inflamed with thoughts of my visits to the past. Normally, having my handsome husband at a game—something that had never happened even when we were dating—would have made my day. But this time, while I was cheering for our team, my gaze kept drifting toward that courtyard, as if somewhere in a parallel world, those old events were unfolding all over again.

My only big, unfixable mistake had been made not long before graduation, right there in that sunny green space.

Was I losing my grip? Or—if those experiences had been real—was there some way I could go back and stay, repeating everything until I finally got the chance to right that wrong? And it wasn't just Will's life—and mine—that might have turned out differently. If that summer had gone another way, Eric might have ended up with someone who truly fit the world he came from—someone he didn't feel the need to re-shape. Maybe he would have been happier, too.

Even so, it didn't seem like I had that kind of choice. Both times I'd gone back, I'd been propelled right back into my life about an hour later. I didn't know what to think or wish for, but I hoped some answers would come with time. Now I had to focus on something I could realistically accomplish—getting a new job and doing some genuine science.

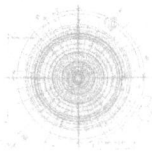

COLLEGE – Designing Hope

April – August 2003

I t was early April our junior year. Will called me at the end of the day on Wednesday, and he sounded even more enthusiastic than usual.

"Lauren! I've been talking to MED-ATL, and I'll be working there again this summer. Guess what—aside from my paid work, they're going to let me do a side project on my own time to try to come up with something to improve underserved people's access to their devices. I'm so stoked."

"Oh Will, that *is* fantastic. Congratulations. I know you've been eager to get your hands on a project like this. Will they assign you a specific problem to solve?"

"Nah, I've worked there enough over the years that they're going to turn me loose. I can work on fixing a known issue with a device, or I can get a start on creating something new or a new feature, whatever I think has the best chance of working. Or I should say 'we,' because they said I can recruit other Tech students to volunteer their time, and it will be a real team. The

company will make it legit by giving them unpaid internships."
I heard some noise in the background, then a door close, and
he was in a quiet area again. "They're giving us limited key
card access to the R&D wing and labs—enough to use the
prototyping equipment and testing stations, but not complete
run of the manufacturing floor. A senior engineer will mentor
us and check in on our progress, but otherwise, we get to work
independently.

"They said our team could use the company's facilities and
materials any day and at any hour, and anything we discover
will belong to MED-ATL, of course. Fine with me, as long as
they put it to use where it's needed."

"How wonderful. I know you can't wait to get started."

"Oh yeah, I've got a million ideas. Finding team members
won't be easy—a lot of the most driven people already have
internships—but I'm going to start calling around. I'll need
a couple of biomed, mechanical, and materials engineers, plus
someone in industrial design who's great at prototyping. Now
I just have to convince them that my wild plan is worth their
time—and keep them from killing each other once we start
working.

"I'm actually about to start recruiting right now, but I had
to tell you first." His voice was electric with excitement. "I
don't think I'll sleep tonight."

"I can imagine. How can I help? Of course I'm not an
engineer, but I'll be around here this summer, taking a special
topics class and working. I'd love to do something. I really
mean it."

"Thanks, Laur. Yeah, I can use all the help I can get, because I want our team to solve at least one problem or make
real progress on something new. Maybe we'll even come up
with something MED-ATL will be interested in and want to
keep working on."

"I admire you and your compassion so much. So really—be thinking about what I can do to help save you time you can spend on this good work. Anything. Computer work, searching journal articles, or even doing unrelated other chores you usually have to do. But don't let me do all your damned laundry and yard work, then catch you using the extra time to hang out on the river drinking beer with your buddies."

He laughed. "I appreciate it so much. There's no one I'd rather have on my team. And I'll try to remember not to abuse you too much on the laundry stuff."

◊ ◊ ◊

As soon as finals were over, Will started his paid job at MED-ATL and also threw himself into the side project with his signature blend of enthusiasm and determination. He recruited a small but dedicated team of students, and together they spent long hours in the lab, testing materials and refining designs.

With his roommates away for most of the summer, I'd started cooking Will's favorite meals and stocking his fridge with individual portions of them and other easy grab-and-go foods, knowing he'd dive straight into the independent project at the end of each co-op workday. Whenever I stopped by his house, I made sure his trash was taken out, his laundry pile wasn't getting out of control, and that his front yard didn't look abandoned.

Early one Sunday morning in June I let myself in to find him sitting hunched over his kitchen table drawing in a notebook with a mechanical pencil, a cup of coffee in front of him. His eyes looked exhausted, but he gave me a smile with that open, earnest expression of his and said, "Lauren, thank you for everything—you're a lifesaver. I don't know what I'd do without you keeping me sane and fed." He started to get up, but I put my hand on his shoulder, feeling the solid strength beneath my fingers. The gentle pressure was enough to convey that he could stay seated, that I was here to help.

"It's the least I can do," I said, meaning every word. I started pulling containers of food from the bag. "What do you want for breakfast? If you're in a hurry, there are bagels and cream cheese, plus a few kinds of fresh fruit. And for dinner, one container is stir-fry, and this one is your favorite—pesto chicken with pasta. If you have time now, I'd be happy to cook you some eggs—spinach and feta omelet, maybe?" I took away his cold coffee and fixed him a fresh cup. I was so glad to see him and get to spend a few minutes with him before he would need to get back to work. Watching him pour his heart into something so meaningful only deepened my admiration for him.

The next time I came to Will's to bring food, I noticed most of the containers from previous visits were clean, drying in the rack by the sink. On the table sat a small white bakery box, with a little piece of engineering paper taped to the top. In block letters, Will had written my name and "Thank you!" For the "o" in "you," he had drawn a smiley face. Inside were a dozen iced cake balls from the fantastic bakery next to MED-ATL. Six were chocolate and six were lemon—my favorites. Will had to be the only person I knew who encouraged me to enjoy life without worrying about calories or anything else.

A couple of weeks later, I found another bakery box on the table—this time with lacy oatmeal cookies, iced in vanilla and chocolate glaze, each half-and-half. A small square of engineering paper sat on top, with a flower Will had drawn in blue pen and shaded with a purple colored pencil. I put the little note in my purse and began to put the food I'd brought into the refrigerator.

◇ ◇ ◇

By early August, after my relentless offers of help, Will was allowing me to collect the notes and test results from the team and organize them for his easy reference for the final reports. He and the group had solved a materials problem with a MED-ATL medical device—one that had originally required specialized imported components, making it too costly for production in developing nations. By designing an alternative using locally available, lower-cost materials that still met rigorous durability and safety standards, they'd made it possible for manufacturers in those regions to produce the device affordably on-site. MED-ATL was already moving forward with the findings, and people were going to benefit from the team's dedication. Until now, I'd never fully grasped the crucial role engineers played in our medical care beyond just instrumentation.

Late in the afternoon on the day he presented the last of his reports and wrapped up the project with MED-ATL, Will turned to me and the engineering students and said, "Team, I think it's time for a party! How about tomorrow night?"

The others were quick to agree. After dinner that night, he and I went out to grab the supplies we'd need. The next day, I helped him get the food and house ready. I baked chocolate chip cookies while we put together a large fruit platter as part of the dessert spread, plus various chips and dips. His neighbors Jason and Rob, always invited to Will's gatherings, came over to help, even loaning him a second grill so he could cook skewers: chicken and vegetables on one, strictly vegetables on the other. By early evening, the project team—many bringing their partners—along with other mutual friends, began arriving, everyone ready to celebrate the success. I'd never seen Will happier than he was that night. Finally, instead of just carrying the weight of the problem, he had been able to do something to change it.

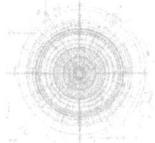

CURRENT – Science Calling

OCTOBER 2023

Monday after homecoming I got up an hour early, eager to get to the rest of my day. I was going to get a real microbiology job. I had done some reading the night before so I could at least speak to Michael halfway intelligently when I got in touch with him. As much as I wanted to leap into this new opportunity, I would avoid calling him the minute he walked into the office. I knew firsthand that at the beginning of the workday, there were a million things vying for attention, and an additional phone call would just be annoying. I didn't want to be one more thing he needed to finish with as fast as possible. For once in my life, I would not give in to my compulsion. I'd call him when he'd had a chance to settle in.

To jumpstart my thinking, I took a quick jog around the neighborhood. I started out feeling great, as if I could go for-ever. But after just over a mile and a half, I could feel my usual leg cramps and exhaustion, which meant I wouldn't last much longer. Maybe I really was running "wrong," as Eric said. But who cared? Today I was ready to move on to other things.

As soon as I'd stopped sweating, I showered and got dressed for work. I planned to sneak in a little more time reviewing microbiology techniques before writing my resume. Did they still use the same type of equipment I'd worked with in college? I'd already looked at a few articles, but figured I'd read some recent journal articles too in case I was called upon to discuss the new job and the knowledge or experience it would call for.

As I pulled into the parking lot, I noticed Dan wasn't at the office yet. Maybe I should call Michael now after all. It would be great to do it without my boss breathing down my neck or calling my name.

When I entered the office, things seemed quiet, so I hurried to the break room to grab some coffee, taking it back to my desk to start my day. The quiet was short-lived, unfortunately, so I didn't try to call Michael. The rest of the morning was busy, including a staff meeting in Dan's office, and it went by fast. I tried not to worry about my call; after all, I had intended to wait a bit, anyway. I was nervous, but I knew this would be the first step toward the career I wanted. Either way, I could barely pay attention to the discussions of everyday things like customers, lab results, and reports. I had an urgent mission to accomplish. My life was about to change.

As soon as Dan said, "Okay, a couple of action items for next time," I knew we were almost out of there. In my mind, I was already halfway down the hall. Finally, everyone stopped talking.

Although some people still seemed to want to linger, I strode back to my space as rapidly as I could. Grabbing my cell phone and a small notebook and pen, I hurried out of the suite, down the stairs, and outside before anyone could call my name.

"Hello," said Michael's prerecorded message. "You've reached . . ."

That was one thing I hadn't thought about—getting his voicemail. I wondered if I should leave a message or just try again in an hour. I decided I'd wait and call again later. Yes, that would be best. Then I'd know for sure what to do next. I needed to calm down and exert a little self-control.

Despite my intention to wait, I began talking once I heard the beep. "Um, hi Michael. This is Lauren Whitman—er, Lauren Mahan. We talked at homecoming? Anyway, I wanted to . . . I wanted to get with you on applying for a job at the new company." I floundered around a little more, then finally gave my phone number and ended the call.

And as soon as I did, I started beating myself up. All right, now he'd either call back soon, or . . . what if he didn't? By leaving that message, I'd lost the chance to try again later. If he didn't call me back, I couldn't just call again. Because I'd left a stupid, stupid message. I checked to make sure my ring volume was turned up nice and loud. I couldn't miss this chance.

As I returned to the office, I passed Ashley's desk. She looked up. "Got lunch plans?"

"No, I'm available. Eager, even. Where would you like to go?" My phone was still clutched in my hand, where I vowed it would remain until I heard back from Michael.

"How about Joel's?"

"That works. Around noon?"

We made our plans, and I went back to my desk to look at some lab results that needed a bit of follow-up. What if I got a real research job like I'd dreamed about when I was younger? I'd need to stay current on all the latest discoveries and techniques and would be more than happy to do it. Maybe I'd even start taking graduate-level classes. A career in science usually required an advanced degree. I wondered if I'd be able to do some online classes at . . .

"Lauren." Dan was standing beside me.

"Oh, sorry. I didn't hear you come up." I gave him what I hoped was a pleasant look.

He had a thick catalog of some kind in one hand. "We're moving forward with the new construction, and I wanted to give you a heads up. Your group will be able to move offices in about three months."

"Oh, great. That's sooner than I thought."

"That's if things work out as scheduled. Anyway, the industrial hygiene lab will be built first, with built-in desks for the lab techs along the sides, and you and Ashley and Joe will have separate offices across the hall."

"Wonderful, thanks." Wow, I'd always wanted my own office instead of this open plan.

"Have a look at this." Dan plopped the furniture catalog down on my desk and opened it to a page where a small Post-it was attached. "I've marked some pages you three can pick from."

My cell phone started ringing. I glanced toward it for a millisecond but couldn't see who it was.

And Dan continued to talk. "Each of you can select a desk, a credenza, and a hutch."

"Great. Thank you." It really was wonderful news—if I'd been planning to stay here. A new office all to myself and new furniture that I'd get to select. Joe wandered up and joined us in looking at the catalog as Dan flipped a couple of pages. My phone was still ringing. Why couldn't we have been doing this at Joe's desk so I could step away?

"Joe, I was telling Lauren, you three can pick out your own furniture for the new offices. Everything on the pages I've marked will match what will go in the rest of the space, and we have special pricing with Stella Interiors. We're getting a great deal."

My phone had stopped ringing, but now it started again. Shouldn't they be saying, "We'll let you get that" and walk away? What if this was important? How did they know it wasn't my doctor? Why not take the catalog to Joe's desk, and I could come and join them later? Somehow, since Dan had come to my desk, I felt as if I couldn't leave.

". . . and you can each pick a chair, of course, and two guest chairs."

"I think guest chairs send the wrong message," Joe said.

My laugh caught even me by surprise. Good old Joe. He despised people trying to socialize with him when he was trying to get something done.

By now my phone had stopped ringing again.

Dan flipped the catalog shut and pushed it toward me, saying, "Just reach out to Barbara when you know what you want to order. The sooner the better, so they can have everything ready to move in when your space is ready. Tell Ashley too." He trundled away.

◇ ◇ ◇

At eleven forty-five, I was finally alone, and I knew I'd be meeting with Ashley soon. But I'd listened to my voicemail, and the call had been from Michael, all right. Trying to be invisible, I slipped out the back of the suite. I wanted to call him before I attracted my coworkers' attention. I took the stairwell to the bottom floor and went straight outside.

This time when I called, Michael answered. I was unsure what to say, but luckily he launched right in.

"Lauren. Great to hear from you. Things are coming along well here, and I think you'd fit right in. But you know, there's bureaucracy everywhere, right? Can you shoot me a resume?"

Definitely. I could get a good start on it, at least—then I'd need to get creative. The educational part would be great, but the work experience . . . not so much.

"It's just a formality. I'm already giving you rave reviews here, of course," he continued. "Smart people who are easy to work with are exactly what we want. You can pick up any new techniques once you get here, so don't worry about that."

He gave me the same email address I already had from his card, and I promised to get my resume to him as soon as I could. As we hung up, I knew I was smiling, glowing even. My mind was full of thoughts about what my new job would be like. Everything in my life would be better somehow. I turned around and saw Ashley on the sidewalk, coming closer.

"Look at you. Whoever he is, I'd say it's true love. I brought your purse, so you don't need to go back in. Let's go to Joel's and you'll tell me all about it."

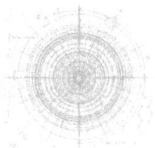

COLLEGE – Sweet Autumn

SEPTEMBER 2003

B y the time fall semester rolled around, I felt like I was
already off to a great start. In mid-August, before classes
began, Will and I took short-term campus jobs helping freshmen move in and settle into life at Tech. The job was easy
and fun, and for the first time in a long time, the semester
ahead felt full of possibility—before the weight of midterms
and responsibilities kicked in. This year, my birthday fell on a
Sunday. After a long workout at the rec center, I walked across
campus, soaking in the buzzing energy of the new semester.
Groups of students filled the sidewalks—talking, laughing,
tossing Frisbees. My phone rang just as I reached my dorm.

"Happy birthday." It was Emily.

"Thanks. It's a good one so far."

"Can I buy you lunch in a little while?"

We agreed we'd meet at Mr. Wang's at noon. I loved their
incredible hot and sour soup, and I was looking forward to a
fun lunch with my sister.

◇ ◇ ◇

After I got back, I grabbed the stuff I'd need for the afternoon from my room then walked back to the rec center. I wanted to spend a couple of hours at the pool. As I made my way over, I thought about the coming months. It was time to consider my life and what I needed to do. I had to apply to grad school soon, and I didn't even know what program I was aiming for yet.

Also, of course, I knew I was playing a hopeless game waiting for Eric to get serious about me, so I vowed I'd start going out with other guys. It was a weird feeling, because Eric and I had never talked about being exclusive—or not. Last year, going on dates with him each week had left me in a strange limbo, where I was afraid to move on, afraid he thought we had had some sort of "understanding" and I'd blow it, yet also afraid I was wasting my life. This year, it was time to do some dating.

By now it was the afternoon of my birthday, and I had no plans for the evening at all. Eric had not called or even emailed, and I'd be damned if I was going to sit in my room all night. He had until four, and then I'd turn off my phone and do something fun.

At six, I decided I'd go up to Will's and see what those guys were doing for dinner. Maybe they were getting a pizza or something. This year, he was only sharing the house with one guy, Adam, a transfer student from southern California, but I assumed he'd have several friends there tonight. There were always a few people around.

I was sure that in another month, I'd probably have a real boyfriend, but right now I was still in a weird place with Eric. I swapped out my shorts for a short skirt. I brushed my hair and put on some extra mascara and lip gloss. It was my birthday, and the night was yet to come.

◇ ◇ ◇

At Will's, Josh let me in with a smile. Melissa and Adam greeted me from the couch, where they were watching the news. Will shouted my name from the hall and said, "Happy birthday. You look really pretty."

"Thanks. How did you know?"

"Last year I think you told me you'd just had your birthday. Can you believe I remembered a thing like that? I got you something." He ducked into the kitchen and came back with a small bakery box. Inside was a beautifully decorated little cake, with lots of brightly colored icing flowers on a chocolate background.

"Will." I was happy and touched and glad I had come there. "Thank you."

"You're so welcome. For some reason I didn't think we'd see you until tomorrow or so. But since you're here, we need to celebrate. Want to start by going out somewhere for dinner?"

"That sounds perfect." And it did.

"Who all wants to go?" he asked Josh and Melissa and Adam. "And when we get back, birthday cake."

The five of us piled into Will's Jeep and went to a new Mexican place just north of Atlanta. Throughout the meal, I was thinking it was the best birthday I'd ever had. We laughed, drank margaritas, and ate fajitas and way too many chips. Will insisted on paying for me. I agreed, if he'd let me get his when it was his turn. We ordered a round of water to drink at the end. We didn't want to spend the night in the Atlanta drunk tank.

When we got back to the house, Josh and Melissa told us they needed to get going.

"No birthday cake?" Will asked them.

"I couldn't eat another bite," Melissa said, "but we'll see you tomorrow. Happy birthday, Lauren."

They left, and it was just Will, Adam, and me. When we got inside, Adam said, "Happy birthday again. I've gotta go return some emails, so you kids don't wait up."

Well, that was odd. I wanted this wonderful evening to go on a little longer, but it looked like everyone was full and tired. I supposed I should leave too.

Will caught my eye. "We have a new bottle of milk. Or would beer be better? Can we finally cut that cake?"

A smile broke across my face. "Sure. Are you going to sing?"

We went into the kitchen, and I put plates and forks on the table while he fixed our drinks. When he took the cake out of the box, I once again felt struck by how lucky I was to have met this awesome guy.

While we ate, he asked, "Any birthday wishes for the year to come?"

"Yeah," I said. "Wishing for a good senior year—to have lots of fun, maybe a little adventure or two, plus academic success, of course."

"I'll do my best to make the first parts happen." Will glanced down at the table for a second, then back up at me. "I'm so glad you enjoyed going out tonight. I know you don't like to be the center of attention, but I decided it would be okay since it was just us."

"How did you know that? You're absolutely right, though. I despise having all eyes on me, but no one else has ever gotten it."

"Maybe I have a special antenna too, at least where you're concerned."

I couldn't put into words how happy that made me or exactly what this wave of emotion was. The feeling of being understood like that was a rare treasure for me.

"You did everything just right," I told him. "And when your next birthday comes, I know what to do. We'll have a minimum of fifty people, and we'll sing to you, and then you'll even have to give a speech."

That won me a big smile. "You nailed it."

We got up and rinsed our plates and glasses. I turned to him, ready to leave.

"Thank you so much, Will. This has been the best birthday."

"Glad you enjoyed it. It has been a great night."

He was standing so close to me that I had to tilt my head back a little to hold his gaze. He reached out and touched my hair, tucking a strand behind my ear, but at that moment Adam's bedroom door burst open.

"Am I too late for some cake?"

I stayed to chat a little while Adam had a slice of cake, then went back to my dorm. I brushed my teeth and undressed, smiling about the pleasant evening as I drifted off to sleep.

◊ ◊ ◊

I woke early the day after my birthday with the sun shining through my window. Senior year was going great, and I couldn't wait to see how the rest of it unfolded. This was going to be the best year of my life. Wasn't that what older people always said? Would I finally be able to forget about Eric? He hadn't called last night, and I was trying to tell myself that everything would be fine even if I never heard from him again. Today was the first day of my new chapter.

The morning went by pretty fast, and Amy and I grabbed lunch at the student center food court at noon. I was about to go into my one-o'clock class when my phone rang. To prove to myself that I had more self-control than last year, I didn't look to see who the caller was. It was still ringing when I crammed it into the bottom of my bag and stepped into the lecture hall.

A few hours later, I had done a little food shopping and was juggling two bags of groceries and my purse while unlocking my room. The phone started up again. Slightly annoyed, but feeling a little prick of interest, I got the key out of the lock and slammed the door and answered.

"Hel-lo." Eric's voice was confident and cheerful.

"Oh, hi." I tried to sound distracted.

"Got back in town late last night," he said.

"Oh, didn't know you were gone."

"I went on a quick getaway. Don't want to be at this place any more than I have to."

I didn't know what to say to that. I was thrilled to be here, plus yesterday had been my damned birthday.

"Anyway, the reason I called—we need to go to dinner and do some partying tonight."

"Yeah?" A smile crept onto my face. So, he *had* remembered my birthday.

"Yep, one last night before my project cranks up. This year is going to be a bitch."

◇ ◇ ◇

When I woke up the next day, I was ready to forgive Eric. Never mind that he'd forgotten my birthday. Maybe he'd never known about it. He never asked me anything about myself, except in-the-moment things, like whether I liked a certain food or wanted to go somewhere.

I was getting dressed when Will called, excited. He, Drew, Josh, Jason, Rob, and Adam had begun to dig a big, long hole in the backyard, and they were going to have a pig roast at the house on Saturday, since our team had an away game that day.

"You did what? What about your landlord? Won't he kill you for destroying his yard?"

"Relax, Laur." Will sounded happy. "I told Mr. Spark I was going to plant a nice apple tree for him this year, and I already got the exact spot he wants it. So we've dug a big hole, and it's almost finished.

"But why would a tree need a long hole like that?"

"After the pig roast, I'll refill a lot of the pit with dirt and plant some grass. Then when it's the right time for it this winter, we'll plant the tree. It'll be fine."

Mr. Spark lived on the other side of the city and trusted Will implicitly. Will often made minor repairs and performed routine maintenance on the house, plus he had leased it for several years and always paid his rent on time. So, the fortunate landlord would not show up at the student rental house on the spur of the moment to try to catch his ideal tenant in some misguided endeavor.

"Well, all right then," I said. "What can I bring? And how can I help? But don't even think about asking me to deal with the star of the show."

"You could bring a side, like beans, or potato salad. Whatever you like. Adam and Josh and a few others are getting the keg. We're going to have a ton of people—it will be amazing!"

Of course I started worrying. What if Eric asked me out for Saturday? I always saw him whenever he was available, because I was all too aware that he would be in another city once the year was up. Well, it was time for things to change. Maybe I'd invite him to the pig roast and take back some of the power in our relationship. Or if he didn't call, he'd soon find out I had been busy and happy with other friends, not sitting around waiting for him.

"Sounds great," I told Will. "I'll try to think of something good to bring. Want me to come help get the house ready tomorrow or Thursday?"

"That'd be so great. We're going to finish digging the pit, line it with bricks, and get some wood. We also need to find a grate for the pig and all kinds of other stuff. Plus, of course, we have to get Mr. Pig himself home Friday morning somehow."

"I'll leave the guest of honor to you guys, but I'll be glad to come clean house a little and see what kinds of supplies we're going to need. We'll have the place looking almost civilized—at least until the party gets underway."

"Thank you so much," Will said, and I could almost see the big smile on his face.

◊ ◊ ◊

Friday night, the guys worked hard—a whole pig was a tremendous amount of trouble to deal with. Getting it marinated (I really didn't want to know how or where this took place), wrapped in burlap and chicken wire, and cooked was a huge undertaking.

The fire had to be checked every hour or so to make sure the temperature inside the pit stayed steady. If it dipped too low, whoever was on shift would carefully dig into a corner and add fresh hardwood coals from the separate pile they kept burning.

Will and Adam, along with Jason and Rob from two doors down, had taken shifts throughout the night to keep the roasting going. They checked the fire, added coals as needed, and stumbled back to their own beds between turns, catching what sleep they could. By first light, Melissa, Josh, and Drew had arrived to take over, allowing the overnight crew to finally get some uninterrupted rest.

By around eight Saturday morning, the early roasting team had things under control, and Amy and I got to work on the indoor preparations. We made enough potato salad for an army, as well as five dozen brownies. Then I scrubbed the old kitchen, plus put plenty of toilet paper in the bathrooms for a change and washed and dried all the towels.

It wasn't too long before Will was up again, excited about the day ahead. While Amy and I continued our indoor prep, he joined Drew and Melissa at the pit, freeing up Josh to help Adam get ice and a keg and set it up on the patio.

Music drifted through the house from speakers in the living room and just outside the back door. Soon more friends showed up, bringing soda, chips, beans, buns, and more bags of ice.

A long folding table had been set up in the yard, already covered in coolers and containers of sides. I carried out the potato salad and brownies and began to organize everything—opening containers, arranging them neatly, and finding the right serving spoons.

I glanced over and saw Liz, Rob, and Will standing together at the pit, Will laughing at something Rob was saying. Liz gave me a quick wave, and I returned it with a smile. We'd had a few classes together, but I really knew her through this group—quiet, sharp, always with a wry comment tucked away for the right moment.

It occurred to me that I hadn't looked at my phone all day. Should I go in and check to see if Eric had called? I was about to turn toward the house, but Melissa came up to me, a Solo cup in one hand.

"How's it going?" she said with a cheerful smile.

"Great," I said. "Everything turned out amazing. You guys all worked so hard roasting that pig! I've never seen anything like this."

"Yeah," Melissa said with a grin, "for some reason, Will has been super excited since the semester began, and you know how that goes. One minute I was just living my life, the next minute we're cooking a whole pig in a backyard pit."

"I've been excited too. I'm determined that senior year is going to be special. And hanging out with all of you—it's almost guaranteed," I told her with a smile.

Melissa tipped her cup slightly, grinning. "Well, we're glad you're here. It wouldn't be the same without you."

The words caught me off guard—simple, genuine, and warm.

"I'm starving. I'm gonna grab some food," Melissa added, already stepping toward the table. "When you're ready, come join us."

I lingered for a moment, going back to arranging the dishes. I was so focused on lining up the containers that I didn't notice Will until he was standing beside me, holding out a cold beer.

"Everything looks great," he said, his smile easy and bright.

I took the beer, savoring the first crisp, cold sip. "Thanks. And I can't believe how amazing it smells out here," I said, breathing in the smoky, rich aroma of roasting pork, garlic, and spices.

"Just wait until you taste it." He nodded toward the pit where our friends were slicing the tender meat.

"Is that garlic, cumin, . . . what else?" I asked.

"You'll just have to help with the marinating next time if you want all our secrets," Will replied with a playful grin.

Melissa and Josh, along with Drew and Amy, had spread out some old blankets on the grass for extra seating. After we filled our plates, Will and I settled in near Melissa. She pulled us into the conversation—classes, favorite professors, the best late-night spots around campus.

I found myself laughing and talking more than I ever had before I met this group.

At one point, I glanced up and caught Will looking at me, his smile soft and warm, a quiet gentleness in his eyes. I must have been smiling too, because his expression lit up just a little more. I knew there was nothing he loved more than bringing people together for a happy occasion. He'd been so excited about this gathering all week, and he had pulled it off.

Much later, I realized I'd forgotten all about Eric for a while.

◇ ◇ ◇

Sunday, I woke up relaxed and happy, thinking about the day before. Then I realized with a start that I hadn't heard from Eric yet this weekend, and that sent my mood plummeting. After this year, he'd be in med school, and I'd be in grad school somewhere, and we might never . . .

With a bit of effort, I shrugged off those thoughts and went for a quick run to the rec center for some strength training, and it helped brighten my outlook a little.

After lunch, I dropped by Will's on my way to get groceries. I wanted to help with any cleanup we hadn't finished last night. He was outside near the pit, using a large shovel. He had chosen the site for its sun exposure and aesthetically pleasing position in the yard with the eventual apple tree in mind. True to his word, he had almost finished filling in the excess length with earth. I helped him put some plugs of grass sod on the end that wouldn't be in the little tree's root area. We would plant it when the time was right.

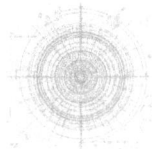

COLLEGE – Helping Hand

September 2003

I was sitting on our usual bench the next Friday just after twelve when I saw Will approaching. He gave a little smile and nod as he got closer, and I scooted down to give him some room.

"How's your morning been?" I asked.

"It's been all right." He got a Coke out of his backpack and met my gaze. "Just had a little detour before getting here." He glanced into the distance for a moment, brushing the hair away from his eyes. "I was planning to make it to campus early today, but when I was about to cross Tenth, I saw this guy, Joey, on the sidewalk. He needed some help. Cars were flying by and no one walking would even look at him as they rushed past. I know it's an everyday thing around here, but there was something about him—he looked desperate and afraid. I couldn't just walk away. I didn't want to leave him on Tenth, so I asked if he could walk with me back toward the house to grab the Jeep, and then we could go to breakfast and talk for a bit."

"How did that go?" I asked.

"Good. He was glad to get some good food and have some-body to talk to. He told me he used to be married, and he had a son, too. He said he made a few bad decisions, and he lost his job and his family. You know, we don't ever stop to think about it, because it would scare us to death to face it, but once that happens to someone, the safety net can disappear fast. He said he's been on the streets for a few years now."

"I bet he was happy to have a kind person to talk to and eat with. And you're so good at putting people at ease, so that must have made it even better. Where is he now?"

"There's a men's shelter downtown that does more than just provide food and a bed—they have job skills programs, case managers, the works. They really help guys get back on their feet. I've known the director there, Brian, for a couple of years because we both help with another organization some-times," Will said.

He turned to face me a little more as he leaned his elbow on the backrest of the bench. "I thought Joey'd be a great candidate for Brian's program if they had room for him. He says he's more than ready to get back to work, but it's been a while, so he'll need all the coaching and support he can get. So that's where I've been. He and I walked around the place, and we talked to Brian. They have a spot open, so now it will be up to him."

I couldn't imagine having the courage to engage with someone I didn't know and to offer to help them, no matter what that entailed or how long it might take. "Will, running into you this morning could be the best thing that has hap-pened to Joey in years," I said.

"I hope it all works out."

"You know you can follow up to see how he's doing."

"Oh yeah, I'm planning to. I told him I'd be checking in. It's not really my business, but once he's settled in, I'm going to encourage him to let his boy know he's okay. It's a special kind of hell, the not knowing." Will looked at me for a couple of seconds, and something passed between us in that glance. I could see how deeply the man's situation had affected him.

"Let me know how I can help you. Remember, I'm your partner in crime."

"Always," he said. "How was your morning?"

"Oh, it was good." I was facing him now. "But—you missed class, and it looks like you don't have any lunch. We can go to my room and get you some food if you have a minute."

"I'm fine, thanks. Just a couple of hours ago I took Joey to a place that has pancakes and eggs and all kinds of stuff that would probably kill us if we ate it every day. I'm only drinking this Coke to be sociable." Now I got that smile from him that I loved so much.

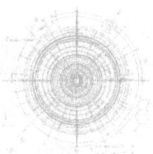

COLLEGE – Trails and Tales

September 2003

Saturday evening, I was at Will's house. The previous night, I'd gone out with Eric, and we'd had our usual anxiety-inducing date and sleepover. Now Josh, Melissa, Adam, Will, and I were enjoying beer and conversation in the living room. Josh and Melissa were on the loveseat, Adam and I on opposite ends of the sofa, and Will was sprawled on the floor, leaning back against an armchair.

"Tomorrow's supposed to be beautiful. Anyone want to go for a hike along Lyman Creek?" Melissa said.

We all agreed that sounded like a great plan. I knew the area was in northeastern Georgia, but I'd never been.

Josh said, "It's been so long. Really will be good to get back up there." He looked at Will. "Okay, so how do you want to do this? Should we caravan, or do you guys want to meet us up there around ten?"

Will said, "Meeting's fine with me. Adam and I can pick Lauren up, and we'll see you there—if that's okay with you, Laur?"

I nodded. Sounded nice and easy to me.

Melissa said, "Okay, great." She looked at me. "If you haven't been there, it's about a seven-mile hike in all, and it's not too difficult, just a couple of places that are a little steep. We always just bring whatever we want for an easy lunch at the top of the trail, and of course, water bottles."

"Sounds good, thanks."

After we'd hung out a little longer, Josh and Melissa left. I stood up and grabbed my purse, ready to leave too, but first I asked Will and Adam, "For lunch tomorrow, I have stuff to make sandwiches, but what do you guys usually bring?"

Will said, "There's a store up there that has all kinds of great cheese, fruit, crackers—whatever you want. They even have small bottles of wine. I say we just stop there on the way. Would that be okay?"

Adam gave a quick nod, and I said, "That sounds perfect. Do I need to wear my hiking boots?" I sure hoped not. They were broken in by now, but they were way too heavy for my liking.

"Nah, I wear hiking shoes just because there can be muddy spots, but you don't need anything heavy," Will said.

Adam agreed. "It's not too rough, but like he said, sometimes there's mud if they've had a lot of rain."

◇ ◇ ◇

Will arrived to pick me up the next morning, and I noticed he was alone.

"Where's Adam?" I asked.

"Oh, he had to run an errand in Midtown when he got up, so the quickest thing was for him to go to Josh's house instead of back here. He's riding up with them."

"All right, then," I said. "Guess that means we can tell our usual tall tales and lies."

"I'd like nothing better." Will pulled the Jeep onto the main road, headed for the interstate.

◇ ◇ ◇

We stopped at the store he had told me about, and the selection was wonderful. We bought cheese, a couple of pieces of fruit, crackers, and some miniature bottles of wine. I was a little concerned about the time, though. We were supposed to meet the others at ten, and I didn't see how we'd make it. It would be awful if they had to just stand by their car and wait for us. I hurried to get into the Jeep.

Will had just opened the driver's side door when his phone rang. He leaned against the Jeep with one hand resting on the edge of the roof, and I could hear his end of the conversation.

"You guys go ahead. We'll be behind you, and we'll see you at the top for lunch."

"Oh no, I guess we're late," I said, feeling a little anxious.

Will laughed. "They're okay. We'll get with them pretty soon."

◇ ◇ ◇

Walking up the trail, there was so much to see that I hardly knew which direction to look. The creek was rushing by on one side, and there were little birds flying between the trees, as well as delicate purple and blue wildflowers growing along the edges of the trail.

Will slowed almost to a stop, looking at the water. "Okay with you if we stop for a minute so we can go off the trail and look around? This is such an amazing place."

"Aren't you worried about catching up with the others?" I asked.

He flashed his gorgeous smile. "I'm sure they're taking time to see everything, too. I always like to explore a little. That work for you?"

"Absolutely." I relaxed almost immediately.

The creek was wide, and the water was flowing fast around and over large rocks, creating little rapids and cascades. As we left the trail and got closer to it, it was even louder, and just standing near it filled me with an instant sense of well-being. I could see that the whole creek bed was lined with rocks big and small, but they were wet and most likely very slippery, so I'd just look from here.

Will stepped from the bank onto a dry boulder, then took another step to a second one. "C'mon," he called me. "Stand on the first rock and I'll get you to this one."

Getting to the first one was easy enough. It wasn't too far from the edge. But from there to the large one Will was standing on was just enough of a giant step that I knew any attempt I made would probably end in wet, embarrassing disaster. "This is fine," I told him.

He leaned toward me, reaching out. "Grab my hand and take that big step, and I'll make sure you land here with both feet. On three, okay?"

It did look really inviting where he was standing. He could probably see a long way down the creek, with all its beautiful wild water.

I laughed and said, "Okay, here I come!" On his count of three I grabbed his hand and took a leap of faith. With his help, I landed right in front of him on the big boulder. After looking down to find my footing, I turned to stand beside him, taking in the beautiful sights and sounds.

◇ ◇ ◇

We eventually returned to the trail. There were a few fairly steep hills, but there were plenty of small roots to provide traction. We were looking around, talking about the scenery as we walked. We crossed a wildflower field that still had some blooms and stretched as far as we could see.

After another half mile, the trail made one more steep climb, then we came to a clearing at the summit, which descended gently toward a drop-off about fifty feet away. I could already see that the view was spectacular. A lot of other hikers were up here. Some stood at a weathered, waist-high dark metal railing, gazing at the panorama below, while others sat on large rocks or small ledges, enjoying their food and drinks as they took in the beautiful vista. I didn't see our friends, but there were plenty of people around, so they were probably there somewhere. We walked over to an unoccupied section of the railing and looked down at the rushing water and the landscape so far below.

"Kind of puts things in perspective when we think something to do with our classes is a big deal, doesn't it?" Will said.

"Yeah, maybe I need to find a picture of this and look at it every day," I agreed.

"I'd love to have one of those too. By the way, there are a lot of little waterfalls here. After lunch, if you want to, we can take a different trail back down and see one or two."

"That sounds fantastic."

"Hey, so you did make it!" I heard Josh say. He, Melissa, and Adam were walking toward us, shouldering their day-packs. Melissa was clutching a half-empty water bottle.

"Sure did," Will told him. "I love it so much. Glad they've kept it wild, but I know that makes it harder for some people to experience it."

"Yeah, it's a tough balance," Adam said, gripping the railing and looking down at the view.

The others joined us at the rail, taking in the view. After a few moments, Melissa tugged Josh's arm and turned to us, ready to go.

"Guys, enjoy your lunch," she said. "We're about to start back down. I've been dying to try to climb one of the little falls, and I think today's the day."

◇ ◇ ◇

After they left, Will and I sat together on a large rock and retrieved the food and wine from our packs. As we ate, we talked about the hike, and he told me a lot of things I'd never heard about trails and creeks and waterfalls in this part of my home state.

Looking out at the horizon, Will said, "How about this—let's come up to this area every weekend until we've explored every mountain and every stream in north Georgia."

"Every—Yeah, sure, let's do that," I said. "But can we take January off if it's bitter cold?"

"Nah, there's great hiking in winter too. Beautiful scenery, if we can get past the snow and ice."

"What will we do about next football season?" I teased.

"You know I'm not one for a lot of planning, Ms. Mahan."

"Okay, we'll wing it. That's how I roll anyway."

He laughed.

I couldn't remember the last time I had been so relaxed and happy.

◇ ◇ ◇

The path we took back out was less well marked but not too difficult, and we stopped to admire several narrow waterfalls rushing down from between huge rocks far above us. As we approached the end and were about to emerge from the lush tree canopy out onto the trailhead and into the real world, Will said, "Later on, would you like to—"

Before he could finish, my cell phone rang. It was Melissa. "We're on the road, but we were talking about going for dinner later. Want to meet around eight at Blue Sushi Grill?"

"Sure, that sounds great," I said. "I'll tell Will."

Once I'd informed him of the plan, I said, "Oh yeah, what were you about to ask me?"

"That was it." He paused for just a beat. "I was about to ask if you thought we should all grab dinner later. Blue Sushi sounds great."

We chatted on the way back. At my dorm, Will asked, "So, what time should I pick you up tonight?"

"Oh, you don't need to do that," I said. It would have been a lot more fun to go together, sure, but I didn't want to inconvenience him.

"Maybe I have a couple of tales you haven't heard yet. Ever consider that?"

I couldn't help smiling. It had been a fabulous day, and he was just so dang cute. I got out of the Jeep and was about to close the door, then I stuck my head back inside. "Seven thirty. Let's not make them wait for us again. At least not today."

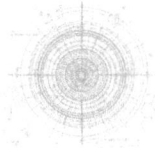

CURRENT – Grateful Heart

November 2023

I t was mid-November, and vivid memories from my college days were flooding back every day. Since Eric and I had returned from homecoming weekend, I'd spent a lot of time reading my old journals, letting the voices and moments from back then emerge and speak to me again. I often found I had a smile on my face as I drove around or went about my routine.

Life had been so satisfying, so full back then. Although there were some good people in my classes and labs, most of my real social life had orbited around Will. Now, with the clarity of hindsight, I could see what I hadn't back then—the subtle signs of Will's deeper feelings for me. He had never hidden that he thought I was special and liked spending time with me, but he had always been respectful, never crossing any lines. I had felt like a treasured friend, not realizing he had wanted something more.

Even when I started to feel something deeper, especially during our senior year, I let my fears keep me from exploring those feelings. I told myself I was protecting our friendship, unwilling to risk losing Will completely. Instead, I stayed with Eric, clinging to the familiarity of that relationship despite how poorly he treated me at times. My naivety and immaturity had blinded me to the potential for a fulfilling relationship with Will.

It was one of my biggest regrets—missing those early opportunities for something real with the person who would become the most important man in my life.

But today, thoughts of the past had to wait. Sean was coming home for the holiday. As I moved through the house—stocking his favorite snacks in the pantry and planning all the meals I wanted to cook for him—I felt a renewed sense of purpose and joy. The house already felt warmer, brighter, more alive, just knowing he'd be here soon.

◇ ◇ ◇

"Mom. Dad. What's up?"

It was the day before Thanksgiving, and Sean was making his way through the front door with his backpack slung over one shoulder and a large duffel bag in his hand. Now our home had come to life. Eric and I hadn't seen him since homecoming, and then it was just for a couple of quick meals. This would be our first opportunity in several months to have time to relax and enjoy him.

I met him halfway across the room and gave him a big hug. Eric gave him a tight little smile and a pat on the shoulder.

"It's so good to have you home," I told Sean. "Tell us all about . . . everything."

He laughed. "It's so great to be here. I'm used to cold gray halls in engineering buildings or the computer center. But school's good, and I've met so many cool people. I'll almost hate for this semester to end." He started telling us about his classes and recent projects, plus some weekend outdoor pursuits—one story after another. Then he stopped midsentence to ask, "What smells so wonderful?"

"Oh, I thought you might like some pesto chicken and pasta for dinner tonight. How's that?"

"My favorite."

How I had missed my happy, sweet son. Life was good again for a while.

◇ ◇ ◇

When Thanksgiving weekend ended, I had my customary attack of the "Smondays," but it wasn't as bad as usual. Now I could look forward to Sean coming home for the long semester break in December. At work, I'd already asked for a few days' vacation before and after Christmas, so combined with the time off the company gave us, I should have plenty of time for baking cookies and enjoying having my boy at home for a while.

Monday passed without too much pain. Business was a little slower because our customers were also taking time off, so we didn't have any meetings or office drama. Instead, I caught up on my work, creating and submitting lab reports.

The day hadn't been so bad at all, I realized as I pulled into our driveway. Maybe soon I'd hear from Michael. Just the thought of that was enough to have me daydreaming of gleaming new labs, interesting new projects, and . . .

When I stopped to get the mail, I saw a thin envelope with the Biolution logo in the upper left-hand corner. I ripped it open to find what looked like a form letter, signed with a stamp or computer-generated signature.

Dear Ms. Whitman:

Thank you for submitting your resume. Unfortunately, we do not currently have any opportunities that align with your work history and skills. We will keep your resume on file for one year, however, in case such a position becomes available. We wish you luck in your future endeavors.

Sincerely,

Krissy Johnson
Human Resources Assistant

And just like that, I once again had no hope for a career. I was a little ashamed by how depressed I suddenly felt. It wasn't as if I was going to starve or live on the streets. I had plenty of every material thing I could ever need, and I had a wonderful son—the best in the world. I felt a lump in my throat as I drove into the garage.

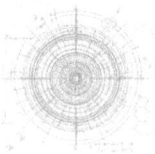

COLLEGE – Shadows and Chemistry

September 2003

Friday after class, I had almost given up on hearing from Eric. Right at five o'clock, I was about to see if anyone from my lab or maybe Will's house was going for beer or something. I had waited long enough. Then my phone rang, and it was Eric.

"Want to go to a party later?"

Oh. I didn't really. A party where I didn't know anyone at all, with a guy who wasn't exactly Mr. Social. It would be an uncomfortably awkward night.

"Sure. What time?"

"I'll pick you up around eight," he said.

"Great. See you then."

At exactly eight, my ever-prompt boyfriend knocked on my door, and off we went. He looked magnificent, like he always did. I was a tiny bit nervous as we drove to the house where the party was being held and parked down the street. To calm down, I reminded myself that the worst that could happen would be that I'd end up talking to some stranger, or rather, listening to him discuss whatever his pet hobby was, all night.

Eric didn't seem to know the guy who let us in, but the fellow greeted us and waved his hand to show us that everyone was at the back of the house, the keg visible right outside. We walked through to the patio, and Eric got us some beer in red plastic cups, then started looking around. He finally spotted his friend, the one who had invited him, and the guy saw him at the same time.

"How's it going?" He grasped Eric's hand in a big shake.

"Jon," Eric said, "this is Lauren. Lauren, this is Jon."

"Hi. Yeah, I met her last week when y'all came to Chad's."

A strange look passed between them. At first, I thought it was an "oh shit" look, where Eric had brought another woman somewhere and didn't want his friend mentioning it. That was enough to send my stomach into a downward spiral. But there was something even worse about it. It was almost as if what Jon had done was rehearsed, intended to shake me up. Why?

Never one for confrontation, I tried to cover my misery with an idiotic smile and nodded as if I didn't understand. I forced myself to look around and say something scintillating like, "Great party."

Eric and I spent the rest of the night drinking too much beer and talking to strangers. Finally, we left. In the car, he asked, "Coming home with me?"

For once in my life, I put up a bit of resistance. I was furious and didn't think he deserved as much as a smile from me, and I was in no mood to be affectionate with him. I didn't want to be treated this way for the rest of my life.

I said, "No, I need to get up early tomorrow."

"Early?" Of course he had to ask. He always thought he knew better than the person who was speaking, even about everyday details in their own life.

"Yes, early. I have to meet someone at seven to work on a project before she goes to work."

"Sucks."

He drove me home. At the door, he poked his lips out to give me a goodnight peck. "See ya."

"See ya," I managed, then slipped into the building and let the door clang shut behind me. I was a mixture of angry and hurt, and I wasn't sure if the anger was more at Eric or myself. Was he making fun of me with his friends? Why would anyone do that?

◇ ◇ ◇

When I woke up, I remembered what Eric had done the night before. A year ago, I would have wasted an hour or more of my life as well as Emily's trying to analyze what had happened, but luckily, these days there were much more important things to do. We had a home game early this afternoon.

Will, Adam, Melissa, Josh, and I gathered at Will's a couple of hours before kickoff to enjoy some food and drink, then we walked to the stadium together. It ended up being an amazing afternoon. We were on our feet for most of the game, cheering for our team and soaking up the atmosphere, and we won. After it was over, we made our way through the crowds and traffic jams back to Will's, where we hung out for a while. Fans were parked in every little space on the streets in the neighborhood, since there was no charge to park on a public road, so there were plenty of cars stopping and going just outside the front window.

Melissa and Josh went home around six. Soon after, Adam left to meet some other friends for dinner. I turned my bottle up to finish it, thinking it was time for me to head home.

"Can I interest you in another beer?" Will asked.

Of course, he would have said that whether he wanted me to stay or wanted some time to himself. I'd seen him entertain drop-in friends when he really needed to be studying because he couldn't stand the thought of disappointing anyone. But in the millisecond before I could automatically decline, he said, "Please?"

"Sure, that would be great." If he wanted my company, it sounded wonderful to me. Comfortable and relaxed, with cold beer and my favorite person. Nothing was better than that.

He grabbed the drinks, handing me one before he plopped down on the sofa, twisting his cap off and spinning it absently between his fingers. He turned to face me. "This might sound kind of random, but I've been wanting to say . . . I really appreciate how you just *get* things. Like, you can always pick up on stuff that most people miss. I don't know . . . you make me feel like I can talk about anything. It's nice." He pushed his hair away from his eyes as he looked at me.

I was caught off guard. I had expected him to joke or talk about some outdoor adventure he wanted to go on. I smiled and touched his arm for a second. "I'm really honored. You usually seem so upbeat, but I love all our conversations."

"Yeah, I try to keep the energy up, but with you . . . it's different. I can just be myself." He looked at me with a warm expression. "And I love hearing what you think. It helps me more than I can explain."

"Well, likewise. You make my life a lot more fun in so many ways," I said. I had thought about this a lot. "That fun energy of yours is exactly what I need sometimes. And you help me do things I wouldn't have the courage to do on my own—you know, like dare to leave my safe little rock and make it to a better one in the middle of a beautiful creek."

"Chemistry," he said, tilting his bottle toward me.

I clinked mine with his. "Chemistry."

It was after meeting Will that I first got interested in personality types. He was an extrovert who lived fully in the moment, never worrying about time. On the other hand, I was an introvert and always uptight about deadlines and plans. On the surface, we seemed like we'd have nothing in common, but we both shared a strong intuition and a tendency toward emotional expressiveness. That created a connection I'd felt even in the first weeks after we met.

Will seemed to be always laughing and eternally optimistic, but he cared deeply about people, and sometimes that got to him. I was touched that he trusted me enough to show me his vulnerable side, even though he tried to keep up a carefree front with everyone else. He'd transformed my life in ways I never could have imagined.

And now he was back to thinking of more fun things for us to do.

"We have a few away games coming up, so we can do some more hiking and stuff, or whatever else you'd like to try. What do you think about Cloudland Canyon? Or would you like to ride horses again if I can manage that?"

"Oh, either of those sound fantastic to me," I said. "Or both. And anything else you dream up." I leaned back on the sofa, resting my head on the cushions and turning to look at him, relaxing in a nice buzz of beer and companionship.

"Foolish ventures would be on the table?" he asked.

"They're still my favorite kind."

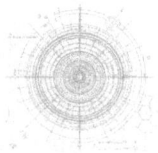

COLLEGE – Magic and Electricity

September 2003

S unday morning, I went to the rec center for some strength training, then jogged back to my dorm. After a quick shower, I called Emily, and we met for lunch in Midtown. There was a place we both loved, Ranelli's, where we could get great half sandwiches and soup, plus enough time and space to catch up on our real lives. We both had a lot of studying to do, but I rationalized that this was a replacement for an hour on a therapist's couch. The alternative was going nuts from stress.

We got started on our analysis of the previous week.

"How's life?" I asked her.

"Oh, too much to do, too much time in the law library. I think today is the first time I've been outside in real daylight since last weekend."

"Any good-looking inmates in the library?"

"Yeah, a couple. This guy Barry is really cute and super funny. But he's so competitive. I think even if we were going out, he'd step right over me or even on me if I fell." Emily played with the straw in her Coke. "Know what I mean?"

Yep, I imagined law school had to be like that. After all that studying and money, only the top few would make it to the firms they really wanted. An undergrad majoring in something like biology or psychology was the same situation. There weren't plentiful jobs for us. We had to aim for a few precious spots in the grad programs we really wanted.

"Maybe you should date a med student. Then he wouldn't be competing with you," I said. Our food arrived, and I tried my tomato basil soup. Perfect.

"On the first day of medical school, I believe they brainwash them to despise all attorneys automatically," Emily said. "But really, I'm happy just going out with my friends on Friday nights, keeping it casual. Once I start applying to work at firms, I don't want to worry about geography. I'll meet someone once I get settled in a city for a while."

I couldn't imagine what would happen if my sister moved far away. What if she ended up working in the Northeast or on the other side of the country and I couldn't see her? Or what if I ended up in grad school far away next year? So far, I hadn't yet figured out what specialty to focus on, so I hadn't filled out any applications, but I had to get going on that so I wouldn't miss the deadlines.

"How about you? How was the party with Eric?"

I told her about what he and his friend had done, and her face grew stern. "He is such an ass."

"I know. I decided it would be a good idea to search for a new contestant."

"Great. Glad to hear it," Emily said, lifting a spoonful of soup to her mouth. "Got anyone in mind?"

"It's too bad; there's one guy I feel a really strong connection with, and I love every second I spend with him, but I wouldn't ever really try to date him. To a little nerd like me, he's larger than life. He's one of those people who is always looking for the next new and exciting experience, and let's face it—being in a relationship with me would not provide that."

"You're selling yourself short," Emily said, tilting her head a little and looking at me with her fond big sister expression. She was only one year older, but she knew a hell of a lot more than I did about the world. "Are you telling me you have feelings for Will?"

"Well of course I love him, but I think everyone does. He's so cute and just naturally flirty and outgoing. Whenever I see him around campus, he always has people around him, girls and guys, laughing and talking. If we started going out and he got bored with me and moved on, or even worse, if I drove him away with my insecurity, I'd lose the chance to enjoy his companionship at all." I saw that I had shredded my napkin, so I reached for another one. "Right now, I feel free to hang out with him as much as I want, and we can talk about anything. It would destroy me if he didn't like me anymore and avoided me."

It made me feel a little sick even to think about that. There was no way I'd ever risk it.

"I just want you to be happy, and life sure would be easier if you dated someone like Will, who actually, I don't know, had a personality. So you could talk to him like a normal person and know what the hell was going on with him, for one thing."

"It can't be Will, but I'll look around. I know what you mean about normal, and it's a great point, but I'm not sure I could settle for normal, easy, simple—that sort of thing. I want electricity, magic, crazy passion . . ."

Emily looked amused. She'd heard this from me before. "Those sound like great qualities for a relationship in a fun beach read, but use that brain of yours. Do you think relationships like that have happy endings in real life?"

Sadly, I didn't know. I wasn't too smart about real life and had seen far too little magic and electricity, anyway.

◊ ◊ ◊

That afternoon, I did my laundry and went for a nice, long walk around campus. The weather was glorious, and once again, I was trying to give Mr. Normal a chance. Whoever he was, all he had to do was show that he was interested in being part of a regular, average couple, and off we'd go.

I looked at the various guys I passed on the sidewalk. They were just humans like me, some nicer looking than others. None of them would ever make my heart pound the way Eric did, and none of them seemed too impressed with me, either. I knew that if I could just be patient, I'd meet someone eventually. I just didn't know what to do with my heart until then.

I finally got back to my room and was pulling off my shoes when my phone rang. It was Eric.

"Hi there," he said, his voice crackling with that Eric confidence.

"Hi." I tried to forget it was the guy with the perfect looks on the other end. I tried to sound cheerful, as if he were just someone who sat across from me in bacteriology class, calling to ask a question.

"You want to grab some dinner later?"

Oh, I wished I had an obligation this evening that I couldn't get out of. I needed to pull away from Eric. I knew that, but for some reason I couldn't make the decision to say no to him.

"Sure."

"All right. What is it, five thirty now? Pick you up at seven." Then he was gone.

Okay, no more searching for Mr. Someone Else, at least for now. I didn't know exactly what had happened Friday night, but maybe that friend of his had been mistaken, or maybe things would get better. It was time to get ready for my date.

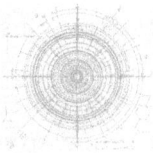

COLLEGE – Foolish Venture

OCTOBER 2003

O n a Thursday in late October, *Seinfeld* was over and the others had left. Adam was out somewhere, and Will and I were in the kitchen finishing the cleanup. I put the last bowl of leftovers in the refrigerator and wiped the table. Time for me to go.

Will turned off the water and dried his hands on a dish towel. "What would you say to a foolish venture?" He leaned against the kitchen counter, his hand resting on the surface as he faced me. "Maybe Saturday?"

"Sure. That's great timing for me; I have no tests anytime soon. What do you have in mind?"

"Anything you like. We can just wing it when we hit the road, if you think that would be more fun. Outdoor stuff, or we could take a drive and explore a new town—whatever sounds good."

"I'd love to do something outside," I said.

"Me too." He nodded. "Okay, should we ask a few more people to join, or would you prefer it to be just us?" He paused, seeming to think. "Maybe this time we should keep it just us? That way, if we see something we want to do, we can just go for it. Total freedom, no need to convince a crowd."

"That sounds perfect to me," I said. I was already getting excited.

"This is a little out of character for me, but I want you to feel comfortable and happy, so maybe bring a change of clothes? Just some extra jeans and a shirt. If we end up hiking or wading through a creek and then want to grab dinner somewhere, being a little dusty or damp might limit our options."

I laughed. "I appreciate the heads up and will definitely do that."

He said, "This is going to be amazing. It's whatever we want to do, so be thinking about it."

I was sure I'd think about nothing else. When was the last time I'd been on a spontaneous day trip just for fun, no structure and no schedule? Never, was my guess.

◇ ◇ ◇

Early Saturday morning Will came to pick me up. "Good morning, Ms. Mahan," he said as I hopped in the Jeep. I buckled up, and he turned toward the interstate. "Where to?"

"I'd like to be surprised," I said, smiling. "Anything you haven't explored yet that you've been wanting to see? Or somewhere you love and want to go back to?"

"I'll start heading north and we'll see what happens," he said.

We pulled away from campus and began leaving the city behind. Traffic clogged many of the parkways and main roads in north Georgia. It seemed like half of Atlanta was up there to see the leaves, but that didn't faze Will. He continued north-east along smaller roads, revealing breathtaking, colorful views as we drove through the mountains. Sometimes we'd turn onto unmarked narrow roads, some of them dirt or gravel, just to see what was there. Even the grasses and vines were beautiful at this time of year, wild nature at its most vibrant.

A few miles down one rutted dirt road, we found a trail-head that looked promising and began walking up the path. The colors of the leaves around us were incredible—red, yellow, orange, bronze, and even purple. The terrain was rough in some areas, with lots of rocky patches, a few fallen trees to go under or over, and some steep inclines, but that just made it more interesting and enjoyable. We used boulders and, at one point, several broken sections of a massive log to cross beautiful creeks. From time to time, Will helped me when I needed it. It just felt natural and fun. We eventually made it to a summit, where we had a breathtaking view of distant mountains, all covered with glorious colors and lit up by the sun.

◇ ◇ ◇

When we left the trail, the sun was setting. Will said, "I don't know about you, but I'm starving."

"Same here," I told him. "It came on all of a sudden."

"Guess we'd better get back to that main road and see what's available."

We stopped at a mom-and-pop-type gas station, and Will asked a couple of locals for advice. Soon, we found ourselves in a restaurant that had been recommended for its delicious fresh food and nice, casual atmosphere.

Our server Tom approached our table almost immediately. "Can I get you something besides water?"

We were at least two hours away from Atlanta, and I could tell Will was about to shake his head and say not for him, so I cut in. "Will, we don't have to drive back tonight unless *you* need to get back. I'm happy to keep exploring."

He shot me a big smile and said to Tom, "Don't ever let 'em tell you there's no such thing as the perfect woman." Turning to me, he continued, "How about a bottle of wine on this fine autumn evening? Let's have a look at this list."

When our wine arrived, Will lifted his glass. "To our first foolish venture."

I clinked mine against his. "First of many, I hope."

His smile widened. "Oh, definitely."

The rest of dinner was fabulous. We talked about our childhood dreams, pets we'd had, ridiculous things we'd done—everything in the world. The warm restaurant lighting caught Will's face as he leaned forward, telling me stories about the backyard adventures he'd had with his first dog. I didn't know when I'd ever had so much fun talking and laughing, and I'd been hanging out with him and his friends for over a year now.

When we were almost finished, lingering over the last drops of wine, he asked, "You're really okay to stay up here and keep playing? I can get us home tonight if you'd like to go back, no problem at all."

"Absolutely okay. I'm having the time of my life, and I don't want it to end," I said.

"Same here. I feel like a different person when I have some freedom like this and can get out and see something new."

⋄ ⋄ ⋄

Outside the restaurant, Will leaned back against the Jeep's driver door and turned to me. "It's still early, but with me being a big planner and all, I thought we'd better talk about where we'll spend the night, in case it takes some time to find a place."

"Oh, yeah, what do you think?" I asked.

"Hotels are probably all booked up, and I can check, but even if they are, I have a buddy who's the manager at one just a few miles from here. He always has at least a couple of rooms that he can't let regular guests have. You know, something needs maintenance, like the safe won't stay locked. Just little things. So, there's that. Otherwise, we could find ourselves a little campsite somewhere and sleep under the stars. I mean that literally, though—I don't have my tent. I do have three sleeping bags in the back. They're clean, just been washed. I use them for when the guys and I ride bikes on the trails and we decide to stay in the mountains and drink beer."

"Wow, sleeping under the stars sounds so awesome," I said. "Without city lights, I can't even imagine how beautiful the sky will be."

"It's incredible out there, especially if you get far enough into the rural areas. I've got groundsheets and thick pads for our sleeping bags, but it'll still be pretty rough compared to your cushy Tech dorm." Will gave me his cute smile. "If we end up just pulling the Jeep into a car-camping slot, it will be nice and quiet, but . . . no restroom, of course. Or maybe we can find a legit campsite that has real bathrooms nearby. They may all be taken this time of year, but we can try."

"I'll be okay. When I was in high school, the only thing to do in my town on the weekends was to camp out with my friends on someone else's land and drink all night—Miller Lite someone's older brother bought, usually. And really, I'd like a more primitive, private site. That way it will be quiet, and no one will hear our tall tales," I said.

"Okay then, I think I know the perfect place we can go. It's a remote mountain road that has car camping, so it'll be plenty dark enough for us to see those stars. We'll stop somewhere before we leave civilization, though, so we can pick up your Miller Lite and anything else you can think of."

I felt a smile of pure joy spread across my face.

◇ ◇ ◇

After being in Atlanta for so long, I had forgotten how dark the night could be. The road we were on was totally black, of course, but Will's headlights eventually showed us a vacant site, and he pulled the Jeep in. We used flashlights to see as we laid out our sleeping bags. He had brought a couple of gallons of drinking water from home, plus some tablets we could use to make fresh water safe to drink. We'd drunk some during the day, but we still had plenty.

As we started settling in, I pulled a little tube of toothpaste and two new toothbrushes from my daypack and offered one to him.

"Wow, I'm really glad you thought of that. You're a lifesaver," he said.

◇ ◇ ◇

Lying there in total darkness, it seemed like there were a million stars floating close to us. I was perfectly comfortable—Will had found a nice, flat spot where we could set up side by side. I wished I still knew the constellations. I was sure I'd learned about some of them as a child.

I told him, "This is so perfect. It's the closest to nature I've ever felt. Total immersion. Makes me want to learn a lot more about our universe."

"Same. I think we need experiences like this more often," he said. "Does wonders for my mental health, anyway."

We lay there silently for a few minutes, looking at the sky. But I knew he'd be getting bored with silence soon, unless he was ready to sleep. The soft swish of his sleeping bag told me he was already shifting around.

"What's the worst thing you've ever done? Only asking for funny stuff—don't have to talk about things that make us unhappy," I said.

He laughed. "Okay, get ready. This one is gonna have a lot of embellishment."

"Good, let's hear it."

◇ ◇ ◇

Later, as we got drowsy and our conversation slowed, Will said, "If you need to get up during the night, please wake me so I can listen out for you. I mean it. If I open my eyes and you're not there, it's going to scare me, and I'll probably call the sheriff and all kinds of stuff that will go terribly wrong."

"I understand. Because then if I don't come back, you'd be in this whole situation where you wonder when it would be okay to leave. Like, do you have to stay until six o'clock tomorrow morning? Nine? Awkward."

He laughed. "Lauren."

"I promise," I said, "And same goes for you."

In my cocoon with my eyes closed, I snuggled deeper and turned on my side toward him, my arms curled comfortably against my chest. I mumbled, "Don't leave me."

"Never," he said.

I drifted off to sleep in the fresh mountain air.

◇ ◇ ◇

When I opened my eyes again, the sun was up, and Will wasn't there. I twisted around and saw that he was coming toward me from the other side of the Jeep. He sat down on his sleeping bag, next to my feet.

"Morning. How did you like cowboy camping?"

"Loved it. I don't know if I can ever sleep in my room again," I said.

"Same here. It was amazing. No hurry, but when you want to get up, I'll take a walk over that way so you can get ready for the day. I'll stay near the road to make sure no one comes up here from that direction, but I'll be close enough to hear you if you need me."

"I'd like to get up now," I said. "Thanks."

He got to his feet. "Oh, the back of the Jeep is a pretty decent spot to get dressed, and I've got some stuff in there to freshen up—plus trash bags. It's unlocked." He headed off.

I appreciated his thoughtfulness. Will surely didn't know it, but I had removed everything except my shirt last night and stuffed it down in the bottom of my sleeping bag. The privacy he was giving me would let me move around freely and quickly. It seemed I hadn't yet invented a way to be awkward that Will didn't quietly smooth over. I loved the way that made me feel.

◇ ◇ ◇

After we fortified ourselves with breakfast at a little diner, we traveled a narrow, extremely curvy road up the side of a nearby mountain in search of more beautiful hiking spots. We soon found a small parking area and a trailhead that led to a narrow path lined with blazing colors from the oak, maple, and hickory trees. After about a mile of steady, gradual uphill walking, we reached a rocky outcrop beside the top of a massive waterfall. There we stood, not too far from the edge, watching the powerful white water tumble to a deep pool far below. I loved hearing its roar. I loved feeling the mist from it on my face, too. This place was heavenly.

"Looks like there's a way to climb down to the bottom if we want to," Will said. "Then we could see the whole thing from down there. It's a little steep and might be wet and slippery in places, but it could be fun. Or I bet if we keep walking up here, we'll discover another trail we can use to go down there. Either way's totally fine with me."

I had a look at the narrow, rocky descent. I was feeling brave today. "I'd like to give it a try." Will was standing next to me, looking down at the path. I reached up and let the tips of my fingers brush the stubble along his jawline for a second. "I like the scruff," I said.

He grinned, eyes full of mischief. "Ah, so you've noticed my 'effortlessly rugged' look," he teased, his voice low and playful. "Good—it's totally intentional."

We got back to the Jeep at around six. While still in north Georgia, we decided to stop at a charming little place for dinner to prolong our experience a while longer. Then we headed back to reality.

When we got to my dorm, Will didn't pull up and drop me off like usual. Instead, he parked near the door.

"Didn't seem right to let you out with a quick 'see ya,'" he said.

I nodded. "Will, thank you so much. This has been the best weekend, and as usual, I can't find the right words. But I'm sure you know."

"It has been awesome," he said. "How can I go home alone to routine and homework when all I want to say is, 'Where do you want to go now?'"

"Me too. And no stars watching over us tonight, either."
I could have sat there for hours talking to him, but I assumed
he wanted to get on with it. "Well, I guess I'll let you get home
and take care of your camping stuff. Be thinking of some good
tales for next time."

"I'll do my best." He reached over and squeezed my hand,
his palm warm and solid against mine. "I enjoyed it so much,
Lauren. We have to do it again soon."

"Can't wait," I said.

◊ ◊ ◊

When I got into my room and took my phone out of my bag, I
saw that I had a couple of missed calls from Eric, one yesterday
morning and one yesterday afternoon. Now I was glad he was
a last-minute kind of guy. If he'd locked down my Saturday a
few days in advance, I would have missed one of the sweetest
and most enjoyable weekends I'd ever had.

Eric called just as I was emptying my daypack.

"Where've you been?" he asked. "You always answer your
phone."

"Oh, I was away yesterday. Sorry," I said. How had I gotten
so many oak leaves in here?

"I was trying to get you. I'd wondered if you wanted to go
hiking today."

"Thanks, but that's not really my thing," I said. "Maybe
we can see a movie or something soon—your turn to pick."

It occurred to me that if I were dating Will, instead of
basking in the afterglow of our weekend, I'd probably already
be worrying about if I had bored him, if he had decided I was
definitely not the one for him, and if he'd ever call again. That
was stressful enough with other, replaceable guys. It could *not*
happen with Will. As I'd told Emily, I was in a good position

right now where I could see him every day if I wanted to. I didn't want to be the shooting star who enjoyed one hot moment, then disappeared.

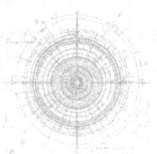

CURRENT – Echoes of Yesterday

DECEMBER 2023

I n mid-December, Sean was coming home for winter break. I couldn't wait to have him with us again for a few weeks, even if it would require a little adjustment. He was sure to have his usual pack of young people coming in and out of the house, and I'd finally gotten used to the quiet after all these months. Still, I was more than ready for any amount of noise and activity if it was Sean's.

As I made a list of his favorite foods to pick up at the supermarket, I got a text from him.

oh yeah we need to move everything out of my dorm room Saturday moving different dorm after the break

It looked like I'd be back on campus for part of Saturday. Did I dare to hope I might have another experience with the past? I didn't know how it had happened or what caused it the previous times. I felt a little thrill of anticipation, although I knew it was silly. Had it happened because of the strong feelings I was having, or could I count on making it work anytime I went into that hall?

What I wouldn't have given for another sweet hour with Will like the one I'd had back at the beginning of the fall semester. But all I could do was go back to that dorm and try to find my way back to him.

◇ ◇ ◇

"Wait a minute. Are you telling me you're going all the way to Atlanta to help Sean move his stuff because you think you're going to have one of those dreams again? Why don't you try to see if there's a medium somewhere who can have a séance?" Heather said during lunch the next day. She laughed as she dug into her Cobb salad.

Her comment was like a sucker punch. Séance? I wasn't thinking about talking to the dead in some spooky service; I wanted to talk to the living, to the man with whom I'd had the most vital relationship of my life. Sure, the interlude had taken place in the past, but there was nothing dead about it.

"Wow. That was kind of brutal," I said. But of course, Heather had no way of knowing how much I loved Will or what a tragedy his death had been to all of us. It had been so long ago that she must think of it as ancient history.

"I'm sorry," she said, wide-eyed. "I didn't mean anything bad. I thought you were thinking you wanted to communicate with Will somehow, or at least hoped you might."

I put my fork down, smiling a little. "I don't know what I can hope for, but I want to be there. It gives me hope, and even gives me a little of the good feelings from those days. I crave that now. It was overwhelming and sad when we first got to campus back in August, but what happened that day really made me happy for a while. *Whatever* it was."

"Lauren." Heather looked directly into my eyes, her face full of sympathy. "Are you sure you don't need to see someone? I'm worried about you. If you're so stressed that you're kind of . . . mixing dreams and real life?"

"Losing my tenuous grasp on reality?" I said, with a bigger smile. "No, I assure you, I'm very much present in real life. I've done nothing but engage in normal, routine daily life since I was last there."

"Okay. I know you can handle it." Heather put her fork down. "Oh—did I tell you what I heard about David Hunter's affair with that OR nurse?" And like that, she was off and running on a great gossip story she'd picked up at the fitness center.

◇ ◇ ◇

Finally, Saturday arrived. Sean needed us at his dorm around ten, because he had the ten-thirty time slot to check out with his resident advisor, so we had to get up early. For the first time in a long time, I felt inspired and excited while getting dressed, almost as if I were getting ready for a date.

On the drive to Atlanta, I kept thinking about Will and the courtyard. I couldn't wait to try to get there again. I was deep in this daydream when I realized Eric was talking.

"Are you asleep? Don't you pay attention to anything anymore?"

"Sorry, just lost in thought," I said, feeling a little irritated at the disturbance.

A few months ago, I would have been alert to even the smallest utterance from Eric. I might have walked around feeling angry or hurt much of the time, but I had been conditioned to anticipate his advice and criticism, to head off his disapproval before it could start. Now, after being with Will for that one magical hour in the courtyard, I found myself caring less and less about my husband's opinion.

◊ ◊ ◊

Finally, we got close to the dorm and pulled over near a campus cop, who waved us toward an area where we could park temporarily. We were supposed to load the car and leave, but if I could go back to talk to Will for a minute, or a million years, I'd let Eric worry about parking.

It was nine forty-five, so we were early. We got out and headed toward the dorm, and I texted Sean that we had arrived.

Since it was move-out day, the door was propped open, and we proceeded inside, with Eric rolling the hand truck in front of him. We went up to the second floor and walked toward Sean's room, but as soon as Eric started talking to him about what to move first, I took off to the spot where I had entered the courtyard back in the fall. I walked down the corridor, scanning the walls carefully for a sign of that ancient door.

It had been on the same floor as Sean's room, which meant I had one floor to cover—and cover it I did. I walked along the right wall, turning at each corner, all the way around to the end. Nothing. Then I walked back, doing the same thing to the other wall, just in case. Occasionally I got the sense that students might be noticing my search, but who cared?

Disappointment washed over me, and I felt the familiar ache of depression seeping in. *Please.* I still had a secret wish that the door would suddenly appear in front of me. If this had been a movie, I would have found it at that moment.

Something, somehow, would have made this beautiful time with Will happen again.

Instead, I stood there miserably, thinking about him. Why had I been so stupid and immature as a college student? A pain grew deep in the center of my chest. Of course I knew logically that, even though I had been afraid and too anxious to tell Will how I felt about him, I hadn't caused his death. He still would have gone on that trip if I'd been his girlfriend, and the accident still probably would have happened. But at least we would have had some time together as a real couple, and he would have known that he was loved.

I stood in that hall and finally allowed all the revelations that had been seeping in over the past few months to become crystal clear. It was a miserable, even agonizing experience, because the time to act on this knowledge had long passed.

As I stood in the dorm hallway, being passed by parents and students going back and forth with belongings and carts and hand trucks, all I wanted was to retreat somewhere and curl up in a ball of sadness. Instead, I somehow shuffled down to Sean's room.

He and Eric were getting the last load of clothes out and letting the resident advisor sign off on the room being vacated. We left the dorm carrying the bags. Eric didn't say a word to me, but Sean was telling us about his past week on campus, and I tried to respond as best I could to his enthusiasm. He made it easy by doing most of the talking.

Once we got to the car and packed the clothes into the gaps between the boxes and other bags, Sean was ready to get his own vehicle and drive it home. Suddenly, I felt I had to see the house Will had rented all those years ago. I had to at least taste the tiniest bit of those golden days. I asked Eric and Sean if we could go up to Fourteenth Street instead of Tenth to get on the interstate.

"Why?" Eric asked. He asked this more than any other question in the world.

"I'm hungry and thought it would be great to grab a sandwich at the Cuban place instead of having to stop for food on our way back."

Hunger, plus a reluctance to stop once he got on the interstate, were concrete things that Eric seemed to understand, so our little family caravan crossed the north part of campus and through the residential area on the way to Fourteenth Street.

I kept my gaze fixed out my window, so as we passed by, I didn't need to turn my head conspicuously to see Will's old house. The apple tree he and I had planted all those years ago was still there. It was now mature, but its limbs were bare, and it looked dead in this ugly winter season. The entire scene was desolate—bare branches, gray skies, dead or dormant grass. I closed my eyes in misery as Eric continued to drive.

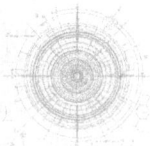

COLLEGE – Midnight Clear

December 2003

A couple of weeks before fall semester ended, I found a good photo of Lyman Creek. It showed an area filled with huge boulders, and in the foreground two of them were nearly touching, forming a natural bridge over the rushing water. Above and behind that were pretty trees and a sheer, rocky cliff face. It was a great image, but I didn't want to just frame a print. I wanted to make it more personal. I got my graphite pencils out and got started.

It took me a few days of working on it whenever I had time. As I drew, I imagined the smell and the roar of the water and the mist on my face. I tried to capture all the feelings I'd had when I stood with Will on that boulder in a different stretch of the creek a few months before. Once I finished the drawing, I signed it with my initials, sprayed it with fixative, and let it dry. I wanted to be sure not to smear anything before I could get it protected under glass.

Friday after my classes were over, I took it to be framed. I had called the shop the day before and asked if someone could do it for me while I waited. The woman behind the counter showed me a selection of mats, and I decided on a sage green to evoke thoughts of the outdoors. Once the drawing was returned to me, I took it back to my room and wrapped it in uncoated, moss-green paper tied with a woven, natural ribbon. I'd add a sprig of holly or maybe eucalyptus as a decoration later. For now, I just had to have the willpower to let it stay safely on my closet shelf.

◇ ◇ ◇

A week later, Eric and I got together the night before he left for his parents' house for winter break. We went out to dinner at Giorgia's, the place he had taken me for our second date. Afterward, we went to his apartment, and it was time to exchange Christmas presents. He handed me a beautiful, gift-wrapped box from Mimi's Boutique. Inside was a cashmere winter scarf. It was very long and very soft, but it was black and bright red with a bold pattern. My coat was tweedy and the color of blueberries, with some little green threads woven in here and there, and the scarf would clash horribly with it. In fact, I never wore red at all, but Eric had probably never noticed that. It was all right.

"Thank you," I said. "This is so soft and beautiful."

He looked pleased. I gave him his gift. He had previously remarked that he liked my daypack because of the way the straps curved, so I had gone by Mountain High and bought a similar one for him.

When he had unwrapped it, he scrutinized it and remarked, "I'm just not sure about these compartments. This may not work for me."

"Luckily there's a gift receipt tucked in there, so you can go to Mountain High and get what you want." I wasn't hurt. I'd heard from plenty of friends that it was hard to buy stuff for their boyfriends because "nothing is perfect." Maybe I was learning how to not be so oversensitive, because I wasn't disappointed at all. In fact, I was getting bored. "You said you got a new DVD from Netflix, right? What is it?"

We watched a movie in his room, and I stayed over as usual. Eric left for North Carolina after taking me home.

◇ ◇ ◇

Emily and I both wanted to stay in Atlanta for most of the break. We were finished with life in a dying small town, or at least I sure hoped so. We had lost our mother a few years before, and now our dad was married to a woman, Catherine, who usually wanted the two of them to spend holidays in Florida with her grown children and their families. They would be home on Christmas Day this year, though, so my sister and I would go to Dismal and make an appearance for dinner, then come back to the city we loved.

◇ ◇ ◇

Two days before Christmas, I called Will. "Hey, are you home and somewhat alone?"

"Sure, you coming over?"

"See you in a minute."

He was going to be leaving the next day to ski in North Carolina with a couple of friends, returning on the 28th, so I was happy to find him on his own on his last day in town. I didn't have gifts for anyone else and didn't want to be rude.

I handed him the green package I had wrapped a couple of weeks before. "Just wanted to stop by and give you a little Christmas present."

"So glad you came. I was going to call you a little later and bring you something," he said, retrieving a beautiful gift from an end table and handing it to me. The paper was a metallic midnight blue with tiny silver stars and had a silver tag with my name on it. We settled onto the sofa together.

"You first," he said.

I opened my present. Inside was an exquisite smoky light-blue-green stone pendant on an intricate gold chain. I looked at Will, at a loss for words for a second, but finally managed to say, "I love it. Thank you."

"You're more than welcome. I got it from an artist at a show in Piedmont Park about a month ago. She called it a raindrop. I'd told her I wanted something for my favorite nature lover, and when she showed me this one, I knew I had to have it. It's the same color as your eyes."

I hoped my face conveyed my feelings, because now I was totally speechless. I picked it up and opened the clasp, ready to put it on.

"Here, let me," he said, holding out his hand. "I can't tell you how hard it's been not to give it to you early."

I turned so my back was to him and lifted up my hair. He fastened the necklace around my neck, his fingers brushing my skin as he did. Then he touched my shoulder lightly. I turned to face him.

"Gorgeous," he said, looking at me. I smiled and got my mirror out to have a look. It was indeed.

"Okay, now you," I said.

He picked up his present and carefully removed the wrapping, then had a long look at the picture. "You did this for me?" His eyes lit up with surprise and appreciation. "Thank you—this really means a lot."

"That's one section of the creek, of course, but if there's another scene you like better, I'll do another one and it can be a series," I offered.

"Lauren, I don't even know what to say. I love it. It's incredible." He was still studying the details of the drawing. "I can almost hear the water." He met my eyes. "I was going to hang it here in the living room, but . . . I think I'll put it in my room instead. It should be the first thing I see when I wake up every day."

We heard a car pull up, and we stood up, looking at one another. I was flooded with strong emotion and didn't know what to do. I thought about what I'd do if a female friend had just given me such a beautiful gift. I asked, "Would a Christmas hug be all right?"

Will held out his arms. "Bring it in."

◊ ◊ ◊

By New Year's Eve, I was still having a great time even though most students hadn't returned from break yet. Will and some other friends were in town, and of course Emily was too. Since we hadn't yet started the next semester, there was no academic pressure, and we had all the time in the world to relax and enjoy life.

Will had said he'd like to have a very casual gathering at his house tonight—just some friends, food, and beer, plus bubbles at midnight. I invited Emily, but she had a similar party to go to with her own friends. About twenty people from our circle said they'd come, so he and I went to buy bottles of reasonably priced champagne, bags of ice, and other supplies. Eric had already told me he would not be coming back to campus until the night before we started class, so for once I could just have fun and not be anxious about possible conflicts.

When we got back to Will's house, we started chilling the bottles and prepping the food. With some recipes we found on the internet, we prepared a few kinds of appetizers we could put in the oven right before the party, so we could have warm hors d'oeuvres yet be free to enjoy the evening. Once everything was ready to go in the fridge, I ran home to put on my soft white sweater—and my beautiful raindrop necklace.

◦ ◦ ◦

I had a great time catching up with familiar people and meeting a few new ones. Throughout the evening, I kept an eye on the tables, making sure food made its way from the kitchen to the living room whenever it was needed. Earlier, I had told Will I'd like to handle that tonight. I loved to see him carefree, laughing and talking, and this was a little gift I could give him. He had always done his best to make things fun and nice for me and everyone else, and he deserved to have someone think of him, too. The sound of his laughter made me happy.

The living room looked festive, with the lights dimmed and candles glowing on the side tables. Music played at just the right volume to create a pleasant background ambiance. As twelve o'clock approached, I started to look at the crowd. Was it mostly couples? When they had arrived, they'd come in groups of a few at a time, so I had no idea. Oh well, as awkward as I always felt as the third—or nineteenth—wheel at a New Year's Eve gathering, surely each of these people would be more concerned with what they were doing at that moment than with what I wasn't doing. It wouldn't be a big deal. I'd just hide in the kitchen.

It took about half a minute before a horrible thought struck me. Was one of these women going to be with Will at midnight? Or maybe more than one beauty, depending on where he happened to be standing at that moment? He was so cute and friendly, there was no telling what would happen. The thought made me feel extremely uncomfortable. I wasn't Will's girlfriend, but that didn't mean I wouldn't be devastated to have to watch him with someone who was or would be. And what would happen *after* midnight?

I glanced at the door, wondering if I could possibly leave right now without anyone noticing and making a big deal. Thinking it through for a few seconds, I realized that would make me even more anxious, worried that Will might notice I was missing and become concerned or even mad at me.

I looked around until I found him in the kitchen, pouring champagne into flutes. He glanced up at me, his eyes full of happiness. "It's almost that time," he said.

"Yeah, it kind of snuck up on me." I turned my back and busied myself pulling a couple of trays from a cabinet. By now I knew Will could read my emotions like no one else could, and I was determined not to dampen his mood with my anxiety.

We carried the filled glasses to the living room. People began to take the flutes from our trays, getting ready to toast the new year. With ten seconds left, someone started counting down, and I started to slink back to the kitchen with my empty tray. I felt so damned lonely.

"Lauren." Will was behind me, holding two glasses. As I turned to face him, he stepped close to me and gave me one. "Happy New Year!" His smile warmed my heart.

"Happy New Year, Will."

He leaned in, giving me a quick kiss on the cheek. His lips were warm and soft against my skin. "This is going to be the best year yet."

One thing was for sure: it was getting off to a perfect start.

◊ ◊ ◊

When I woke up midmorning New Year's Day, I realized how unfair my worries had been to Will. How could I have thought I'd be left in an awkward position right there in his home, when we had happily worked together on party prep much of the day? He was always attuned to the people around him and would never have let someone feel excluded if he could help it. Everyone was important to him. Whenever he saw someone sitting alone at any social event, he'd go talk to them or ask them to help him do a little task like getting more chairs or something—whatever he thought would help them feel comfortable. He had understood me from the very beginning, allowing me to ease into social events with his group, doing fun activities that didn't require a lot of small talk, until I knew everyone a little better and things came more naturally. And he was kind enough not to ever mention it.

Not long after I'd met him, I'd come to trust him with my sensitive soul, and he had never given me reason not to. So, if anything had changed, it was me. I had almost let jealousy and anxiety take over last night, and I needed to remember to relax and have faith in him like I always had, or I might really blow it someday.

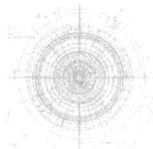

COLLEGE – Roots of Forever

January 2004

On the fourth Saturday in January, Will called around ten and invited me to help pick out the apple tree we'd plant in the backyard where the pig pit had been. This time of year, the sapling would be dormant, and we knew that was best, so it would have time to establish its root system before springtime.

"I have to work with Carl for a while," he said, "and I'm headed over there now. Can I pick you up at three?"

"Isn't that too late in the day to get started?" I asked.

"Nah, we'll be okay," he said. "This is going to be amazing, planting a new tree! So . . . is three okay for me to pick you up?"

If it was all right with him, it was all right with me. He was the one with the landlord who was expecting this to happen.

By four, we were at Martin's Nursery, and there were so many choices I didn't know how to help with the selection at all. After we looked around a minute, Will engaged an employee in a friendly conversation, and soon the man proudly showed us the young tree he thought was the best they had.

He assisted us with some other things we would need, such as compost, mulch, and some nutrients to add to the soil.

Back at Will's house, with the sun beginning to set, we focused on the end of the old roasting pit that got the most sunlight each day, digging out enough earth to leave a shallow area for planting. We cleared weeds and grass from the dirt, then unloaded the Jeep, walking around the side of the house to the backyard with our purchases. By now the sun had set, but we had streetlights and moonlight, and our task would be straightforward enough.

Looking at the slender sapling, I started to wonder if there was anything else we should have done or if we should have read up on it before today, but before I could ask, Will rested his hand on my shoulder for a moment and gave me an easy grin. "We won't mess this up, Mahan. Promise."

I was used to carrying the entire mental load for everything in my life—something a lot of people, especially single ones, did. But I noticed how the usual hum of tension in my mind dissolved when I heard Will's words. It was nice that I had a partner for some things now.

We got to work, and in near darkness, Will and I planted the tiny tree. We took our time, spreading out all of the delicate roots before we placed a mixture of soil, compost, and fertilizer around them. We covered all but the top portion, leaving them barely peeking out, then watered the area thoroughly and added a layer of mulch, careful to keep it away from the trunk.

As we stepped back and dusted off our hands, Will said, "Could I tempt you with some spaghetti and meatballs? The sauce is already made."

"Sounds great. Who did the cooking?"

"You're looking at him."

"Sure," I said. He must have done it last night, since we'd had the usual potluck gathering on Thursday. I looked away for a second, wondering who he had made dinner for. If it had been a gathering of our usual crew, I assumed I would have known. Of course, it was none of my business who he had entertained here.

When I glanced back at Will, he was looking at me. He said, "I was out last night, but when I got home, I made a pot of homemade sauce with meatballs. I got the idea when it was too late to call you, but I was hoping we could plant the tree today and have dinner after, so I took a chance you'd want to."

◦ ◦ ◦

Will turned on some music and we grabbed a couple of cold beers and put water on to boil. We chopped veggies for a salad and heated up the sauce while the pasta cooked. The incredible aroma of garlic, tomatoes, and herbs filled the kitchen. When everything was ready, Will opened a bottle of Sangiovese and poured a glass for each of us with a playful flourish that made me smile.

The food and wine were exquisite. "Okay, now I am *totally* blown away," I told him, "And in fact, I'm a little bit embarrassed about the things I've been bringing here on Thursday nights."

"Oh," he said, "thanks, but you're good as far as the Thursday stuff. This sauce was my grandmother's recipe." He leaned in closer, his voice dropping a little, beautiful eyes full of humor. "I've been saving it for if I really wanted to impress a girl."

I couldn't help but laugh. "Consider it a total success."

After dinner, we washed the dishes. When I was alone, I disliked cooking and cleaning up afterwards because it was boring and there were so many other things I wanted to do with my free time. But here with Will those chores were fun.

By the time we had enjoyed laughing at a couple of stories and singing along with a few songs from his playlist, we were finished, and it was probably time for me to go. Since he had picked me up, I assumed he would take me home. I turned to him, ready to ask about that, but he must not have been tired of me yet.

"Guess we're kind of full of food and wine now, so we probably don't want to go dancing," he said, "but how about we watch a movie here? I have a bunch of them, plus I just got some from Netflix."

"That sounds wonderful."

Standing by the TV in the living room, we looked through the stack of DVDs together.

"Aww, *Seabiscuit*," I said, pulling it out to have a look. It was one of his Netflix selections. "Would that be all right?"

"'Course it is," he said. "I think we'll love it."

We settled on the sofa together to watch. Will slung his arm across the back of the sofa behind my shoulders, and I relaxed into the cushions. I thought I needed to run errands with him on Saturdays more often.

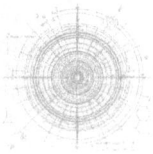

COLLEGE – Two Valentines

FEBRUARY 2004

I t was late afternoon the second Tuesday in February, and Valentine's Day was coming up on Saturday. I had just let myself into my room after a day of class and work when Will called.

"Hey, Lauren. Since it's been way too cold for our usual outdoor lunches lately, I was thinking—how about we grab dinner instead? That way we can catch up on all the tall tales we've missed. Maybe Friday?"

"Sounds great," I said.

"I said Friday, but you know, I was assuming you . . ." He trailed off.

"Yeah, Friday's great," I said. It would be nice to be able to relax knowing we didn't have class the next day.

"We'll make it an adventure," he said.

I found myself smiling. My day had just improved by 100 percent.

◇ ◇ ◇

Friday after work, I took a shower and put on a little more mascara and sheer lip gloss. It had been a long day, and I was ready for a fun evening. I chose my soft ice-blue sweater in order to set off my raindrop pendant.

At seven, Will picked me up. We had decided earlier that we would go to Kin Khao Kan, a new Thai place we'd heard about. When we arrived, I was surprised to find that Will had made a reservation for us. I guess it showed on my face, because he laughed and said, "Yeah, that's a first. But I wanted us to sit where we can see the city lights."

The restaurant occupied the top floor of a low-rise building in a mixed-use area, and the dining room was softly illuminated, with candles on the tables. The place was casual, but the glow of the tiny flames and the vista made it feel enchanting.

Will had requested a table by a big window with the best view. It looked out at a spectacular skyline scene, with beautifully lit buildings spread out as far as I could see. We ordered a bottle of wine and began studying the menu. Will looked as happy as I felt.

"I just love this," I told him. "Those twinkling lights out there definitely add a touch of magic for our adventure."

"I was hoping you'd like it." He gave me a smile. "You look beautiful, by the way. How's your week been?"

Wow, I hadn't been expecting that. "Oh, thank you! And as for the week, I mostly got tales of DNA and such, but I'll dress them up to make them fun," I said.

After I told him a little amusing story from class, I said, "What have you been up to this week, besides planning this wonderful adventure?"

"Got lots of embellished stories to tell, but first, here's a true one you'll love. Remember Joey, the guy who was on Tenth Street and went into Brian's program?"

"Yeah. You get an update on him?"

"Sure did. He's doing great. He's working at an office now, living with some roommates, and making his way back. He still gets coaching from Brian's place, to make sure he keeps making progress and knows how to handle whatever situations come up. Although he'd made some mistakes before that cost him his job and family, it wasn't anything illegal, so it wasn't too hard to find an employer willing to give him a chance."

"Will, that is fantastic. I'm so glad you saw him that morning and helped him."

"I'm glad it's turned out good so far. One day soon I'm going to talk him into calling his son."

Our food arrived. We'd ordered things we both liked so we could share everything, and it was all fantastic. While we ate, we talked a little about the food and did some more catching up, including laughing at a few ridiculous tales. As always, the time with Will seemed to go so fast.

◇ ◇ ◇

At the end of the night, he took me back to my dorm and parked in the lot.

"Just wanted to give you a little something," he said.

He handed me an art journal, cloth-bound, the cover featuring an image of delicate flowers and leaves in soft colors. He had tied a dark green ribbon around it. Inside the front cover, he had written, "Lauren, Take this with us on our next adventure, and fill it with your beautiful work. – Will"

"Will, thank you. This is so thoughtful and perfect," I said. He always blew me away with how much he got me and appreciated me.

"I hope it's the right size and everything. I thought this would be handy for you to carry when it's time to draw some nature scenes."

"It's absolutely right in every way. It will be the first thing I pack for our next adventure," I said. He had even made sure it had the best kind of paper for graphite pencil work. "Got a little something for you too." I pulled his gift from my purse, where I had managed to wedge it before leaving my room. It was a small travel journal.

"Lauren!" Will gave me a big smile when he saw the cover. It had been personalized with the words "Foolish Ventures," and just inside, I had written, "Here's to many more fun foolish ventures. – Lauren."

As a first entry, I had written an account of the trip to northeastern Georgia we had taken in October, including the hikes, dinners, cowboy camping, and our climb down that big waterfall. Beneath it, I had drawn a little rough sketch of the waterfall as well as I could remember, including two tiny figures standing on some rocks near the bottom.

"Thank you so much," he said.

We looked at each other for a moment, and he started to lean toward me a little, but then he stopped. "How about I walk you to your door?"

Once we were just outside the dorm, I stepped toward Will without thinking. He opened his arms, and I walked into them, my head nestling just below his chin. That wonderful hug lasted only a few seconds, but while it did, I felt like I was exactly where I belonged.

"This has been a pretty good little adventure, hasn't it?" he said.

"The best. Thank you for everything, Will."

"'Night Lauren." His voice was almost a whisper.

◦ ◦ ◦

The next day was Valentine's Day. Eric took me to dinner at an elegant-looking place in north Atlanta. The food and wine were great, and we managed to carry on a conversation about what we'd been up to, since we hadn't seen each other the last few days.

He had been accepted to a few med schools but had decided to go to Duke. His parents would pay, so he could devote himself to studying with no worries about loans. As soon as he graduated from Tech, he would move back home with them until it was time for classes to start. I wondered what kind of doctor he would turn out to be. Hopefully a surgeon or anesthesiologist.

When we got back to his place, he had a gift for me. I was surprised. Last year he hadn't acknowledged Valentine's Day at all, maybe so I wouldn't get the "wrong idea" or something. From the shape of the package, I could tell it was a book, and my interest was piqued. I did love to curl up with a good book when I could. I tore the paper off and revealed the cover. It was called *Getting Things Done: The Art of Stress-Free Productivity*.

Last year, I would have been upset to get a gift like this from my boyfriend, but this year, somehow my main fear was that I'd laugh. If there had been a way to transmit the scene to my sister, I would have done it.

"Thank you, Eric. I can't wait to dig in."

"You always seem so worried about time, so I thought this might help," he said.

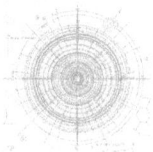

COLLEGE – Instinct and Impulse

MARCH 2004

It was finally getting to be springtime. After class on a beautiful day in the first week of March, I walked up to Will's house for a little exercise and to deliver some old notes and a book I had promised to one of his younger friends. She was taking freshman chemistry and needed some more study materials. The walk was especially nice because the shrubs in some of the yards were blooming with sweet-smelling, pretty flowers in pink, white, and purple.

As I reached the house, Adam's car pulled up fast, brakes squealing a little. He and Will climbed out, Adam slamming his door harder than he meant to. His face was pale, hands still gripping his keys like he hadn't realized he hadn't let go.

"You won't believe what this crazy bastard did. I thought I was about to watch him die."

Will brushed his hair back from his forehead with the heel of his hand. His eyes found mine, steady, and he smiled. "Nah, it's not my time yet."

The casualness in his tone made Adam spin on him.

"What happened?" I asked, my voice sharper than I meant.

"Oh, a lady and her kid were in a little fender bender, but when they opened their car door, their dog bolted and started to run across Fourteenth Street. This idiot here—" Adam jabbed a finger at Will, his hand still shaking, "—jumped out of my car at the red light and ran into traffic to catch him."

Will's grin softened. "Well, he's safe now, isn't he?" He rolled his shoulders.

Adam ran both hands through his hair and let out a shaky laugh. "Maybe he is, but I think it took ten years off my life. You're insane, man."

"If you have a chance to save a life, you have no choice. It's a no-brainer, isn't it?" Will gave him a friendly clap on the shoulder.

Adam let his breath out hard, then shook his head again. "Yeah, yeah. I guess so. I hope you're prepared to share that ridiculously overpriced bottle you keep bragging about, though. I'm definitely going to need a drink after that heart attack you just gave me."

◇ ◇ ◇

Two days later, I went out to the courtyard with a turkey club and a soda. As I sat down, I saw Will walking toward me. I found myself smiling, the way I automatically did whenever I saw him, even though the morning had been a little stressful. My biophysics prof had assigned term papers a few weeks earlier, but this morning she had told us she was going to require individual presentations in her office as well, along with possible oral exams. I couldn't think of anything more terrifying.

"Hey there," I said, scooting from the middle of the bench to one end to give Will some room. "How's the morning been?"

"Good," he said. "So glad it's Friday."

"Seriously." I caught his eye. "Can I ask you something?"

"Anything," he told me, tugging a sandwich and Coke from his backpack.

"You make your decisions so fast, and it seems like you never look back. How do you do that? In my case, I think someone could ask me if I wanted a glass of water and I wouldn't know the answer until the next morning."

"Hmmm . . . well for one thing, I love looking around and thinking about what's possible, instead of focusing on what's already there. And yeah, I'm not always as interested in the details as I should be, and I don't reflect much afterward." We both smiled. He was right about that. "But I usually know exactly what I want long before anyone asks me." Will turned toward me, his elbow on the backrest. Light slanting through the courtyard trees caught his eyes, making them look almost silver-green, like ripples glimmering on a wave. "For someone who's told me several times that she can't think fast, you sure do rip through the math problems quicker than anyone I know."

"Well sure, because a math problem has one correct answer and all I have to do is solve for it. But with a lot of choices I get paralyzed by all the possibilities," I said.

Will nodded. "For some things, I think you might be getting overwhelmed by other people's feelings. Maybe sometimes you know what you want, but you get caught up in thinking about how it will affect others or what they'll say?"

"That's definitely some of it."

"I have to admit, I take feelings into account too, so I get it," he said. "But I've learned it's okay to say, 'Let me think about it.' You don't always have to give an answer right away, especially when it's a big decision."

"That's the thing." I turned to face Will a little more. "If I don't know the answer immediately, I tend to just say no to avoid feeling trapped or pressured. Like if someone asks me to commit to something on the spot, my default is to say a fast no. But sometimes I say that quick 'no thank you,' then I think, 'Damn, I really did want that beer after all.'"

The look in his eyes showed that he got it. "With the beer example, maybe you thought you should say no because it would be more convenient for the person who asked? But if you were in a room with a cooler full of icy brews and there were no other people involved, you'd know very well you wanted one, and you'd grab it."

"Oh, hell yes. Maybe even two."

He rapped the top edge of the backrest with his knuckles. "Okay, let's start small. We can quickly get you out of the habit of that automatic 'no thank you' that's keeping you thirsty. I'll help you practice. Be ready to say yes to some good food and drink tonight, all right? I'll get a few more people to join us, and we'll go out and make it a nice, stress-free decision-making training lab."

"Deal," I said. "I mean yes." I broke into a smile.

Will had been cheery as usual when we talked about the "no thank you" problem, but now he grew a little more serious and seemed to think for a minute. "One more thing that's kind of related, and you didn't ask, but since we're close, I feel like I need to share something I've sensed. Is that okay?"

"Yeah, I want to hear it," I said, feeling a little anxious about what was coming. But I knew whatever it was would be delivered kindly.

"When we first met, you didn't have all these doubts, did you? You knew what you wanted and were going for it. And before that, getting out of that small town and into the biology program at Tech was huge. Lately, though, it feels like you're second-guessing every little choice. Did something happen that made you feel this way? Maybe one decision didn't go as planned, or someone's been too critical?"

I nodded. That sounded like me. I had been avoiding the thoughts of *Why did I do that?* or *I wish I hadn't* at all costs. It was probably why I couldn't decide which graduate programs to apply for. Had I thought the right one would just send me an acceptance letter out of the blue?

"If you make a bad decision, remember you're not stuck with it forever," he said. "It's like buying expensive shoes that end up hurting your feet. Just because you spent the money doesn't mean you have to suffer in them until they're worn out. *You can ditch them anytime.*" He rested his hand on my arm for a moment and looked at me intently. "You don't have to wait for life or anyone else to make your choices. You're incredible—smart, capable, and beautiful. I just want to see you take charge again."

I knew it wasn't at all the point of what he'd just said, but I couldn't help feeling a little shot of pleasure at one word he'd used. No one but Will had ever called me beautiful, and while I knew he was effusive with his compliments, I'd take it.

"Thank you for all the kind words and for sharing that insight," I said. "You're right about my fear of making bad choices. For the past year or so, I've felt almost paralyzed by the fear of doing the wrong thing, thinking I should just wait and see what life brings. But that's pretty dumb, isn't it?" I couldn't help but throw in an awkward joke. "Maybe I should get one of those Magic 8 Balls or something."

The humor came back to his eyes. "Right, *that's* what I was trying to tell you, to get one of those."

We chatted a little more while we watched people walking around, then the whistle blew. As we stood up, Will said, "All right, I'm looking forward to tonight. Let me know who we should invite and if there's anywhere in particular you'd like to go. I've got a couple of spots in mind with food and drinks even you won't be able to say 'no thank you' to."

Sounded fantastic to me.

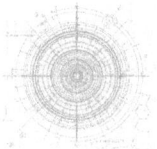

CURRENT – Decision Time

FEBRUARY 2024

It was now late February, and I was fully aware that the existence I had been living all this time was artificial and shallow, but there was no way to fix it. During my senior year, I'd finally understood the difference between genuine love and the crazy infatuation I'd felt for Eric, but the summer after our graduation I married him anyway, because I didn't have any other good options.

I had become pregnant the last week of class. I didn't realize it right away because I was on the pill and had skipped periods before, especially when I was stressed. Once I found out, I wanted to give my baby the best life I could. Eric was dismayed when I told him, but he agreed to get married. His parents urged us to have a quick wedding in Aspen, far from the scrutiny and gossip of their friends, and since he had been counting on their financial support for med school and help with expenses for the next four years, that's what we did.

Once we were married, Eric was nice enough to me, and we were sufficiently compatible to live together, but I knew he didn't love me. At the time, I had tried to tell myself I was going to be all right with how my life was turning out—if I could smother my grief. I would have my baby and the companionship of a husband who was smart and reliable and good-looking. Leaving Atlanta sounded like a relief, as the city was full of reminders of Will. But any hope I'd had of a real career in science was over. I stayed home with Sean for a few years, then once Eric's training was over and we moved to Green Valley, there was nowhere good for me to work.

All these years later, I still had no choice but to make the best of my situation, as I had done for so long. Once again, I tried to immerse myself in various diversions.

Over the next couple of weeks, I dug into my online work twice as hard, taking on more coaching clients and writing long blog posts almost every evening. This made the site busier than ever and provided a mental escape for a while. But eventually, some part of my brain gave me a nudge.

One night, I dreamed of Will. I didn't know where we were, because I didn't notice the background objects, but he was standing in front of me. He turned and walked to an elevator. He got on it, keeping his eyes on mine, and the doors slowly began to close. I stood there helplessly—I was frozen, paralyzed. I knew I couldn't let him get away. I tried to yell and run to him, but my voice and legs were useless.

I woke up, my heart pounding. The message was clear and urgent now, in the dark, with none of the distractions I usually hid behind. I had to do something. I had to try. If there was even the tiniest chance that I had really visited the past last fall, I at least wanted to go back one last time and have another chance to talk with Will. I had to do everything in my power to figure out how.

Everything I'd read said that even if we somehow found a way to travel to the past, there would be no way to change events or outcomes, because doing so would change everything that followed. Still, if I could, I would warn Will not to go on that damned trip. And even if I couldn't change what I said this time, I was at least going to reach out and touch his hand, keep my big mouth shut, and let him say what he wanted to say.

Considering that I was contemplating planning a trip to the past, it should have felt as if I were just pretending, but that wasn't the case. Once I allowed myself to consider that I might be able to change what had happened to Will, I could feel the tension that had been gripping my body begin to relax. I had a goal, and I needed to make a plan. Finally letting go and allowing myself to focus on the past—and the future I hoped for—made me feel better than I had in years. I knew that to some, my determination might look like a betrayal. But the truth was, Eric also deserved someone who fit seamlessly into his world, and maybe in a different version of our story, he would find that person.

As I lay in my bed, I considered the possible consequences. Even if I got back to a day when I could talk to Will, I might not be able to change it and would once again have to live through the conversation where I'd stupidly shut him down. That would be horrible enough. I still remembered the aching sense of loss I'd felt that day. To think I'd see it coming and be unable to prevent it was awful. But much, much worse would be knowing he was going to die yet being unable to warn him. To live like a puppet, going through the motions but unable to change anything.

Thinking about those terrible outcomes gave me a temporary flash of a feeling that I couldn't do it. But that was mere selfishness. If there was any chance of saving Will, or at least making him happy for a moment or a month, I had to do it. He would have risked everything to save a life—stranger or friend, human or animal. To him, it would have been a no-brainer.

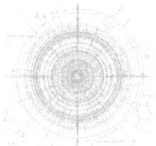

CURRENT – Key to the Past

MARCH 2024

Now I had a goal, but I didn't know how to figure out what I needed to do. Although the past was where I wanted to go, I didn't need a physicist to talk to about theories of time machines and what it would take for them to exist. What I wanted was someone who was really intelligent and open-minded who could help me figure out what the hell had happened, and especially how I might talk to Will again.

It occurred to me that Will had had that super smart friend, Carl Simmons, who he'd partnered with to create custom software. Will had the vision and imagination to dream up and invent new products and know who to sell them to, and Carl had the patience and coding skills to follow it through.

Carl had dropped out of college early because all he wanted was to create; he had no interest in pursuing more theoretical education in computer science. I knew that the two of them had been close, and that Carl was unconventional and quiet, but extremely nice. He didn't need something to be in a main-stream book or journal to give it some serious consideration. I had a look at Google to see if he was still around the Atlanta area.

◇ ◇ ◇

Carl turned out to be easy to find. Still programming, he wrote custom software for various clients, and although he didn't have an elaborate website, he included his phone number and email address on his Contact page. He was now living outside the 285 perimeter, in Gwinnett County.

He didn't sound surprised to hear from me, once I re-membered to use my maiden name, adding that I'd been a friend of Will's and had met him a long time ago. I told him I'd had a strange experience and I'd like to talk to him about it. As someone whose goal it was to earn my living online, I was sensitive to the fact that some people wanted me to work for free, and I certainly wasn't expecting that of him. I knew he was a consultant, and I asked him if he would allow me to pay him for some of his time.

He chuckled and said that was unnecessary, but that he would really appreciate it if I would stop and get five chicken burritos and two large Mountain Dews from Taco Bell. Hell yes, I could do that.

Once I made it to within a few miles of his house, I went through the drive-through to get the burritos and drinks. I loved Taco Bell and would normally have gotten a soft taco for myself, but my stomach was in knots with a mixture of anxiety and anticipation. This was one of the most important situations I'd ever been in, and I worried that if Carl couldn't point me in the right direction, I'd be at a dead end.

A little flame of hope was still alive in me, though. I wondered what Carl would make of my story and if he might think I was just another attention-seeking crazy. I parked in the driveway behind his Acura.

Carl still looked much the same. The main difference between now and twenty years earlier was that he was balding, with only a fringe of dark hair remaining.

"Hello Lauren," he said, blinking in the daylight.

Nervous as ever, I greeted him and held out the bag of food and the drinks. "Here, I brought your lunch."

He smiled. "Actually, that's *our* lunch. It will be nice to take a break and have someone to eat with. I often get so wrapped up in my coding that I don't leave the house."

He invited me inside. His living room had a large window, which provided natural light. Apparently, he liked to do at least some of his work here, because there was a comfortable-looking chair on the left with a laptop in the seat and a table beside it. Against the back wall stood a large glass-topped desk with a backlit keyboard, mouse, two monitors—one horizontal and one vertical—and a custom-built tower below. There were whiteboards on the walls on the left and right sides of the room, covered with formulas and programming code written in every color of marker.

Carl pushed the keyboard and mouse toward the back of the desk and set out the food. He gestured to a chair for me and sat down in the one beside it.

I took a seat, putting my purse on the desk, and stuck the straw into my drink. I saw that Carl was looking at the old key ring I'd clipped to the bag's hardware a few days ago. I caught his eye, and he said, "I apologize for staring. Will had a key ring with a Möbius strip sculpture like that when we were freshmen. I remember he lost it, and we nearly tore our room apart looking for it. I was wondering if he found it after all and gave it to you."

Now it was my turn to stare. I took a moment, touching the little shape on the key ring and feeling a rush of emotion. "This was his," I whispered more to myself than to Carl.

"Yes, it was custom-made for him by an upperclassman in the machine shop when we first got to Tech," Carl began. "Will's fascination with topology started in high school. He had a physics teacher, Mr. Dukes, who recognized his gift for math and his tendency to spend too much time trying to make other people laugh. To engage Will and give him something to really sink his teeth into, Mr. Dukes introduced him to topology—things like the Klein bottle and Möbius strip, which seem to defy everyday intuition."

"Mr. Dukes!" I couldn't help interrupting. "Will told me about him during our junior year."

Carl paused, a little smile beginning on his face. "Will told me he was hooked right away, spending hours reading topology books and discussing concepts with Mr. Dukes. When he got to Tech, he shared that enthusiasm with me. He especially loved the Möbius strip—how it formed a continuous loop with only one side. I remember him telling me, 'The Möbius strip is a physical representation of infinity. It reminds me that what looks impossible may just be a matter of perspective.'"

I nodded, reaching out to touch the key ring again, feeling the threat of tears as I ran my finger over the little sculpture. The knowledge that Will had carried it with him and attributed such meaning to it fit perfectly with what I knew of him—his optimism, sense of adventure, and dedication to pushing beyond constraints.

I fumbled for what to say. "The thing is . . . Will didn't give this to me in college. I have to tell you something crazy."

While Carl began eating, I told him about my experience the day Sean moved to campus. "Oh, and just before I got out to that courtyard, I found this"—I pointed to the key ring—"in the passageway. I'd forgotten about it, but it surfaced in my purse a few days ago, so I attached it here. Just looking at it reminds me of that wonderful day."

Carl leaned forward slightly, his eyes widening, but his voice remained quiet. "Tell me more, please."

"My son Sean is a freshman now, so I came to campus to help him move into his room. Er, that's in Dell Hall." I told him everything I could remember. By the time I finished, he looked extremely interested and already had something to tell me.

"Dell was where Will and I spent our freshman year."

"Oh. I guess I never thought of him in a dorm—I thought he'd always had the house."

"Yes, freshmen were encouraged to live on campus, and of course, coming from high schools out of state, neither of us knew where else we would live, so we found it easy to move into Dell. We were strangers when the housing office put us together, but we got along very well and became friends almost immediately. By the end of that year, I decided to leave school, but he left his unique mark on the place." Carl gave a soft chuckle. "I was always surprised the administration didn't board up room 259 permanently after we left. Will was quite a character."

I was astounded. "My son was in 259 for the fall semester."

"Curious." Carl still looked unruffled. I felt encouraged that he'd stick with me and help me analyze this.

I told him the rest of the story about my first visit as well as about getting back there again on the Friday of homecoming weekend, but that on move-out day for winter semester, I had not been as fortunate.

"What time of day was your first successful visit?"

"Time of day? Oh wow, I don't . . ." As I spoke, I remembered Sean and Zach had been told they had a floor meeting at twelve, so I had left. "It was almost noon. I guess I left their room at ten before the hour, because I didn't really know what time it was, but then the whistle blew while I was in the hall."

"Interesting. And the second visit?"

"It was almost four on the Friday afternoon of homecoming weekend. I was going to pick up some things from my son's room, and I needed to do that after he was back from class."

"What about the third visit? The one when you were unable to find the door to the courtyard."

"That last one was at ten on a Saturday morning. And it was totally unsuccessful. At least on the second visit I made it to the portal, as I'm calling it to myself these days, but on the third visit I didn't. Do you think it was because it was morning instead of afternoon?"

"I don't know if the hour is significant," Carl said. "But what does interest me is the fact that both times you were able to visit the past were on weekdays right before the hour. Did the whistle blow on your second visit before you saw your door?"

"Yes, in fact, it did. I had been searching the hall for it and had just about given up. I was heading back to Sean's room when it sounded, and I knew that meant I'd better hurry. Then, at the same moment, the door appeared. What could that have to do with it?"

Carl nodded slightly. "The whistle was of significance to Will during our freshman year for some unknown reason. You know how he could immerse himself in a subject if it was of interest to him."

I smiled. Oh yes, I knew he'd get obsessed with his ideas, all thousands of them, but what was this about the whistle?

"Will had been interested in the whistle and the old buildings on campus from the beginning, but something terrible happened to him at the end of that first fall semester. He never told me what it was, but I got the impression that someone close to him from back home had died. He seemed to lose all his usual happiness and vitality and wasn't the same person during that time." Carl had stopped eating and was leaning forward a little with his hands on his knees.

It broke my heart to think of sweet Will suffering like that, losing his usual brightness. "What happened next?" I asked.

"During winter break, he filled several notebooks with technical drawings—intricate plans of our dorm building. These weren't standard blueprints. They contained passages and doors that weren't really part of Dell. The draftsmanship was exquisite, every impossible angle and gravity-defying corridor extremely detailed. Will had sketched them meticulously, with precise measurements noted, but the layouts defied physical reality."

I didn't want to interrupt Carl, but I must have looked confused, because he went on to explain, "The passages seemed to loop back on themselves in impossible ways, like they were bending back through spacetime. His cross-sections showed hallways turning at angles that should have intersected with existing rooms but somehow didn't. Most remarkably, the drawings showed doors opening into spaces that couldn't exist—corridors and rooms extending far beyond the building's physical boundaries, as if the normal laws of space had been bent or forgotten."

"Wow. I assume he poured himself into creating those detailed drawings as a way to distract himself, at least temporarily?" I asked.

"That's what I thought at first, but sometimes, especially when the dorm would get too noisy or crowded, Will would grab his notebooks and disappear for hours. Even if I looked for him immediately, I could never figure out where he went."

Carl paused, seeming to collect his thoughts. "By springtime, when he seemed to be feeling better, I asked him where he had gone back then, and he said he had built an 'escape hatch,' and that during the few seconds when the whistle was blowing, he could circumvent the constraints of spacetime. He gave me a smile and a broad wink at that point, so I assumed he was joking, that maybe he simply had a friend down the hall whose room he would visit. That, and a few other isolated events, made me almost sure that Will thought the whistle had some special power."

At my open-mouthed silence, Carl added, "Well, the whistle is quite important in the lives of students. We know it can cause even a long-winded professor to stop talking and end class, and it blows to celebrate football wins. Maybe it is a bit magic." He smiled. "It makes me happy to think that Will could be creating these experiences for you."

That thought was lovely, and I knew if it was possible for Will to do such a thing, he would. Something dawned on me. "So, the day I went to move Sean out of his room for winter break—it was a Saturday, and no matter how long I hung around, the door to the old hallway never appeared. And it wasn't going to, was it? Because the whistle doesn't blow on Saturdays."

"Our sample size is too small to say for sure, of course," Carl said, "but I would guess you are exactly right. If I were you, I would try going back to campus on a weekday during class hours and go to that spot a little before the whistle blows. Maybe you can find your door again."

Oh wow. This all fit just right. Will had probably outgrown his fascination with the whistle just like he had a lot of his ideas, because I didn't remember him ever mentioning it to me. But now at least I had time targets to aim for with my next attempt.

"Carl, do you think this all started because of me? Or do you think maybe I just stumbled on a portal to the past that's always there for anyone to find?"

"I don't know for certain, but I would think that in a dorm full of intelligent, inquisitive students, someone else would have found that door and made the information widely known if it were available to anyone other than you. Now, whether this has to do with your son moving into our old room, or whether it was merely your own presence in the dorm, perhaps coupled with your high emotional state, I do not know." He put his thumb and index finger to his chin and frowned, looking deep in thought. "That's assuming—Will didn't know your son, did he?"

"No," I said, feeling my anxiety mount again. "He'd been gone for months by the time Sean was born." I was breathing deeply to stop my gut from contorting.

"Still, Sean is a part of you. Perhaps his moving into our room was enough to trigger . . . whatever this event was."

After all these months of having no information and hardly any hope, this was a lot to take in. But it fit. After a moment, I said, "These ideas are so encouraging. Thank you so much. Thank you for believing me and not dismissing me."

Carl gave me a pleasant look and said, "I want very much to think that this is a genuine opportunity for you to speak to Will and spend time with him. I wish I could talk to him too, but I believe he has chosen you."

"As much as I'd love to talk to him for the sheer pleasure of it," I said, "I mainly would like to tell him not to go on that trip. I don't know if I can change the past. I know about all the reasons we're not supposed to. But I must tell you, that is my goal. To tell him to do anything else that weekend but go to Utah. Then maybe he can have the rest of his happy, productive life. Maybe the universe will let me do that. I know the entire world would be better off if he had lived," I said.

Carl looked at me for a moment. It wasn't an uncomfortable silence; he appeared to be thinking. It occurred to me that maybe he would like to know how this story ended. Will had told me that Carl was passionate about science, but he only chased the questions that truly intrigued him. It was clear he wasn't driven by money—he was far smarter than many guys I knew who wore expensive suits and had huge mortgages. So, since he wouldn't take payment for his time, I wanted to do something I thought might be great for him, something only I could give him.

"Carl, I can't thank you enough. I've learned a lot, and I have genuine hope now that I can get back there and try to save Will. And if it works, if I ever manage to do what I want to do, I'm going to email you or come back to see you and tell you every detail of exactly what happened and how I did it, so you'll have some knowledge other scientists don't."

He said, "If you're able to get back to that time and do what you intend to, this meeting we're having today will never take place. But best of luck to you, Lauren. Godspeed!"

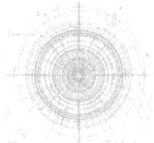

CURRENT – Engineer of the Impossible

MARCH 2024

S topped at a red light on my way home from Carl's, I glanced at my purse, which I had tucked in the center console. Will's key ring caught my eye. I reached over to trace the twisted surface of the metal sculpture, my fingers following the endless loop. I remembered from our study sessions in college that Will had always enjoyed the patterns and insights he found in math, especially calculus and topology. But this was different. The Möbius strip had been his compass in life, a symbol of his refusal to accept conventional limitations.

My mind wandered to what Carl had told me about Will's drawings, his design for a lifeline to cope with whatever had happened during freshman year. Although he and I had grown so close, he'd never mentioned anything about it to me. Will was almost always upbeat and full of energy, making the impossible seem achievable. When I saw him unhappy, it was usually because of others who were in distress, but instead of remaining sad, he jumped straight into action to help. It was hard to imagine, but something had overwhelmed him to the point where he needed an escape hatch. Then all these years later, that same pathway had become available to me—just when I needed it, too. And he had been right there somehow, talking to me and making me happy again for that wonderful hour.

It was incredible to think about. Will hadn't just stumbled into that mysterious hallway like I had. He'd designed the passage and engineered it to pierce the veil of spacetime itself. For the first time since his death, I felt more than desperate longing. I felt fierce hope—almost certainty. Will had left a breadcrumb for me to follow, and I believed I finally knew enough to find my way back to him.

As much as I wanted to, I couldn't rush to campus without proper planning. I had to be smart about this. I'd come to realize that both times I'd found the escape hatch, I had arrived in the courtyard on the same day of the month and the same time as I'd entered the dorm, but twenty years in the past. That meant I had to find the right moment to make my attempt.

If I went to the dorm at random and hit a lot of wrong days or times, I'd make myself conspicuous, especially as—now that Sean had moved out—I didn't belong there at all. I shouldn't squander any such opportunities on times when Will wouldn't be in the right area of campus. I needed to figure out when to go.

My best bet would be to examine my journal entries to find some days he and I had sat in the courtyard together. Since I had lived close by, I'd often brought food out there to enjoy in the fresh air, but Will's classes were all on the other side of campus, so he'd probably only come on days when he wanted to take a break and relax with me during lunchtime.

Back then, I really hadn't noticed a pattern. I'd always been glad to see him, but I'd never wondered what brought him all the way over there on any given day. It had been an ideal time to talk and share our thoughts one-on-one, instead of as part of the group at his house.

◊ ◊ ◊

Once I got home, I texted Sean.

I may come to campus one day soon. Need anythg from home?

Something dawned on me. I hoped Sean's presence in the dorm wasn't a necessary catalyst for me to find that portal, because he had moved during winter break. But almost as soon as I had that thought, I realized that, no, this wasn't about him. It was about Will and me. He'd shown that door to me, and I was going to go back and talk to him when I found the right time.

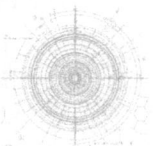

COLLEGE – Fleeting Harmony

MARCH 2004

T he third Saturday of March was a beautiful day, and Eric had found a little music festival in a park east of the city he wanted us to go to. Bands of several genres would be playing from early afternoon through the evening, and the article he'd seen said there would be lots of people in attendance, as well as many varieties of beer and food for sale.

We got there at around two and started walking around in the crowd. The air smelled like a mixture of beer, gyro meat, and I'm not sure what else, but for me it added to the festive feeling. There were a couple of stages, placed at opposite ends of the park, where the bands would be performing. Eric had already found and printed a list of who would be playing where at what time, so we could make a semieducated guess on where was best to hang out. We chose the indie rock band that had started playing at two. Armed with a beer for him and a can of hard lemonade for me, we found a space on a grassy hillside where we could see them while sitting comfortably.

About an hour later, although I was enjoying the loud music and a bit of a buzz from my second hard lemonade, Eric called my attention to a little sunburn I was developing on my face and arms. I gave a half shrug, not concerned at all. But then he pulled sunscreen from his fanny pack and began applying it to me with meticulous care.

What else did he have in there, I wondered, remembering the long list he had given me of things to bring on our day hike when we were juniors. Emergency flares? A first-aid kit? Anything for any disaster that could possibly happen, I supposed, and thinking of some extreme examples having to do with angry squirrels and sword-wielding bad guys made me laugh. Eric glanced at me but didn't ask. He was probably used to me being kind of weird.

The last band of the night was on a stage with flat ground all around it, where all we could do was to stand in the middle of a huge mob to try to see. To my surprise, following the example of a lot of guys in the crowd, Eric invited me to sit on his shoulders. I didn't want to be annoying to all the people behind us, but there were girls on shoulders in every direction, so up I went. Wow, the night air was so nice, the music good, and the vantage point couldn't be beat. This had been the best time I'd spent with Eric in months. It was all fun, with none of the usual feeling of pressure for stilted small talk.

I stayed over with him as always, and the next morning at breakfast we once again found ourselves in long silences punctuated by superficial remarks. Maybe we were both so deep in our own heads that connecting verbally felt nearly impossible. Some couples might thrive on that kind of quiet, valuing their introspection. I had always enjoyed occasional *comfortable* silences with friends and family, but with Eric, they felt awkward and strained. It was probably because I was constantly trying to force things to fit. All my efforts to keep our conversations on life support were probably irritating to him. Maybe we'd both be happier if I stopped.

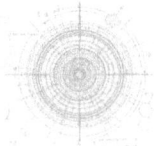

COLLEGE – Wild at Heart

MARCH 2004

When I got home from Eric's on Sunday morning, I went to the rec center to exercise, then after a long shower, I studied most of the afternoon. Around six, I parked at Will's and went for an early dinner with Adam, Josh, and Melissa. It was so good to see them and have our usual light-hearted chitchat. Will wasn't with us, because he and Dave and Nick had gone to north Georgia that morning to rent ATVs to ride on the trails up there.

After dinner, we returned to the house, where Adam let me in to wait for Will. He then left to work on a group project, and Josh and Melissa went home, saying they both needed to study and get ready for the week ahead. I grabbed my bio-physics book from the car and headed back inside, settling onto the sofa. I was hoping to get a chance to say hi to Will if he returned before it got too late, because I hadn't seen him all weekend.

I'd made it through a few pages when I heard him pull up and saw his lights through the curtains. I had a quick look in my little mirror and smoothed my hair with my hand. After a minute, he came in, carrying his cooler and a small daypack. A film of dirt coated his arms and legs, his clothes, and even some of his face, but he looked happy. His light brown hair was windblown and streaked with dust, and his T-shirt clung to him in places where sweat had cut through the dirt.

"How was it?" I asked.

"Oh, it was amazing!" Will said. "So much fun. We totally acted like complete idiots. Let me get cleaned up real quick and I'll tell you all about it."

I wondered if there was more stuff in the Jeep he needed to bring in. "Do you need any help?"

His face lit up with a playful expression. "Sure. There's a spot right in the middle of my back I can never seem to reach with my loofah."

I turned to watch him disappear down the hall.

Less than ten minutes later he came back to the living room clean, with damp hair, a bottle of beer in each hand. "Hey Lauren, I hope I didn't make you uncomfortable or anything. I swear I wouldn't have made that comment in front of other people. I'd never want to embarrass you."

I feigned confusion. "Why would *I* be embarrassed? I'm not the one who suddenly smells like Axe."

He laughed. "Mahan, I love how you always surprise me. And it's not Axe—it's Dial for Men, Wild Adventurer scent, if I'm not mistaken." He sat down close beside me, his knee gently resting against mine, setting the bottles on the coffee table. His skin was still warm from the shower, and I could feel the slight dampness of his shirt sleeve against my arm. "Now will you put that book down so we can tell some tales? What have *you* been up to today?"

"Gonna have to make up a lot of it," I warned.

"Perfect," he said. "Make me the hero." His outdoor fun had apparently put him in a mood that was even more exuberant than usual.

"Of course," I said. "In the following tale, the Wild Adventurer totally saves the day and gets the girl."

His sitting so close to me, or maybe it was the Dial, had gone straight to my head.

◇ ◇ ◇

That Friday night, Jason and Rob were having a party, and we were all invited. After class, I had changed into a casual black sundress with narrow straps that tied on the shoulders, plus my raindrop necklace. The crowd was mostly familiar, with a few new faces. I grabbed a beer and was on my way up the hall when Will approached. His eyes met mine, then flicked briefly to the raindrop pendant resting against my collarbone before returning to my face. A smile played at the corners of his mouth, and something in his expression softened.

"You know you still owe me the end of that story. The Wild Adventurer saved the day all right, but you'd said he'd get the girl, too," he said.

"Yeah, who knew Adam would get home at that minute. Then I didn't want to tell the end of it with him right there when he hadn't had a chance to hear the beginning." I pushed my hair off my shoulder with my fingers. "This way I'll have a little more time to figure it all out. Maybe there are some obstacles," I said, not really knowing what the hell I was talking about. Sometimes the part of my brain that came up with words seemed to have no connection to the part that did the thinking.

"If the hero is any kind of hero, he can easily conquer most of those obstacles, inspired by just one of his girl's enchanting smiles," Will said.

I couldn't help but laugh at him and his nonsense. He was such a cutie.

"Hey, guys!" Drew was approaching us, with Amy, Rob, and Liz right behind him. Liz flashed me a quick smile, balancing her drink in one hand while tucking a loose strand of hair behind her ear. She had this effortlessly cool vibe—like she was watching the world with a private punchline in mind.

Drew turned to Will. "Will, haven't seen you in a few days. Is your project coming along okay?"

"Yeah," Will said. "We're in good shape. How 'bout yours?"

Amy and I exchanged quick smiles, but we'd seen each other earlier in the day and had had time to chat between classes. As Drew, an electrical engineering major, started talking about his team's work and the others chimed in, I sensed Will looking at me. Our eyes met, and a brief flicker of something like a private joke passed between us. I wondered how much he'd had to drink before I got here.

◇ ◇ ◇

Later, when I was going for another beer, I ran into Will alone again. He stood close to me and said, "I'm beginning to think the only way a guy can hear a tall tale with no interruptions is to be on a mountain in the middle of nowhere."

"Just remind me next time we're up there." I gave him what I hoped was a carefree look.

He smiled, but his eyes held mine for an extra second, and there was something else there I couldn't quite read. "We'll figure it out," he said, quieter this time.

I knew he was just having fun and probably talked this way with dozens of people, but I didn't do a lot of flirting and playing except with him, and it was becoming a little too important to me. I had to remind myself that I couldn't afford to fly too close to the sun. Aside from all my other fears, there was a reality I had to face. He had an interview coming up with a company in California, and I assumed he'd get the job. He deserved it. This beautiful time was running out too fast.

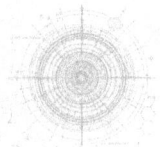

CURRENT – Sifting Through Yesterday

MARCH 2024

Since the day I moved Sean in at Tech, I had read through the electronic diary of my last two years of college many times. The first had been an experience of painful guilt and sadness, and I'd felt a renewed, bittersweet grief each time I saw Will's name. But after that, and especially since the day I'd decided that I had to go back again, I had begun to read the journal with more and more enjoyment. What I'd written about Will now brought back happy memories of his irresistible laughter, his unwavering compassion, and that crazy connection we had shared. Now it was time to use my old writing to try to navigate my way back to him.

To plan my visit to Tech, I needed to examine my long-ago senior-spring semester. After the break in March, we'd spent our last weeks together before graduation. And after our last day of class, I never saw Will again.

I searched the entries for the end of March and found that, unfortunately, I had mentioned no lunches with Will in the courtyard. There might have been some, which I guess I would have considered routine back then, but on weekdays I had mostly written about class and hanging out at Will's, as well as my growing annoyance with Eric. There were other activities, like a little day hike and a party with Will and the gang, in the journal, but I knew I wouldn't be able to transport myself to those off-campus sites by going through the door in the dorm. I had to find the right time to visit the courtyard.

Once I got to April in the diary, I found a day that looked like a great candidate. I tried to control my excitement as I checked the calendar to make sure it fell on a weekday this year. It did. I grabbed my phone and set a reminder to ask for that day off from work, my hands trembling slightly as I typed. I needed to get up, move around, maybe make some tea to calm my nerves.

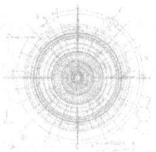

COLLEGE – Crossroads and Compasses

April 2004

I t was just after twelve on the first Friday of April. Will and I got to our bench at the same time. I knew he'd been to California for his interview a couple of days ago. I wondered how it had gone, but I didn't want to bombard him with my intense questioning right away.

"How's it going?" I asked, trying to be calm and casual.

"Good," he said. "You get through your presentation and exam all right?"

"Yes, thank you *so* much for reading my paper and pretending to be Dr. Tanaka for me the other day. You came up with some tough questions—I was still terrified this morning, but at least I could retrieve my words a lot faster than I might have otherwise."

"Glad I could help. I was blown away by your work, but I've always known you're as brilliant as you are beautiful."

"Ha," I said. "You know, I was gonna bake you some cookies anyway."

He grinned. "Chocolate chip? Please?"

"Of course." I looked around, more conscious than ever that the way of life I loved so much was going to be over soon. "Can you believe we'll be out of here for good in just a few weeks?"

"Yeah, it's wild," Will said. He turned toward me with his arm draped over the backrest of the bench. "Have you decided what you'd like to do next?"

"No idea. Since I never decided what to specialize in or where to apply, it sure as hell won't be grad school. Maybe the Magic 8 Ball would have told me what to do, if I'd gotten it in time."

"You'll find something that's just right for you. I'm sure of it," he said. He paused to watch a guy run by to catch a Frisbee. "You know what I'd do if I were you?"

"What, stay here and just keep taking classes?"

"Nah, more studying isn't going to tell you anything new." He brushed his hair off his forehead and seemed to be thinking. "What if you applied for a position in a different lab at the bio school? Maybe try molecular biology this time? It'd give you more exposure to the research and might help you decide what to pursue. Plus, it'll still look good on your grad school applications if you want to apply this fall."

"Yeah. How nice would that be, working at Tech without the pressure of taking classes at the same time. I enjoyed being around the labs these last couple of years, but I always felt like I needed to hurry and get back to my studying." I looked around at the people walking by for a second. "I think I'll see what they have open. Thanks for the idea."

Now I *had* to ask about California, although I was sure I already knew. How could they not want him? He was talented, innovative, personable, and loaded with work experience too. "How did your interview in Concord go?"

Will looked at me and took a few seconds before he started talking, like he was trying to figure out what to say. I waited, wondering what the deal was. "It was good. California is beautiful, of course, and the job is cutting-edge, with a huge budget, so I'd probably be able to do anything I could dream up. Oh, and the team seemed like nice people, probably a lot of fun."

I said, "Sounds terrible. What's up?"

"I guess it's all getting a little too real. When I applied for this job, I was just thinking about the cool work and having fun in California. But back then I didn't care if I left Atlanta anyway, because..." He trailed off. "Well, anyway, MED-ATL has already made me an offer, and they're giving me a couple of weeks—actually, until five o'clock on the last day of class—to answer." He looked at me for a moment. "If the California job extends one too, I'll have to decide whether to leave or stay."

"What do you want to do? Not California anymore?" I asked, trying to keep my tone light and relaxed. "You're the guy who usually knows what he wants, right?"

Once again, he seemed to hesitate. "What do you think about it, if I get the choice?"

"Me? I don't think you want *my* advice," I said. He and I had counseled each other about all kinds of things, but this was too important for him to listen to someone like me. And I certainly couldn't be objective.

"Yeah, I've wanted to talk to you about this. What do you think? If I stay here in Atlanta, the job at MED-ATL would be fine," he said. Noticing my stare, he smiled and added, his voice a little lower, "Maybe over the past couple of years I've discovered there's more to life than cool startups."

That caught me off guard. The whole time I'd known him, he'd talked about jobs at new, innovative companies where he could bring his big visions to life. He had worked so hard for years, and now he would consider giving that up just to stick around Atlanta? After a few seconds of floundering, I finally said, "How about one of these next few nights I help you weigh your options? We can make a complete pros-and-cons list for the new job."

He nodded, his gaze steady on mine. "We'll figure it out."

I knew I would hate it if he moved away, and I didn't want to think about it. But if there was anyone who needed the freedom to build his big dreams, it was Will. He had to decide what he really wanted to do, and I could never tell him not to go.

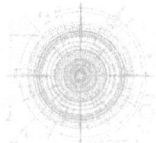

COLLEGE – Well-Worn Path

April 2004

We had five more days of class left in the semester, but they would be tough ones, with finals looming right after. Now pretty much all the enjoyable parts of senior year were over, except for graduation and any parties that might bring. Will had been offered the job in Concord and kept asking me for my thoughts, but I deflected by turning the questions back on him, like, "What do you think you'd like best about your role at each of the companies?"

I believed he might regret it for the rest of his life if he didn't take the California job. He deserved to be happy and live his best life, and I wanted that for him. Maybe I should have told him my opinion, but I couldn't. Deep down, I couldn't imagine living without him, and selfishly, I couldn't bring myself to urge him to go. Instead, I let the turmoil build inside me, anxiously awaiting his decision, knowing it had to be his alone. Just like with the Atlanta job, he had until close of business on our last day of class to let them know.

I'd continued to see Eric, and we had a date tonight. I was still going through the motions of my routine, my stress ramping up more every day, and I was acutely aware that the next few weeks would bring life-altering changes.

I snatched a simple sundress from the closet, slipping it on before he picked me up. For now, despite Will's excellent advice a few weeks ago, I was just doing what I knew—an easy choice in a time of uncertainty and tension.

◇ ◇ ◇

The next morning, I was still at Eric's, and he cooked breakfast. While we ate, we made our usual small talk about things we'd each done the previous few days, the finals schedule, and the local news. My mind was wandering.

As we were finishing our coffee, he said, "Gonna be really busy the next few weeks."

"Yep, me too." I set my cup down.

"I'm going to pack up my apartment and move out right after finals," Eric said.

"What about graduation?"

"Not staying for that. I hate this place. They can mail my diploma."

I didn't even know this guy, and I never really had. We had spent hundreds of hours together over the past year and a half yet had never talked about anything that mattered.

He patted my arm. "You gonna be okay?"

For some reason, a huge smile spread across my face. "Yeah, I think so. But I have an awful lot to do. Would you please take me home?"

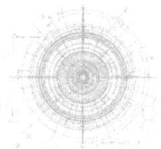

CURRENT – High Hopes

April 2024

The day I had planned to go back and talk to Will finally arrived. My drive to Tech was easy enough. Once I was on I-75 heading south toward Atlanta, I was free to listen to the radio and daydream. "The Search is Over" by Survivor came on. Wow, this had been an oldie even when I was in college, but today I felt every word. I sang and drove and thought about Will, and soon it was time to get off the interstate.

I parked in the large visitor lot at the center of campus. Although I was wearing jeans and relatively comfortable flats, I wanted to change into my running shoes so I could walk faster if need be. Timing was everything with this venture. I opened my trunk and grabbed the runners and socks I always kept there just in case.

Soon I was striding down the sidewalk. I felt a little nervous, but I'd made it with no delays, so I tried to relax and do what I'd come here to do. Passing the library, I hurried down the oak-lined streets in the older part of campus. I stopped to sit on a bench under some trees until it got closer to noon. I couldn't kill twenty minutes standing in the hall of a dorm where I had no business.

At 11:50, I began walking the last stretch to the dorm that had been Sean's. And Will's. There were students walking around and talking in small groups in the little courtyard, but the doors weren't propped open, and of course they would be locked. I kept moving toward the building. Surely someone would be coming or going soon, and I could hide in the crowd.

As I approached, I felt conspicuous among all the young people, although no one was really looking at me. I saw some movement through the glass door, but would a student let a stranger come barging in as he exited?

I got out my phone and put it to my ear. "Honey, I'm here if you'll come downstairs to get me. Oh, there's someone coming out. Maybe I can save you a trip." I looked away from my pretend conversation to the young man coming through the door. I reached out my hand to hold it behind him, and he was cooperative and quiet as he passed me. He might not even have noticed I was there.

I kept the phone to my ear for cover as I went to see if I could find the portal.

◊ ◊ ◊

It was now six minutes before noon, and I couldn't have been more tense. In one minute, the whistle would blow, and I might have the chance to see Will again. The thought gave me a thrill of anticipation that I tried to push down.

Five minutes until noon. Okay, any second now. I waited. Maybe my watch was a minute fast? I looked again. It was now 11:56. What happened? Had I missed it? That couldn't be. I'd been on campus for more than a half hour and hadn't heard it. I stood around a few more minutes, but at 12:01, I slowly started walking away.

Just outside the dorm, I approached a young woman with a long dark braid hanging down her back, earbuds in her ears. "What happened to the whistle?" I asked. "I guess I expected to hear it just now." I could hear how awkward and strange I sounded.

"Um, they sent out a text. It's out for maintenance."

"Maintenance? On the whistle?"

"Yeah, and the steam plant. It's a planned outage," she explained. "They texted to warn us not to be late to classes, that the whistle would be out for a while."

"When will it be working again?"

Her expression changed a little, and she took a step back from me and started to walk away. "Sorry, dunno."

I felt so helpless. With no way to find the door to get to Will, I *was* helpless now. If I couldn't get to him before the last day of that senior year, it would be too late.

◦ ◦ ◦

Once I got back home from Tech, I closed myself into my office. I didn't have time for any interruption from Eric or anyone else. My whole body was uncomfortably tense. I rushed to open the journal on my computer. After the day I had just attempted to return to, there were ones in there that didn't mention Will at all, and I skimmed through them. Pretty soon, the entry for the last day of classes would come up. I dreaded getting to that page.

It was the day I'd been so paralyzed with anxiety and fear that I wouldn't even talk to Will. I didn't want to read the account of what I'd done, but I realized it was the last time I'd ever seen him, and my last opportunity to try to find him now.

I found the date at the top of that terrible page and saw that the talk in the courtyard had happened sometime between noon and one. It would fall on a weekday this year too. So, I could try to get back to that moment when the whistle blew at five minutes to twelve. I had to put everything I had into getting there and doing it differently this time.

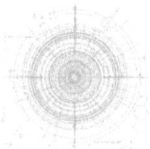

CURRENT – No-Brainer

April 2024

It was the afternoon before the big day when I'd try to go back and find Will. I was at the office as usual but had asked for tomorrow off. The work went by somehow, but it was all I could do to keep my mind even halfway in the present.

When it was almost quitting time, my group started talking about going to happy hour at River Run Brewery, a new place nearby. Usually when I had an important event coming up, I said no to optional activities right before. Since I'm a worrier, I wouldn't want to take a chance on a stupid thing like a car accident or sprained ankle hijacking my big plans for the next day. Now, I surprised myself by saying yes. I was grateful for the chance to spend the next couple of hours with a pleasant buzz in friendly company, and most of all, I was happy for an excuse not to attempt to make conversation with Eric over dinner.

It wasn't even four thirty when Ashley came by and gave me a meaningful look—we were about to head out to freedom.

I shut down my computer and threw my phone into my bag, following her down the stairs.

Over the next few hours, we enjoyed beer and appetizers and lots of inside jokes and silly gossip. It was good that no one had brought their partner, because we would have bored them terribly. As the group broke up and we headed to our cars, I took a quick peek at my phone. There were three missed calls from Biolution and two voicemails.

First, there was a message from Michael. "This is it. I'm sorry this took so long, but we have the perfect spot for you. And you can start June first if that works for you. Mr. Peters has to sign off, though, so we need you to get in here tomorrow before he goes to Europe. I think the admin is setting up your interview. Oh yeah, listen, no suits or anything here. We're strictly on the casual side of business casual."

Next up was a voicemail from Mr. Peters's assistant. "Ms. Whitman, please come to our office at ten o'clock tomorrow morning. Mr. Peters will be here briefly around that time, then he'll be going to Europe for the month. We believe you are the candidate we're looking for, and he would like to meet you and get to know you a little."

Oh, that was a blow. I had already accepted that I wouldn't get the job, but now they were dangling it in front of me again. In fact, it sounded like I might finally have a real chance to be a microbiologist after all these years. But tomorrow was the last chance I had to try to save Will. I had to go to campus.

I was not stupid. I knew there was probably no way to go to the past, and I'd had plenty of disappointments and failures already. In fact, it was crazy for me to think I could really do it. But armed with what I'd learned about Will's escape hatch and the whistle, plus my journal, it was a shot I had to take. I could live with missing out on a job, but I'd never forgive myself if I didn't give Will everything I had tomorrow.

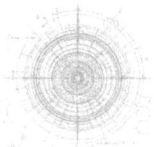

COLLEGE – Final Countdown

April 2004

I t was late April, the last day of class before finals and graduation, and I had a lot on my mind. If I had looked at things logically, the smartest thing would have been to stay in the biology building all day. That would have given me time to process everything that had happened and feel a little less anxious so I could act a little more normal. But today, like many before it, I didn't approach things logically; I just reacted to my feelings.

Hoping a little time outside would help me stop worrying and let me focus on the studying I needed to do, I went to the courtyard to walk around. There were a few people on the sidewalk, but no one was playing. Most had backpacks on their shoulders and serious looks on their faces.

A few minutes later I saw Will emerge from between two buildings, halfway jogging toward me. His face lit up as he approached.

"Hi Will." I tried to sound happy to see him, but my anxiety was ramping up and my face felt like a mask. He reached out to put a gentle hand on my elbow.

"Hey Lauren, I'm so glad I caught you. Can we talk for a minute? I know it's not the time or the place, but it's kind of important."

"Sure."

We walked to a small set of concrete stairs on the side of a red brick building. They led up to an old, narrow door, but there were plenty of other stairs and walkways, so no one would need to get past us for the next little while.

We sat down on the top step, turning to face one another. Will was staring at me, then looked down and then back up at my face. *Oh no,* I thought, *please don't talk about what I think you're going to talk about.*

"Lauren, I'm sure you know now," he said, giving me a tender, almost shy smile, "but I thought I'd better say something just in case." He looked down again for a second, then straight into my eyes. "I've never met anyone like you, and I know I never will again. But I've been so stupid—"

"Wait. No, please." I interrupted. "We really can't do this. Let's not talk about it. You're my very best friend. You know we have something special, and I can't stand it if we make it all weird."

His eyes betrayed the hurt he must be feeling. "Okay, then. I'm sorry, I thought—well, anyway, I wanted to make sure you know how I feel. Our friendship means the world to me, too." He took a deep breath. "But I need to answer these job offers by the end of the day, and there's only one person I'd turn down the position in California for, to stay right here and see what happens." He reached for my hand and said, "No pressure at all, I promise. I'd just take the one here in Atlanta and we'd be able to see each other like normal people."

"Oh no—see, you can't do that." The words burst out of me with more force than I'd intended, but I blundered on. "Once you finally got bored with hanging out with me, you'd hate me forever for making you miss out on your dream job."

I was trying to sound carefree and normal, but my heart felt like a big rock was sitting on it. I couldn't think fast enough, but I was sure of one thing: even if Will and I started a romance for the ages, I'd somehow blow it in no time with my insecurity and anxiety. It would break my heart if I ruined our beautiful friendship. Plus, a job like the one in California was something he had wanted for a long time. Who was I to take that away from him? There was no way I could let him even think about turning down his big opportunity.

"Sure," he said, keeping his voice steady. He stood up, a pleasant look masking whatever else he was feeling. "I'll see ya, Lauren. You take care. And by the way, whoever is stringing you along is a damned fool."

Then he was gone.

The whistle shrieked, going on and on. For the first time, it sounded mournful, like it could rip me open. The stress I'd felt before had been trivial compared to this huge aching pit of loss that now resided where my heart had been. I'd never felt so alone in my life.

I wanted to run after him, but I didn't move, because the only thing worse than letting him leave would be letting him stay for me and having him realize I was dragging him down. Watching that beautiful light in his eyes slowly dim as he grew tired of dealing with my insecurity. Having him stay with me out of obligation.

So I let him walk away, taking my heart with him.

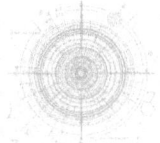

COLLEGE – Hindsight

MAY 2004

We'd all graduated three weeks ago, at the beginning of May. Will and Eric had moved away, but I was still in the area, at least for now. I had found a full-time lab position working at Tech, and that was a dream come true. Every day I was exposed to incredible scientists and groundbreaking research, even though my part in it was tiny. Just being their technician gave me the opportunity to learn more about the work than taking an additional class or two ever would have. I was renting an apartment in one of the houses north of campus, so I could walk to work. That part of life was perfect.

However, the rest of it wasn't so ideal. Eric was being his usual jerk self, except from far away. I'd get emails describing fun things he had done, always with tantalizing hints he had not done them alone. By now these messages had become an annoyance, although I still stopped short of telling him we didn't need to stay in touch anymore.

Will also emailed me, mainly newsy type stuff. He liked his new job, had met some fun guys, and was looking forward to having some outdoor adventures when he got time. He didn't mention anything personal. His birthday had been a few days ago, and I'd emailed him with good wishes and told him I remembered I owed him a big celebration with lots of people. He'd replied, thanking me, but that was it.

Meanwhile, I couldn't get my mind off him. What if he had confessed his feelings earlier? Maybe then I would have had time to process it, and surely I would have responded affectionately, even if I still encouraged him to pursue the best job opportunity for himself. The worst decisions I'd made in my life had come from having to give an answer on the spot. Usually, I didn't know how I really felt about things until a thought woke me up in the middle of the night much later. Usually too much later.

All I'd been able to think about while he was trying to talk to me was my fear. I couldn't absorb the fact that he really wanted to be with me—that he already knew all my flaws and had chosen me anyway.

One thing that hadn't hit me until much later was Will's parting remark to me. He'd thought I wanted to be with another guy instead of him. He hadn't realized my protests were just my anxiety and fear boiling over. If he'd been talking to me about any other subject, he would have known exactly what was going on and easily sliced through my craziness to communicate with me. But since he was putting himself out there, he had his own feelings to worry about and protect. And he had had only a few more hours to decide where to live and work, as well as other issues on top of that.

I was ashamed of my behavior and horribly sad that I had let him down. He had needed empathy and warmth from me, but I'd been too consumed with my own emotions. My heart ached for him, and I wanted so badly to put my arms

around him. No one except Will and me knew how emotionally loaded those moments had been or how much we had lost
at the end, despite how few words had been uttered. If I could
have remained calm and talked to him about the job and our
feelings instead of blowing up with what he probably thought
were weak excuses, we would have been fine. But my damned
anxiety had made that impossible.

Oh, how I wanted to make this right, but I didn't know
how.

If I phoned him, it might leave things worse than before.
He'd probably be guarded, and I was awful at expressing myself
verbally. I wished so much I could talk to him in person. When
he and I could see each other's faces and body language, we
knew everything, without words.

I supposed I was adequate at expressing myself in writing,
so maybe I could use email. The first line would have to be, "I
don't want to be with anyone except you," in bold, so he'd see
that much even if he took a glance at the rest of the letter and
decided he didn't want to read it.

Emily would have had the best advice, but she and a few
classmates had left town right after their finals and were traveling around Europe for a few weeks. She had worked and
saved for it for a long time, so although she'd still been in
Atlanta when everything happened with Will, I hadn't told her
anything. I'd kept things light and joined her in her excitement
about the trip. She'd be home in another week or so, and I'd
give her some time to catch up with her normal life before
dropping my problems on her and begging for her thoughts.

◇ ◇ ◇

Amy was still in town for the summer, although she was going
away to grad school in the fall. We were at Luna Cantina

taking advantage of happy hour specials, or at least Amy was. Something, probably stress, had made me feel a little queasy lately, so I was sticking to Sprite. I tried to tell her about the increasingly urgent need to talk to Will I'd been feeling the last couple of weeks.

Looking at me over the rim of her margarita, she scolded me a little. "This isn't fair to Will. You already told him you didn't want to hear it. Now that you're done with Eric, you want to see what it would be like with him. Am I right?"

Amy didn't know how I felt about Will. He and I had always had an easy, relaxed friendship, but that had changed. Even as my feelings for him had grown so deep during the past year, I hadn't kept her updated. And my emotions were so volatile right now I didn't really know what to say.

"No, I promise. It sounds like that, but it's more that I'm finally growing up. I had a monster crush on Eric after I first saw him, as you know, and for quite a while I thought that meant something, but now I know it was only physical attraction, not real love at all." I used my straw to punch through the ice left in my glass. "It was all my own ignorance and my fault. I can't even blame him, because I did all the chasing."

Still, she was right. I shouldn't call Will and open this wound back up unless I was positive that it was the right thing to do. It would be awful if he made a big change in his life based on my unstable mood.

"Okay," Amy said, "if Eric called you tonight and asked you to marry him, you'd tell him to get lost?"

"Oh yeah, I'd totally tell him to take a hike. But at one time I thought he was the one, as you know, despite the way he treated me. After that display of terrible judgment, now I'm kind of afraid to trust my own feelings and decisions."

I had an idea. "How about this? I'll do my best to wait until the end of the summer. If I'm still feeling this way about Will, I'll ask him if he'd like to date long distance. I assume, since he seemed to have strong feelings for me, he won't be replacing me too fast for me to have time to figure this out." I tried to laugh, but it didn't quite work. Why did I always try to make light when I was talking about something that upset me?

Amy shook her head. "Girl, I hope it works out. You always take the hard way, don't you?"

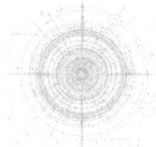

COLLEGE – Lost Light

MAY 2004

I hadn't had any big plans for Memorial Day weekend, but that Sunday I went on a last-minute tubing trip with Savannah and some other friends who'd had chemistry classes and labs with us our freshman and sophomore years. We had been getting together for beer once or twice a semester all this time, and they hadn't graduated yet. It was always wonderful to relax in the sun, although it was a bit more difficult for me to do so today. I felt compelled to call Will as soon as possible, and I had deliberately come here to keep myself away from the phone while I tried to think of the best words to use.

He was a kind person, so I assumed he would let me say at least a couple of sentences before he would try to get away. I wouldn't waste that opportunity on small talk or telling him I'd been an anxious mess the last time I'd seen him. I had to convey the crucial messages first. Then he could lead the conversation in whatever direction he wanted. I knew he was on Pacific time, so I was going to wait until at least nine or ten EDT tonight, when he might be home from whatever fun thing he was probably doing today. I knew myself; it would be hard to wait now that I had decided to do this. I'd stay with this group as long as possible today, keeping myself distracted. I didn't want to start calling his phone every half hour like a lunatic, and that's exactly what I'd do if I got started too early.

When we all got to the take-out point on the river, we dragged the tubes out of the water. Once we'd put them into one of the trucks we'd left there, we rode back to the other cars. After making plans to meet again at seven for dinner, we headed home to get ready. I got a ride from my old lab partner Phil and his girlfriend Leigh and sat in the backseat and relaxed as we made our way to our neighborhood, contributing to the conversation occasionally but not feeling pressured to do so.

◊ ◊ ◊

Once they dropped me at my place, I took a nice hot shower and washed my hair. Rinsing off felt fantastic after spending the day covered in sweat and sunscreen. Back in my bedroom, I turned on my computer. Taking the towel from my hair, I started to comb the tangles out.

Once I got into my email, I saw a message from Josh urging me to call him immediately. I dug through my bag and found that I had missed five calls from him and had a voicemail saying the same thing: "Call me as soon as you get this." His voice sounded . . . well, *grave* was the only word I could think of to describe it.

I couldn't imagine what could be so urgent, as I hadn't seen him for over a month, but I pressed the button to call him back.

I wondered what could be wrong with him. "Lauren, Will is dead."

Immediately, I doubled over, feeling as if I'd been punched in the gut. Some part of me understood the news, and the other part thought I had simply misheard. I clutched the phone to my ear. "What?" I whispered.

"Well, he and a couple other guys were riding ATVs in Moab, Utah. And they say he tried riding in the dark and accidentally went over a cliff."

"That can't be. Wh-wh-what was he doing in Utah?" I asked.

"It was just a long weekend thing. They told me he and some coworkers got the last-minute idea to fly there and do some riding in the desert, some other outdoor stuff... I don't know. I don't know why they were trying to do that in the dark. I can't believe it myself," Josh said.

Although I had asked a reasonable question on the surface, my mind was still rejecting this news. I felt numb but supercharged to do something, to do anything. "Are they sure it's him? Maybe there's a mix-up?"

"No, I'm so sorry. His friends knew what had happened as soon as he went over. A recovery team found his—found him, and they've brought him back up. It's him. He loved you a lot, you know. I wanted to tell you the news before you heard it some other way."

I barely heard him as he told me he would stay in touch about arrangements or a service or some other unthinkable thing that simply shouldn't be happening. How could Will be gone? Had there ever been a more lively, lovable, friendly, beautiful, kind human being in the world?

I thanked Josh, and we hung up. Suddenly, I felt hot saliva flood my mouth, and I only made it to the trash can before I threw up. I went to wash my face and brush my teeth, then somehow got back to my room and crawled into bed. I was shivering from the shock and keening like a wild animal. Finally, still shaking, I felt myself drift off into a crazy sleep. I withdrew into it as far as I could, willing myself to stay there.

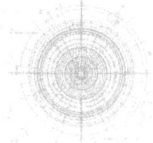

CURRENT – Last Chance

April 2024

Although I'd barely slept the night before, I was full of energy when I woke up. I could hardly wait for Eric to leave so I could be alone with my thoughts and excitement. This was the day I hoped to see Will and maybe even stop him from going on that stupid trip.

I went into the bathroom and started the shower.

When I was ready to get dressed, I went to the back of my closet and retrieved a small wooden chest where I'd kept my personal treasures since I was a teenager. Inside were a few pieces of jewelry that had belonged to my mother, my class ring from Tech, and—wrapped in linen, tied with the green ribbon from the art journal Will had given me over twenty years ago—my raindrop necklace. The sight of it sent a surge of bittersweet emotion through me, but I wanted to believe that today I might find Will again. Wearing the necklace felt like carrying a part of him with me, a symbol of the connection we'd shared. I put it on, thinking about the long-ago day when he had fastened it around my neck.

Right after eight, while I was staring at the necklace in the mirror, I received a text from Sean.

You said you wanted to know—No whistle today. They sent announcement POTUS coming today and they don't want it making noise

I wanted to sit down and cry. Instead, I felt the scorching sadness inside and didn't shed a tear. It was over. There would be no way to save Will. No loving, wonderful, magic guy for me and the rest of the world. I would miss him for the rest of my life, but I had to keep going, as I had done for almost twenty years.

My teal dress was clean, and so were my pumps and businesslike purse. I had an interview to get to.

◇ ◇ ◇

Since I knew that my worst enemy was always my anxiety and tendency to panic, I had left home with plenty of time to spare. I couldn't afford to have my emotions hijack my brain. I needed every bit of insight and intelligence I could scrape together. What happened today might have more impact on my life than anything else in a long time.

After I got into my car and started it, I found Biolution in Google Maps. I had already looked at its location and website many times over the past few months, but I wanted to make sure I avoided any traffic jams. Plus, it might help to hear the turn-by-turn reminders so I wouldn't go into a fugue and drive all the way to Tennessee.

I began to think about Will again. How could I have reached the last possible opportunity, then have been forced to give up like this? I needed the whistle, and it would not be blowing today.

Soon I saw the turn to the new Biolution building up ahead. This part of the area was brand new and looked like it would be an exciting place to work. Taking a few deep breaths, I tried to smile and get into a positive mood. It was time to think about my future.

I was growing more nervous every minute. At the last second, I made my decision. Driving right past my turn, I cut into another office park and exited, now going in the opposite direction from before. Even though the whistle wasn't scheduled to blow today, I needed to try to go back to Will.

Once on the interstate heading south toward Atlanta, part of me wanted to race ahead as fast as the car would go. But I drove a few miles an hour over the speed limit and tried to be careful. The first part of the drive was uneventful, except of course that the full importance of this trip was hitting me like never before. Today my attempt would either work, or I would fail and the tragedy would be final. There would be no more time for crazy hopes or figuring out any dreams. I had never been under more pressure in my life, but I was determined to keep my mind focused. For Will.

Since I had lost time by going to Biolution, I intended to park in the visitors' lot on Spring Street, which was close to the interstate. From there, I could walk the half mile or so to the dorm in no time flat, no matter how many people were on the sidewalks. Unfortunately, traffic ground to a halt right after I got off the interstate, and I was stuck in traffic near Atlantic Station, north of campus. I tried to stay calm, but there was a time to be calm and a time to get something done. I couldn't let time run out while I was sitting here.

Because we were at a standstill, I looked at Google Maps. My route was dark red, indicating the slowest of slow traffic all the way down the road I was on, following the eastern boundary of campus. In fact, it looked like even the side streets leading into the northeast side of the campus were just as congested. Oh, right. The president was here. Why did it have to be today of all days?

I managed to edge my way onto Sixteenth Street. Then I couldn't turn left into the campus because of the backed-up traffic. I struggled west for a few more blocks, but I was getting farther from the dorm with every foot I drove now and could see no fast way to turn back. I put on my signal and found a place to veer over to the curb, stopping in a No Parking zone.

Now about a mile and a half north of the dorm, I got out, grabbing my purse, and started walking fast toward the nearest intersection. Remembering my running shoes, I wheeled around and strode back to the car. I hurriedly threw my pumps into the trunk, stuffing my feet into the runners and tying them tightly. Luckily, my dress had a relatively full skirt, so I'd have plenty of legroom to walk or run as fast as I was able. Once again, I started trotting to an intersection where I could cross the busy street with a light and start working my way south.

I was afraid I'd never make it in time. I was no athlete, and of course there were red lights and traffic stopping me, too. So many things that were usually insignificant were chewing up the clock. Although I didn't want to give up, I feared that my body would doom this venture to failure. I hadn't run fast in a long time, and it didn't matter how much I wanted to succeed. My muscles could only do so much before they got exhausted and failed. And for that matter, what chance did I have of entering that portal at the exact day and hour I needed to right the wrong from twenty years ago?

I hadn't been on foot in this area in almost twenty years, and I hardly remembered some of the buildings and little streets. I kept running, but I could feel my legs slowing. The scenery had changed. Many houses looked different than they had years before because of new paint jobs or other updates. The street curved a little, and I hoped I was still heading south and toward the dorm, not west and away from where I needed to be, wasting precious minutes and energy. I checked a street sign to make sure I was still on the right road.

The next sign I saw coming up was Will's street. I could hardly believe it. I could see the apple tree. It was right there, lit up by the sunlight, so tall and healthy. It looked almost as if it were cheering me on. My mind and body instinctively responded. It was probably a shot of endorphins, but suddenly I could really run. I turned on the speed and pumped my arms and legs, sprinting for the dorm. Now all I needed was to cross Tenth Street, then I'd be on campus and could travel diagonally across parking lots, green spaces, and all the other familiar areas I'd run in when I was young.

I dared to feel some elation. The impossible now seemed within reach.

Students I passed looked up at me, then went about their business. Nothing was shocking in the big city, after all. Running across campus, I continued to the street where the dorm was and slowed my pace. Now I was walking briskly against a tide of people who were heading the other way, and I kept my eyes on the building up ahead on the left. My heart was hammering against my ribs. This was a life-or-death matter, and although I wasn't sure I could change anything, I was going to do everything I could.

I must have looked like a crazy woman with my determined face, speed walking toward the dorm. A student kindly stopped and held the exterior door for me. I thanked him and hurried up to the second floor, where I would look for the old door that might save a life.

As I found the right hallway, I forced myself to slow down and put a calm expression on my face. The last thing I needed was for someone to challenge or stop me here. I walked along with what I hoped was a casual, purposeful look, when in reality I was scouring every dark corner for an ancient yellow door.

It was now six minutes before the hour. It may have been that the whistle was necessary for this mission, but unfortunately I couldn't do anything about that. This was my best and last shot. I would know in a few seconds.

I whispered, "Foolish ventures are *still* my favorite kind."

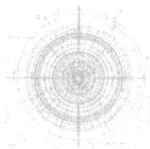

CURRENT – Resonance

April 2024

S tanding in the hall, full of hope and anxiety, I was astounded to hear the most beautiful sound in the world. The whistle was blowing. And just as it did, I found the old door to the passageway I hoped would take me to Will. With a quick glance around, I pulled it open and slipped inside, and the whistle gradually faded away.

By now I knew the way and walked as fast as I could in the darkness. Soon I saw the hint of light ahead, just as I remembered.

As I emerged from the dark hall, I found myself in the courtyard, just as I had hoped. My eyes immediately went to the bench where Will and I had always sat, but instead of Will, there was a young woman there I'd never seen before. She was reading and using a pink highlighter to mark up a textbook. Had she gotten to the bench first, so maybe he'd gone somewhere else? I had to find him.

I walked to the center of the courtyard to try to look for him from there. Forcing myself to take it slowly, I turned and studied every person and every group, but I didn't see him. Finally, I spotted Josh. Thank God. Please, please let him lead me to Will.

"Hey Josh," I called.

"Hi Lauren. How's it going?"

"Oh, pretty good," I lied, "but I'm looking for Will. Is he coming out here between classes?"

"Nope. Our one o'clock was canceled, so he probably went somewhere to study. He may not be on campus again except to take finals, and of course for graduation."

Oh, no. Oh no, no, no. I had to find Will and try to save him from his horrible accident.

Although my face felt stiff with tension, I tried to smile at Josh and said, "Okay, then. I've got to run—see ya." I wondered how far I could walk or travel and still stay in this world. I realized that I should have a cell phone in my backpack. I could call him.

I dug into my bag and found my simple phone. It took a few precious seconds to scroll through my contact list, but I found Will's name. I hurried to start the call. It went straight to voicemail, to the stupid voice with the stupid message that was more annoying than getting nothing at all.

"The mailbox for this number is full. Please try your call again later."

I threw my phone back in the bag and kept up my search. I began racing to the edges of each nearby building trying to see if Will was around anywhere, then running or stumbling to the next. By now, I was crying and praying. He was almost certainly going to die, to miss out on the rest of his life, and it was too horrible to face.

"Lauren, what's wrong?"

Suddenly, Will was right there in front of me, his hands on my shoulders. His face showed deep concern. With a last gulping sob, I threw my arms around him. He put his arms tightly around me too, probably thinking to himself that he had picked a bad time to run into me. Being held by him felt so good. Now I had to try to blurt out my message, which might change everything.

"Will, you can't go to Utah this summer."

"What? All right, what's going on?" Still holding me, he leaned back a little to look at my face. He was so kind and respectful, even though I was raving like a psycho.

"Promise me you won't go on a trip after graduation. Please, do that for me, even though it sounds crazy."

"Well, sure, I promise. No Utah for me. But can we talk for a minute?"

Will and I left the main sidewalk and went to a quiet area beside a brick building. He gestured toward the same set of concrete stairs as he had the first time we had this talk, and we sat down, angling our bodies to face one another. He hesitated, looking a little nervous. "I planned what I was going to say, but after last night . . . I think you know." He looked down, then back up at my face. "I never wanted to risk our amazing friendship, but if there's any chance at all that you'd want to—"

At that point, I reached out to hold his hand, and I gave it a squeeze. I allowed a happy smile to break across my face for the first time in a long time. My heart was full as I gazed at this man I cared for so much. I barely let him say another word before I told him, "I love you."

At that point, the world—other people, traffic noises, and everything else—melted away. After all this time, we were going to be together.

Will said, "I love you too, Lauren," and leaned closer to kiss me. I felt that kiss all the way down to my toes. I wanted it to go on forever. We wrapped our arms around each other again.

Then I heard the whistle starting to blow. Where had the last hour gone? I didn't want to leave him. But if this was the end of my brief interlude, I would always treasure it. My primary goal had been to save Will's life, after all. If he could live and be happy, that was all I could ask for.

I held him tightly and kept kissing him, and the whistle continued to blow.

As the sound faded away, I kept my eyes closed for a moment longer, savoring the feel of Will's arms around me. A small, irrational part of me was afraid that when I opened my eyes, I'd find myself back in the dorm hallway without him. Instead, my first sight was Will's loving smile. He stood up, gently pulling me with him, as he'd done many times before on hikes, but this time he didn't let go of my hand as we started down the sidewalk. This felt like a miracle, but I'd never been happier.

Since both of us were finished with classes, we walked to Quick Bytes, the little sandwich shop near the administration building, for lunch. Instead of sitting across the table from me, Will took the chair on the adjacent side, angled so we could be as close as possible, our arms and legs touching. We had a lot to talk about.

"Will, I know you have to respond to those job offers today. If you'd like to take your dream job in California, we'll make it work. I'm totally flexible. Please don't just toss away your opportunity."

He smiled. "I really am happy right here, if you are. Working at MED-ATL has been great, and I bet I can get them to allow me to do some more side projects to help the people who need it most. Main thing is, I'm the luckiest man in the world."

He put his hand on mine, and I could see the love in his eyes. It had been there for a very long time, but I'd been too fearful and insecure to see it. He leaned closer to me, his voice a little lower. "We won't mess this up, Mahan. Promise."

I thought my heart would burst, I was so happy.

◇ ◇ ◇

After lunch, we started walking toward my dorm.

Will said, "I want to let you get started studying for finals, and I'll make those phone calls. Think you can take a break for a little date tonight, just something simple, so I'll have another excuse to kiss you?"

I laughed. "Absolutely. By then I might think of an excuse to kiss you, too."

"Oh, and after graduation, how 'bout another foolish venture before we start our new jobs?" he said.

"Sounds a lot like planning, coming from you."

"Get used to it." He squeezed my hand just a little.

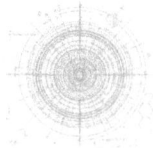

COLLEGE – Missing Page

April 2004

There was only one important day I'd neglected to write about in my journal all those years ago. I didn't make it back to my room that night, and the next morning, I was in a big hurry to get off to class, so I didn't write anything then either. And that next day brought plenty of big events of its own. After that, I decided to let this one thing be a sacred memory, almost afraid that by recording it I would lose some of it. My writing certainly couldn't do it justice. I never even told Amy or Emily about it. I didn't find out until later how important that day would be.

It was the day before the afternoon when Will wanted to talk to me about the future. It started off like any other end-of-semester weekday—going to class, listening for any hints the prof would give about the final, and scurrying off to study like crazy before my brain got saturated and refused to take in another thing. I stopped at six to eat a quick dinner, a salad made from what I could find in my dorm room fridge, including lettuce, tomato, mushrooms, and a couple of ounces of Gouda.

I was back to studying when Will called at around seven. It was so good to hear his voice. I never wanted to go more than a day without talking to him. That night, something was different, though. He was nice as usual and asked me about my day, but I could tell something was wrong. I asked what was up.

He told me that his dad had died, and he'd found out during a call from one of his father's friends late that afternoon—a week after the fact. I didn't know what to say, but I told him I was very sorry. After we hung up, I went back to studying for about thirty seconds. Then I flipped my notebook closed and put my sandals on. I brushed my teeth, brushed my hair, grabbed my purse, and was out of there.

◦ ◦ ◦

Adam answered my knock. He said Will was in his room with the door closed and had been telling people he was fine but wanted to be alone right now. Of course, Adam said I was welcome to go back there if I wanted to give it a try.

I walked to Will's door and knocked softly.

"C'mon in," he said.

I stuck my head in and said, "Hi," smiling just the faintest amount—what I hoped was a sympathetic smile. I couldn't look at him without smiling at least a micron or two.

Will was lying on his back on his bed, hands behind his head, but he was looking at me. He gave me his own flicker of a smile. "Hi Lauren."

I entered and closed the door, then I sat on the edge of the bed.

"I'm okay," he said. "You should be studying. I should be too—there's really nothing I can do for him anyway." His voice sounded so lost, so lifeless, so totally un-Will-like. "I hadn't seen my dad in years. I'm just kind of stunned."

Motioning for him to scoot over a little, I kicked off my sandals and lay down beside him, also facing the ceiling. "What was he like?"

Will told me his dad had been a friendly and charming guy who was a great salesman but had always hopped all over the place, chasing any shiny object or opportunity that came his way. He could never settle down and stay with a job—or with his family, for that matter—for long. Eventually, after he'd taken off the last time when Will was a teenager, Will knew there were no hard feelings and tried to keep living his life without thinking much about his father anymore. He missed him, and he worried about him, but he'd learned not to be disappointed or take it personally when he didn't show up.

"I'm so sorry, Will," I said. "I imagine you must be grieving the dad you had and maybe also the relationship you'd always hoped to have with him." We'd been lying side by side, our arms barely touching, but at this point he took my hand. I squeezed his, just a little.

"Thanks. Yeah, it's complicated. And worse because I didn't have any warning," he said.

We talked for a long time, and I was glad that he seemed more relaxed than he had been. At times there would be silence, then we'd start chatting about something slightly different, just a sentence or two. After a while it grew dark, and the only light in the room was the glow from the streetlights outside. I dozed off a couple of times, although I fought to stay awake. After all, Will had just found out he'd lost a parent. I believed he would get some comfort from having a friend with him right now. And to be decent company, I figured a minimum requirement was that I be alert and present.

I woke up in the dim room, still lying on the bed, now curled on my right side facing the door. I was alone. When Will came back in, I kept my eyes closed, a combination of being ready to drop right back off to sleep and not knowing what to say or do. Did he expect me to leave? I was dead tired. But what if I was keeping him from going to sleep? Maybe he had a hard time sleeping with someone else so close by. I could go to the living room and stretch out on the sofa.

But then I decided maybe I wasn't overstaying my welcome, or at least maybe I was distracting him from his sadness, because I heard his footsteps approach, and he spread a light blanket over me and kissed the top of my head. Then he went around and climbed onto the other side of the bed, and I felt him get under the blanket with me. I drifted off within a few seconds.

Later, I woke up again. I could tell Will wasn't asleep, because I'd hear him scratch his arm or swallow occasionally, and his breathing was quiet instead of deep. I hated that he was lying there awake in the middle of the night, alone with his thoughts. I turned toward him, and in the dimly lit room, I could see that he was on his side, facing me. I scooted close to him and put my face and hand against his chest, my head right under his chin. He was wearing a soft T-shirt; I remembered from earlier that it was blue, and his chest felt nice and warm through the fabric. Breathing him in, I found comfort in his clean, familiar scent. I didn't say anything, but I knew I didn't have to.

Will kissed the top of my head again and put his arm around me outside the blanket. The closeness felt so good. We lay like that for a few minutes. Then some powerful feelings surged through me. Without opening my eyes, I tried to kiss him but ended up catching him on the jawline, his stubble grazing my lips. He found my mouth with his. A jolt of physical urge shot through my body, and I answered that kiss, reaching up to touch his face.

We kissed slowly, deeply, and I felt him smile against my lips before his hand slipped just under the back of my shirt, warm against my lower back. A few minutes later, our clothes were on the floor. Will's hands moved over me gently as we explored and sometimes played. The warmth of his skin, the way he pulled me closer—it all felt exciting and new, yet familiar and completely right. We took our time, savoring every moment. Aware that we were not alone in the house, we communicated with whispered words, soft sounds, and sometimes quiet laughter. Often, our eyes would meet and hold, adding to the raw intimacy that would have been unthinkable with anyone else. It was the most beautiful and profound experience I had ever had.

◇ ◇ ◇

I awoke again after eight thirty because the sun was streaming in through the window. Oh no. I had class at ten, and of course what I'd rather do was stay right there with Will. But he'd have class later too, and we both needed to get ready for finals. He was still asleep, and although I wanted to kiss his sweet face, I made an effort not to wake him as I got up. He hadn't slept much at all, I realized. Plus, if I left now, it would save us from an awkward moment of vowing that we would never mention this again or wondering if we had harmed our friendship.

I understood that last night had been a unique occasion because of extraordinary circumstances, and I hoped we could continue to enjoy doing fun stuff together and not feel uncomfortable or avoid each other. The last thing I wanted was to start acting needy and weird around him, or for us to become a couple and have it end badly, taking our special bond with it. There were plenty of guys in the world, but there was only one Will, and I couldn't screw up our treasured relationship.

I pulled my clothes from the pile where they had landed a few hours earlier and got dressed. After tearing a page from the little notebook I carried in my purse, I wrote him a note:

Sorry to have to rush out, class at 10. Hope you have a good day!

Then I hurried out to my car.

When I got to my dorm room, I showered and dressed, grabbing a chocolate SlimFast from the fridge to drink on the way to class. Scooping up the notebooks I'd need for the day, I hurried out the door.

And I forgot to take my pill.

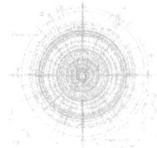

CURRENT – This Time

MAY 2024

Today I got away from the lab early, so I was able to get started on my husband's favorite spaghetti sauce, the recipe we'd perfected over countless cozy evenings of cooking together. As I stood at the stove, I looked around the home we'd created, marveling at how it reflected both of us so perfectly.

Everything was a blend of beauty and comfort, just like our life together. Colorful paintings hung on the walls. A couple of them had been done by artist friends of ours, while we'd bought others at various festivals and shows, simply because we loved them. Will's latest invention sketches were tacked up in his study alongside my nature drawings, a visual echo of the way our lives had intertwined. On his desk, nestled between engineering journals and technical drawings, sat a framed photo of me on the day I defended my dissertation. My face was lit up with joy, caught mid-laugh as he wrapped an arm around my waist, pride shining in his eyes.

Just across the hall, my own study held a matching treasure. Among my research notes and shelves of well-worn books was a photograph of Will standing in a sunlit clinic, surrounded by doctors he had trained on his latest medical innovation. His hands were mid-gesture, his face alight with the passion he poured into his work. I had framed it myself, wanting a daily reminder of the man who never stopped finding ways to make the world better. That same drive to help others—to leave the world a little brighter than he found it—was one of the things I loved most about him.

The hardwood floor felt good under my bare feet as I moved around the kitchen we'd designed together. Nearby, a set of stainless steel bowls held water and kibble for our dog, Charlie. Our geriatric cat, Susie, watched me from the back of an oversized armchair in the next room.

The front door opened, and Will came in. The smile that lit up his face when he saw me was the same one I'd fallen in love with all those years ago, and I felt my own automatic grin spreading in response. He slung his laptop bag onto the living room sofa, gave Susie her expected head scratch, and closed the space between us to wrap me in a hug and kiss. I looked up at his handsome face and marveled at the fact that I was married to this kind, brilliant man who was perfect for me in every way. Those beautiful gray-green eyes still held the same warmth and mischief they had when we first met, but now they also held a depth of love and understanding that could only come from a lifetime of shared joys and challenges.

"Smells amazing in here," he said, keeping one arm around my waist as he reached for a spoon to sample the sauce. Just like always, I gave his hand a playful swat.

Will laughed, then turned at the sound of the door opening again. His arm tightened around my waist. "Look who's here."

Sean.

He had taken his last final. His smile—so much like Will's—radiated excitement, ready for a summer of freedom and adventure. He bounded into the kitchen and wrapped both of us in a big hug, squeezing tight. "I missed you guys," he said, his voice brimming with warmth. "I can't wait to tell you all about the crazy projects we worked on this semester and the awesome camping trip we took last month. Oh, and—I'm starving!"

"We missed you too, buddy," Will said, ruffling his hair. "And great timing—your mom's making enough food for an army."

Charlie, who had been dozing in a patch of sunlight, trotted over to greet Sean with a wagging tail. Even Susie stretched and began to descend from her perch.

Watching Will and Sean, my heart was full of gratitude and love.

Their presence filled the house with warmth and energy, just as Will's home had been a place of fun and friendship back in college. Will caught my gaze, and for a moment, the world slowed. His eyes softened as if he, too, was feeling the weight of everything we had been through to get here. He lifted our joined hands and pressed a kiss to my knuckles, wordless but full of meaning. In that simple gesture, I felt the echo of every tender moment we'd shared, every challenge we'd faced hand in hand.

I squeezed his hand back, our old signal that meant "I'm here, I'm with you, we're in this together." And we were, in every possible way.

Life was so good.

This time.

Acknowledgements

I want to thank my editor, Dylan Garity. He took my roughest of rough drafts and somehow understood exactly what I was trying to convey—teaching me how to translate my ideas into the story we have now. His insightful guidance showed me where to develop my characters and deepen their connections, turning my scattered thoughts into a cohesive, meaningful story. I couldn't have asked for a better guide on this fun journey.

All mistakes are my own.

Dear Reader,

Thank you for joining me on this journey of love, loss, and second chances. Will and Lauren's story is a testament to the enduring power of connection, the magic of possibility, and the belief that some bonds are truly meant to be.

If you enjoyed the book, I'd be honored if you shared it—whether by recommending it to a friend, a book club, or anyone who still believes in second chances.

To my friends in the Tech community: this novel is my love letter to you and to our beloved Institute. I hope you enjoyed the tale and the Easter eggs, and perhaps even heard the whistle in your heart as you read. While I've taken some creative liberties (especially with how much free time everyone seems to have!), every detail was chosen with the hope of crafting a story filled with emotion, meaning, and hope. You are—and always will be—a part of something extraordinary.

With gratitude and warmest wishes,
C. M. Burdell

P.S. If you love slow-burn stories with a bit of science, soul, and friendship, I'm thrilled to share that more is coming—set in the same world, with familiar faces and new adventures ahead.

About the author

C. M. Burdell writes emotional, slow-burn novels where love, a touch of magic, and the power of friendship collide. Her stories delve into second chances, the ties that define us, and the bravery required to reshape a life.

She grew up in Atlanta and graduated from Georgia Tech, where her fascination with science and her deep appreciation for enduring friendships took root. When she's not writing about time-bending adventures, nostalgic college days, and emotionally intricate engineers, Burdell can be found exploring nature, geeking out over the latest scientific discoveries, or cherishing time with her family and friends. She believes in the magic of second chances, the power of connection, and the idea that it's never too late to rewrite your story.

This Time is her debut novel—but it definitely won't be her last.

www.ingramcontent.com/pod-product-compliance
Lightning Source LLC
Chambersburg PA
CBHW050010120726
47903CB00006B/1714